STILL

Long Slow Tease, #1

Ann Mayburn

The unauthorized reproduction or distribution of this copyrighted work is illegal. Criminal copyright infringement (including infringement without monetary gain) is investigated by the FBI and is punishable by up to 5 years in federal prison and a fine of $250,000.

Please purchase only authorized electronic editions and do not participate in, or encourage, the electronic piracy of copyrighted materials. Your support of the author's rights is appreciated.

This book is a work of fiction. Names, characters, places, and incidents are the products of the author's imagination or used fictitiously. Any resemblance to actual events, locales or persons, living or dead, is entirely coincidental.

Still

By Ann Mayburn

Copyright © 2013 by Ann Mayburn

Published by Honey Mountain Publishing

All rights reserved. Except for use in any review, the reproduction or utilization of this work, in whole or in part, in any form by any electronic, mechanical or other means now known or hereafter invented, is forbidden without the written permission of the publisher.

**DISCLAIMER: Please do not try any new sexual practice, BDSM or otherwise, without the guidance of an experienced practitioner. Ann Mayburn will not be responsible for any loss, harm, injury or death resulting from use of the information contained in this book.*

Acknowledgements

I would like to extend a super huge thank you to my Beta readers, and to all my friends and fans that gave me the courage to self-publish Michelle and Wyatt's story. You are, as always the wind beneath my wings.

I'd also like to thank my editor, Ekatarina Sayanova. I loved the conversations we've had while whipping *Still* into shape and your insight has been invaluable. I also appreciate the fact that you think there is nothing strange about yelling at my kids that zombies can't talk while I'm on the phone with you. ;)

My little brother, an active duty Marine with more tours of the sandbox under his belt than should be legal, played an integral part in this book in making sure I got my shit right...well right with a little bit of dramatic license here and there. To him I would like to say a big and heartfelt thank you. I wish with all my might that you weren't getting ready to deploy to that shit hole yet again and you and your family are always in my heart and prayers.

To my super awesome fans, thank you so much for once again giving me the opportunity to entertain you. A story with no readers is like a body with no heart.

Ann Mayburn

STILL by Ann Mayburn

Dear Beloved Reader,

The seeds for Michelle and Wyatt's story were sown during a conversation I had with some fellow military wives about PTSD. They were dealing with everything from their husband being unable to ride in the passenger seat of the car because he thought everyone pulling up next to them might be a bomber, to another woman who had to learn how to sleep with every light in the house on the moment it got dark outside. And if a light burned out and they didn't have a spare bulb, a major panic attack would ensue.

These were all things that we'd never even imagined we'd have to deal with in our role as a military spouse and it wasn't just my group of friends. All over the US our men and women in uniform are coming home with an army of psychological demons in tow.

So, we got to talking about what we could possibly do to help them and one woman quipped that she'd just have to become a Dominatrix and whip his ass into shape because he only seemed to respond when she yelled at him. We all laughed, but later I kept thinking about what she said and the first chapter of Michelle and Wyatt's story came to me that night.

STILL by Ann Mayburn

While this story does have threads taken from real life events running through it, it is still a romance and in romance land a happily ever after is guaranteed. In the real world you have to make your own happily ever after, and it is fucking hard work. For those struggling with PTSD and the people that love them, I've included a list of resources that I urge you to use at the back of the book.

Remember, you are not alone, there is hope, and there is help if you're brave enough to ask for it.

Kisses,

Ann- Sailor wife, Army daughter and granddaughter, and proud United States Marine Corp sister

STILL by Ann Mayburn

Other BDSM Romance by Ann Mayburn

Club Wicked Series

My Wicked Valentine

My Wicked Nanny

My Wicked Devil

My Wicked Trainers

My Wicked Gypsy (Coming Soon)

Virtual Seduction Series

Sodom and Detroit

Sodom and the Phoenix

Blushing Violet

Bound for Pleasure

Sensation Play

Peppermint Passion

The Breaker's Concubine

Prologue

Present Day

Michelle Sapphire closed her eyes and counted to ten, straining with every ounce of her formidable self-control not to launch herself at the asshole secured in the restraint chair in front of her.

Grinning at her.

"Yes, Officer, I know this man."

Oh, she knew this man all right. Wyatt Maverick Callahan. Also known as Marine Gunnery Sergeant Callahan, "Gunny" to the men and women in his unit, and darling boy to his doting mother. A decorated war hero with six tours of the Middle East under his belt. During the last tour, he'd been part of the security detachment assigned to her regiment. She'd been sitting next to him in the M-ATV when the mortar ripped through his troop transport and inflicted the wound that sent him home, essentially ending his military career and winning him another Purple Heart.

Now, here he sat wearing a vintage Pink Floyd tee shirt probably older than he was, faded, grass-stained blue jeans that fit like they'd been painted on, and scuffed boots desperately in need of a polish. He had a good two to three days growth of beard that accentuated his knife-sharp cheekbones. And he still, somehow, managed to look hotter than fucking sin.

"Ms. Sapphire," the older policeman standing next to Callahan started to say before Wyatt lunged forward as much as he could while strapped down to the chair.

"That's *Doctor* Sapphire to you," Callahan snarled and Michelle's right fist ached with the need to beat his ass.

Ignoring the female officer trying to block her, Michelle got right up in Callahan's face, nose to nose. She didn't care if she was in her Hello Kitty pajama pants and a faded pink tank top, or that her hair was hanging loose around her shoulders in a blonde frizz. This motherfucker's phone call woke her up to come bail his sorry, drunk ass out of some two-room jail south of Austin after she'd worked a twelve-hour night shift at the clinic. And she hadn't had any coffee before leaving the house.

He was a dead man.

"Hi, Callahan," she said in a sugary sweet voice.

Up this close she could see the flecks of green and gold in his now bloodshot hazel eyes. He had long, thick dark lashes, the kind women would kill for, and a full, sensual mouth. His dark hair was longer than she'd ever seen it, but then again they'd both gotten out of the military about a year ago. Sorrow flashed through his gaze and, for a split second, she got a glimpse of the suffering man behind the wise-ass persona.

He smiled that panty-dropping smile that had every female within a fifty foot radius fluttering their lashes. "Hi, Doc. You said, if I ever needed you, I could call you."

"I did." Nailing him with her gaze, she enjoyed how he fidgeted. "Well let me inform you of something, Callahan. Right now, I really regret saying that if your idea of help is me bailing you out of the drunk tank."

Wyatt glared at her, his perfect upper lip curling in a manner that made her want to bite it. Sweet Mary, mother of God, put her in his presence for more than five minutes and her whole body ached for his touch. She'd hoped that their time apart would have lessened the impact his presence had on her but, if anything, it had grown stronger. Electricity, sharp and biting, arched between their bodies as their gazes locked. He was so very, very angry beneath all that sorrow, a storm of emotion battering him from the inside out.

He needed her.

"Ma'am." One of the deputies touched her

shoulder.

Not breaking eye contact with Callahan, she said, "It's all right, officer. I've got this. Callahan isn't going to do anything to piss me off any more than I already am because he knows that he doesn't want to see me really angry. Right, Callahan?"

His lips twitched the slightest bit and his angry gaze softened into that familiar devilish gleam. "Ma'am, yes, Ma'am." Michelle was sure if he'd been able to stand up, he would have saluted just to be a smart ass. The all too pleasant image of Callahan doing mountain climbers while nude flashed through her mind. Forcing her libido to calm down, she made herself focus on this moment, on him, and gave him one hundred percent of her attention. Because, God knows, Callahan could be a right stubborn bastard when he was in the mood.

She leaned forward the slightest bit, the scent of the crushed grass on his jeans mixing with his alcohol-saturated sweat. "Now, you will behave. You will do everything they ask in a polite and respectful manner. You will not disgrace me by acting like a fool in public. Do you understand?"

The rest of the anger slowly drained from his gaze and something deep inside her tightened when he was the first to look away, to acknowledge her dominance. That gesture was as old as time and always implied the same thing, submission. When he met her gaze again, he'd rebuilt some of his mental walls, but she'd already seen what she needed.

She knew what was inside his heart.

He swallowed hard. "Roger that, ma'am."

She gave him the smile that he'd always seen right before she laid the smack-down on him. His pupils constricted and his muscles tightened, an unconscious reaction to her emotions. She longed to soothe him, to tell him everything would be okay, but that only worked in fairy tales. In the real world, she had to take charge and *make* things right.

Fortunately, she rather enjoyed being a cold bitch in the right situations.

"Now then, can you please tell me the nature of his charges?"

The older officer motioned her away from Callahan to speak to her privately. Behind her she heard the officers talking to Wyatt, and he was as well-behaved as could be. While she still didn't know what she was going to do with him, she did know she would do everything she could to get him out of jail and someplace to heal. Preferably at her home.

"Well, Dr. Sapphire, we got a complaint about a drunk and disorderly, but it wasn't what we were used to."

"What do you mean?"

He leaned closer, near enough so she could smell the faint scents of coffee on his breath and the dry cleaning solution clinging to his uniform. "He was in a local cemetery. Scared the crap out of the caretaker. The old man was doing his last rounds through the property, getting ready to lock the gates, when he saw Wyatt sitting on a grave with a nearly empty bottle of whiskey."

He had her undivided attention now. "Was it Mt. Zion?"

"Yeah. I-uh I guess you know whose grave it was."

She knew, but she needed confirmation. "Aaron Winters?"

"Yeah."

She closed her eyes and took in a deep breath, torn between the need to choke Callahan for being so reckless or hold him. "Was he armed?"

"Yes ma'am, but only with a big Damascus knife he uses for whittling." He looked uncomfortable and his mustache twitched. "See, Callahan's a local boy. His dad used to be a detective next county over before he retired and opened his carpentry business. We know Wyatt, and we know his family."

Empathy filled her but she kept her expression carefully neutral. "Why did he call me instead of his family?"

Now his cheeks turned a deep red that made his blonde mustache stand out in an almost comical manner. "Well...I'm married to his sister and if I called their parents about him being drunk I'd be spending the next two months sleeping on the couch. Besides, nothing we've done seems to help and we've tried everything we can think of to get through to him." He pursed his lips, his mustache pushing forward like a walrus looking for a kiss. "See, he's talked about you before, usually when he's drunk."

She arched her brow.

"Nothin' bad, just how much he admires you and I figured you bein' a doctor and all, well maybe you can reach him."

She blew out a harsh breath. "Are you going to release him to my custody?"

"If you feel comfortable taking him. He really isn't that drunk." The officer leaned forward and lowered his voice. "Between you and me he's lucky if he gets four hours of sleep a night. The man is exhausted, but he can't outrun his nightmares."

A headache began to form behind her eyes as her heart ached for Callahan. "Okay, I'll take him, but, Officer," she looked down at his badge. "Phelps, since you're family, you should know, I've got a couple of conditions of my own."

He gave her a solemn nod. "Call me Gary."

"Gary," she said with the sweet smile that had always made her troops flinch, "I'm going to want Callahan to sign a contract to stay with me for a month. Think of it as a personal rehab."

"Uh, Doc, I don't think I can do that. It's not legal."

"I'm not asking you to force him and I won't approach him with it until he's sobered up. If he doesn't sign I take him home for one night to sleep it off, then he goes on his merry way. If he does sign..." she smiled in a way that made Officer Phelps swallow hard, "I guarantee in one month's time you will have a changed man. But I'll need you to keep the rest of his family away. He needs to decide for himself that he wants to live, not for his mother, not for his sister, but for himself."

Tilting his head to the side, Officer Phelps studied her. "You were a Marine, too, weren't you?"

"No, I was a Navy doc. We were the ones who got to patch the Marines up."

They were interrupted by the female officer escorting Callahan. As Michelle looked closer at him she saw the telltale physical signs of exhaustion. He looked much older than his thirty-six years, and there was a darkness in his gaze, something worn and guarded that hadn't been there before. She remembered him as being brash, larger than life, her rock, someone she could always rely on. Now, he just seemed so...lost.

"Ready, Callahan?"

"Sure thing, Doc."

After his cuffs were removed she motioned to him, "Let's go."

He looked at his brother-in-law and rubbed his face. "Man, I'm *really* sorry."

Phelps shook his head. "Wyatt, just get some help."

Callahan glanced over at Michelle. "I'm trying to."

She turned away and started walking, swinging her keys, leaving Callahan the choice to follow. Or not. Letting him see her empathy and compassion for him would not be helpful at this point. During the majority of their time together, she'd outranked him and that feeling carried over now as he walked escort behind her down the hallway. A flashback of him shadowing her in Afghanistan, always watching her back, made her dizzy for a moment.

They left the brightly lit hallway of the small police station and she continued on to her car, not saying a word to him. It scared her to the bone to think about him sitting at Winters' grave, drunk, carrying a knife while mourning the best friend who'd lost his battle with PTSD and killed himself six months ago.

Clicking the alarm on her keychain, the Corvette chirped to life. One of the many nice things about living in a snowless part of the state was that she could drive around with the top down on her car pretty much any time of the year. Right now she needed the wind in her face to help clear her head.

Callahan made a low whistle and circled around the back of the car. "Nice ride, Doc."

She traced her finger along the curve of the driver's side front quarter-panel, the deep sapphire blue custom paint glimmering faintly in the parking lot lights. "You puke on her, you even sweat on her and I will hang you from my rafters and beat you like a piñata."

He laughed and slid into the passenger side

with a sigh. "Just take me back to my place and I'll be out of your hair."

She entered the car and adjusted her mirror as she turned the key. The deep, throaty purr of the big engine always made her happy. "No can do. They released you to my custody for the night. You are staying at my place in Austin."

He tensed and turned to look at her. "Doc, take me home."

Ignoring him, she turned out onto the main road leading to the highway. The scent of the desert whipped through the car and she took a deep breath, purging her lungs. Next to her Callahan leaned his head back with his eyes closed, but every muscle on his body stood out in sharp relief. He was so wound up he looked in danger of snapping.

She turned on her stereo and pressed the button to play her Enigma CD. The smooth, almost luscious beats soon blended with the wind. The combination of the music and the soft desert air began to relax them both. Callahan took a deep breath and let it out, his body almost deflating. She wondered what had set him off tonight. Flashback? Panic attack? Whatever it was, she would find out later, but right now Callahan needed to sleep.

They pulled out onto I-35 N and began the drive

that would take them north of Austin, then west to her ranch. After retiring from the Navy she wanted to go someplace warm, someplace where she didn't have to deal with six months of winters so cold it felt like hell had really frozen over, and snow deep enough to bury a one-story house. She'd had enough of that growing up near Chicago.

Callahan kept looking at her, stealing glances out of the corner of his eye. He would look like he was about to say something, then reconsider. For now, she had to try to distract herself, to keep her desire to own him under control. God, how he'd haunted her thoughts over the last year. She was honest enough with herself to admit that Callahan living near Austin had led to her taking a job at the charity sponsored hospital. The work gave her a sense of purpose and she loved Austin.

Keeping her eyes on the road and off of Wyatt was much more difficult than she'd anticipated. Even in his sorry, worn down, and altogether sad state he still made her pulse race. She had to get her hormones under control and get her mind off what his ass would look like after she'd given him a couple dozen good spankings. Despite her resolve, her mind lingered on how she imagined his butt would flex beneath her blows, all rock solid and masculine. Biting into his ass would be like biting into a crisp apple with the slight crunch of his skin breaking beneath her teeth. Callahan shifted next to her and her gaze was drawn away from the road and down to his long, strong legs encased in velvety soft, worn jeans.

Good lord, this man was going to drive her insane.

She wanted to laugh, but she needed to be in the right headspace for the big ass headache in front of her. With Callahan that meant not letting him get away with anything. He was the kind of guy that if a woman gave an inch, he'd have her under him, give her a series of life-altering orgasms, and all while whispering the things women wanted to hear from their men. Then he'd leave her smiling and barely able to walk the next morning, with a vague promise to call her sometime, leaving her craving his touch for the rest of her life.

Callahan turned down the radio. "What are you thinking about?"

Could he somehow sense that she'd been having wicked thoughts about him? "I was thinking that if you keep pushing your luck I'll chain you to the foot of my bed and make you sleep on the floor with only a pillow and a blanket for company as punishment."

"That doesn't really sound like too terrible of a punishment."

She knew that his response to her answer would tell her everything she needed to know. "Oh, yes, it is. You will be allowed to look at my body but not touch. You will be allowed to attend to me, see to my comforts, and make me feel good...but that's it. And only I will decide when, or even *if* you've earned the right to kiss me, to bend to my will, to make me come."

His stunned expression sent a bolt of satisfaction through her and confirmed she was on the right track. Half of her hoped he would push it, while the other half was telling her she was treading dangerous waters.

What she knew about Callahan personally was gleaned from observation. She didn't know shit about Callahan sexually. On very rare occasions, their interactions had tread dangerously close to flirtation. But neither of them was willing to break the strict military code outlining permissible and non-permissible conduct between male and female military personnel, especially between commissioned and noncommissioned officers. And even the idea of sexual relations between superior officers and their subordinates? Um, no. They had risked one kiss since they both got out, but that had been...different.

"Doc, can I ask you something?"

"Go ahead."

STILL by Ann Mayburn

"Why are you taking me to your house?"

"Because you need to get away from the bullshit excuses you've surrounded yourself with and pull your head out of your ass." He started to talk and she held up her hand. "I just picked you up from jail at three in the morning drunk off your ass, Wyatt. Think about it." She didn't mention the fact that he'd been playing with a knife in a graveyard. He wasn't ready for that type of confrontation, yet.

He didn't answer, just turned to look out the window and eventually his head rested against the seat, his eyes half closed. Slowly, he stretched his legs out and laced his hands over his stomach as he looked out the window with barely open eyes. Michelle felt a sense of relief as his eyes closed and his even breathing indicated he finally slept.

Chapter 1

Nineteen Months Earlier

Gunnery Sergeant Wyatt Callahan surveyed the organized chaos of his company unpacking and setting up at their new assignment, in this case, a shit hole on the outside of Marjah at Forward Operating Base Garmsir in Afghanistan. While it was certainly better than the last shit hole he'd been in down by Kandahar, it was still one of the last places in the world he wanted to be.

Ever.

Unfortunately, Uncle Sam decided his ass needed to be in Afghanistan so, here he was, on his sixth combat mission and getting near the end of his rope. For at least the next six months he'd be the Weapons Company Mobile Section Leader at the hospital base instead of doing guard work for the EOD guys. Months of crawling down shitty streets through towns infested with Taliban, looking for explosive devices on the roads had sucked ass. He was pretty sure his asshole was permanently clenched from all the close calls he'd experienced.

"Callahan!"

He looked in the direction of the familiar voice and happiness filled him. His childhood friend, Aaron Winters, was waving as he crossed between stacks of equipment. His normally Irish-fair face was as red as his hair thanks to the strong desert sun. On the edge of his collar gleamed his new

Master Gunnery Sergeant pin. When Aaron got close enough Wyatt clapped him on the arm and pulled the other guy into a quick hug.

"Winters, those crazy turban-wearing bastards haven't managed to kill you yet?"

Aaron laughed and clapped him on the back. "Not yet. Come on, man, let's get some chow and catch up."

"Give me a second to get this shit squared away."

Wyatt checked in with his men and made sure everyone knew what they were supposed to be doing before he rejoined Aaron and they walked through the bustling base together. Instead of the tent cities that Wyatt had lived in at his previous forward operating bases over the past nine months, this US mobile hospital base had actual buildings.

Not only that, there were females.

He had never and would never hit on a military female, but fuck, it was nice to see a woman not hidden behind yards of blue fabric and terrified of Americans. Though the men still far outnumbered the women, he tried hard not to stare at the few women he did see like a hungry dog looking at a juicy, and very off limits steak. A cute brunette passed them and he desperately tried not think about how her breasts bounced with her walk. The first thing he was going to do when he got back to Texas was find some pretty young thing to ride him until he was raw and smiling.

"Put your eyeballs back where they belong, knucklehead."

Wyatt grinned at his friend. "How's Jody doing?"

Aaron's smiled slipped. "She's good. Just misses me. You know, fuck, since we've been married, I've been deployed longer than I was ever around her."

That was one of the reasons Wyatt had never settled down with anyone. He couldn't imagine leaving a wife behind or, worse, a wife and kids. He knew it ate at Aaron to be away from his family and he felt sorry for his buddy. "Just think about how happy she's gonna be when you go home next month."

Aaron let out a deep sigh and nodded. "I'll make it up to her."

"I'm sure you will." He sniffed the air, the scent of something resembling good food making his stomach rumble. "How's the chow?"

"Great. Nothin' like mom's home cooking, but better than that shit they feed you out in the field." He stopped at a pair of double doors and led Wyatt inside the canteen. "We even have a couple of fast food joints set up. There's a Burger King, Taco Bell, and even a Pizza Hut."

His stomach growled at the thought of a huge slice of greasy pizza. "Shit, if I'd known this place was a resort I would'a got myself shot to get here earlier. I could eat a whole large pizza by myself. Lead the way."

They laughed and Wyatt had to keep from drooling once they entered the area of the canteen where the civilian food was served. Wyatt found himself suddenly starved for fresh produce and he ordered an enormous chef salad in addition to his pizza. Following Aaron through the maze of crowded tables, Wyatt was hailed by some of the men in the room that he knew. It seemed like everywhere he turned there was a face he remembered and something in his heart eased a bit to know they were still alive.

After chowing down half the salad he paused and looked up at Aaron, ready for his friend to start briefing him about the base. Before he could say anything a hint of gold caught his eye. His world stopped and his focus narrowed on the exquisite face of the most beautiful woman he'd ever seen.

Her pale blonde hair was pulled back into a tight bun no different than the look worn by the rest of the women on the base, but a strand had escaped and curled against her cheek. A bit of softness in the harsh, unforgiving desert. She was tall, probably a few inches shorter than his six foot height and, even in the baggy utilities, her legs seemed to go on forever. She turned from where she'd been talking to her friend and his heart thudded. A smile still curved her full pink lips, revealing straight white teeth that must have been some dentist's pride and joy. His gaze traveled upwards, taking in a pert nose and high cheekbones, before reaching the bluest eyes he'd ever seen.

She raised her eyebrows and gave him a look that was like a mental slap upside his head. Clearly, she'd seen the way he'd been staring at her. Embarrassment flooded him when he realized she'd caught him gawking like some dumb boot. Still, he couldn't look away as he gazed into her bluer than blue eyes. They were the color of the sky, but not the sky here. Something about the desert seemed to fade out the sky in Afghanistan until it seemed almost insubstantial. Her eyes were the color of the sky on a perfectly clear fall day back in Texas.

Something in her expression shifted and her look turned from 'don't even think about it' to a more predatory gleam like that of a lioness looking down from her sun-warmed rock. Jesus Christ, his brain must have been roasted in his helmet because he knew better than to stare at a female like he wanted to fuck her. Especially a complete stranger at his new base, not to mention an officer.

He quickly looked away and busied himself with shoving food into his mouth. When he looked up again she was gone, but Aaron was grinning at him.

"So terribly sad. Another fool falls hard – helpless victim to the charms of our esteemed Lieutenant Sapphire."

"What?"

"That officer you were drooling all over? The tall blonde that has you blushing like a pretty little school girl? That's Lieutenant Sapphire."

"Fuck you," Wyatt grumbled in a low voice. "I wasn't staring at her."

"Yeah, right. You've loved blondes since we went to junior high together. If I remember right, your first girlfriend was the fair-haired Mary Olsen."

He looked up at his buddy with a grin. "Ah yes, Mary Olsen. The girl who taught me how to French kiss." Laughing, Wyatt leaned back. "Come on, man, you know me better than that. I always toe the line when it comes to the females, especially ones that outrank me."

"Good, 'cause I need you to keep an eye on her."

"Why?"

"Because she's a damn fine doctor." Aaron

lowered his voice and leaned closer. "And she's the daughter of Senator Sapphire from Illinois who's chairman of the Senate Appropriations Subcommittee for Defense. Not to mention her granddaddy was also a Senator and a General in the Army during World War II."

"Huh. What the fuck is she doing over here in this shit hole? PR for daddy?"

"Not as far as I can tell. She mostly keeps to herself and doesn't talk at all about her family." Aaron shrugged. "Sapphire can be a royal bitch, but she is one of the best doctors I've ever seen. She's brought men of mine back from the dead, I swear to God...but she's a bit hard to work with."

Wyatt groaned. "What the fuck are you saddling me with? If anything happens to her you know my ass will be on the line."

"It's not that bad. You just have to do things her way and you're good to go. Some of the surgeons don't like her because she questions them on some of their medical decisions. But thing is, she's always right. Some of the male surgeons don't give a fuck if she's right or wrong, the fact that she even questions them puts their panties in a bunch. They think they're god's gift, so to have a woman call them on their shit really pisses them off. It also doesn't help that ass kissing doesn't get anywhere with her. I've seen more than one 'god's gift to women' doctor slink away with his tail between his legs." He listlessly picked at his food. "Just keep an eye on her, help her out when you can. Develop a professional relationship with her and let her know she can count on you. And I do mean professional; don't give anyone anything to use against either you or her."

"So you're basically assigning me to be her bitch?"

Aaron kicked at him under the table. "Be your usual charming self and everything should be fine."

Two Months Later

Stepping over to the side, Wyatt tried to not see the blood stains on the floor from where the last man had been brought in. A Marine transport vehicle had hit an IED, and then, when the corpsman went to help the injured, snipers had opened up from the hills around them. It had been a total Charlie Foxtrot. They'd gotten five of the guys here and he didn't think most of them were going to make it.

They'd lost too much blood. When someone bled out it always shocked him just how much liquid the human body holds. Enough to fill this hallway and he could only imagine what the OR looked like. His stomach tightened and he tried not to breathe through his nose, hating the metallic, wet iron smell of fresh blood.

He passed someone in scrubs cleaning up the still red splashes, and he had to steel himself against the rush of empathy that tempted him to really think about those men who had just died. These were not faceless Marines, but someone's son, husband, brother, father. Gritting his teeth he forced himself to bottle everything up and went in search of Lieutenant Sapphire. He had a package of much needed meds that had just arrived, and he knew she'd want them right away.

He stopped close to the entrance to the women's dressing room where Sapphire would probably be cleaning up right now. She'd been in the thick of the action, frantically working to keep the men alive long enough for transfusions and surgery. He'd been one of the people who'd helped bring in the wounded from the helicopter landing area and knew exactly what she'd been through.

Hopefully, this package would cheer her up. If that didn't work, he'd reveal that his Mom had sent him more chocolate chip cookies.

He wasn't sure how much time had passed, but when Michelle came out of the dressing room looking as perfect as ever, he noticed right away that something was very wrong.

He took a step forward. "Lieutenant, I have the meds you requested."

She walked right past him, her jaw clenched hard enough that he could see the strain from the muscles extending down into her neck. Alarm bells went off in his head and he quietly followed her outside. She paused as the sun hit her and he hoped that might snap her out of it, but she just looked away and made a straight, stiff bee-line for a supply tent.

The young boot guarding the tent said something to Sapphire and she briskly nodded her head once in return. As soon as she was inside he came up to the young Marine still standing guard.

"Hilbert, no one comes into this tent until Lieutenant Sapphire comes out. Got it?"

Something about Michelle must have worried the boot because he nodded with a grim look. "Don't worry, Gunny, the lieutenant will have her privacy while she looks for supplies."

Giving the kid a nod he moved into the stuffy interior of the tent. Boxes of medical supplies were stacked almost to the ceiling, forming walls like a maze. He walked through the boxes until he found her.

She stood stock still, almost like a statue, and stared at one of the boxes. A fine tremor ran through her and he mentally cursed. Something had happened with those men today that had hit her on a personal level. He'd seen it before. Someone who looked like your best friend, or your wife, or your brother would get hurt and the shit would get real personal real quick. It was funny how the mind could so easily imagine terrible things.

"Hey, Sapphire, your meds came in."

She quickly turned on him, her lovely lips drawing back from her teeth in a snarl. "Get the fuck out of here!"

Narrowing his eyes, he stood his ground. "Fuck you, Sapphire, I ain't going anywhere."

He took a step closer and she trembled. God dammit. If she was a guy he'd have no trouble calling her out and giving her a chance to work off the stress and adrenalin in the fight ring. But she was a female, soft and vulnerable. He could never hit her.

To his shock, she slapped him across the face. "Get out!"

His cheek stung and he saw her brace in preparation to throw a punch and he immediately dropped the package and caught her upraised hand. When she moved to strike with her free hand, using the hand he held as leverage, he spun her around and held her tight against his chest.

She struggled against his restraint, her strength surprising him. The fact that she wasn't screaming for help or doing anything to attract attention let him know how out of it she really was. He'd never seen Michelle like this. She was always the ice queen, cool and collected, but this hell cat in his arms was spitting fire.

"You better fucking let me go, Callahan."

She tried to kick his shin and he took her to the ground. There was no fucking way he was going to let her use him like a punching bag. He kept his weight on her, giving her something to fight against, to let loose her rage. She bucked and writhed beneath him, panting, not saying anything other than an almost constant stream of cursing him out under her breath. After about a minute of this she began to tire and stopped cursing, instead, panting as she pushed listlessly at his arms.

"It's okay, Sapphire. I've got you. Let it out. You're only human. If you keep that shit bottled up, it'll destroy you from the inside out and you'll be no good to anyone, not your patients, not even yourself. I've seen it happen to many good men, killin' them a little bit at a time. Let it go, darlin'."

Finally, she began to settle, then stilled. A moment later the first wrenching sob came and his heart ached at the utter misery of her cry. He rolled to the side and managed to get them both up. The moment they were standing, he let her go and her legs buckled almost sending her to the floor before he had a chance to grab her. Her weight fell against his body and he held her as tight and close as he could, letting her use him for comfort. It killed him to see her like this. After she'd soaked his shirt with her tears, she began to take those hitching breaths that usually signaled the end of a hard cry.

The strength began to return to her body, and as it did, he lessened his hold until it was more of an embrace than a hug. Michelle must have noticed a difference as well, because she slowly slid her arms down from around his neck, her fingertips trailing over his banging pulse, and down to his collar. She stepped away, and he was grateful because he was getting an erection and didn't want her to see it. She'd trusted him to comfort her like a friend, something he'd done for countless numbers of his men over the years. Many of those confrontations had ended with the Marine breaking down as Wyatt gave him a hug, but it had never ended with lightning sparking through his blood.

Fuck, she'd been so soft, so warm against him. Her hair smelled like peaches and vanilla, an entirely too edible scent that made him think about the soft, peach-like cleft between a woman's legs, hot and wet for him to eat. It had been a long time since he'd had the simple pleasure of a woman's body in his arms and he missed it.

Straightening her uniform and blotting the tears off her face, Michelle refused to look at him. He watched as she slowly rebuilt the defensive walls that would protect herself from the soul-killing hell that was daily life here in the sandbox. He cleared his throat but his voice still came out rough. "Lieutenant mind telling me what set you off? I'm askin' 'cause I want to make sure if you're faced with something like that again, I'll know in advance."

"This won't happen again."

He wanted to kick her in the ass for being so stubborn. "You're not a robot, Sapphire. Regardless of if it will or won't happen, I don't want to have to go around worrying about you."

She cut her gaze to him, raw emotion battling with her aura of cool disdain. "You worry about me?"

"Well, not like I'm your fucking mother or anything, but yeah. You keep my men alive, and take care of everyone around you. I've got to make sure that you take care of yourself as well."

She looked away and spoke quickly, so fast he had a problem making out the words. "He looked like a man I used to know. Owen. He had the same freckles over his nose and deep auburn hair."

"Good enough. If any gingers come through I'll make sure to shave 'em bald before you see them. Then you can just think of Doctor Evil."

Closing her eyes, she shook her head. "Callahan, I swear your mother drank when she was pregnant with you."

"That's a good possibility. I was conceived after a Pink Floyd concert."

Taking a deep breath, she squared her shoulders and turned the full force of her gaze on him. The icy shields guarding her heart were fully back in place and once again he was confronted by a woman who seemed to radiate control and power. But now he knew about the fire hidden beneath that icy surface, and he found the contrast almost impossible to resist.

He was so fucked.

"You had some meds for me?"

"Oh, yeah."

He bent down and fumbled for the bag where

he'd tossed it and swore he heard Sapphire give a little moan of appreciation. Trying to keep a straight face while he mentally attempted to get his semi-hard cock to stand down, he handed her the bag.

She took it, careful not to let their fingers touch, and lifted her chin. "Thank you, Callahan."

Hearing her say his name for the first time did funny things to his stomach and he tried to keep from smiling. "Most welcome, Sapphire."

She shook her head and blew out a weary breath. "Okay, Marine, this never happened. Got it?"

"Yes, ma'am."

"Good." She turned and walked back towards the entrance of the supply tent, her perfect ass swinging in a rhythm that matched the pounding of the blood rushing to his cock.

He absently wondered just how he'd pissed off the karma gods to deserve this kind of punishment, the pain of having almost constant blue balls, and a woman he'd love to fuck for days within reach but totally off limits. Yeah, this had to be his own personal hell. The scent of her soap still clung to his hands and he took a deep breath, knowing that he'd be jacking off and thinking about all the raw, dirty things he'd like to do to her all night.

Four Months Later

The big M-ATV that Wyatt was driving eased through another tooth-rattling pothole, one of many littering the road where IEDs had either been removed or had exploded. He was nearing the end of his tour and, while he couldn't wait to get back to the States, he sure would miss the woman sitting next to him in the passenger seat.

Lieutenant Sapphire stared out the windshield, her gaze unfocused and unseeing. They rode in companionable silence, chatter coming from the back of their vehicle as the supply caravan they were in made its way west of Kabul. Sapphire had been tapped to replace some dumb fuck doctor who'd been sent back stateside to serve a couple months in the brig for negligent weapons discharge. That stupid fucker had somehow managed to accidentally shoot a Marine while fucking around with his gun. Wyatt would be there for a couple weeks to help refresh everyone on weapons safety, then he was finally going to be done with this rotation from hell. This would be their last ride together and he almost welcomed the mind numbingly slow pace they were keeping because that meant he got to spend a few more moments with her.

He stole a glance at her out of the corner of his eye, trying to memorize her features. Rumor had it she came from big time serious money back home and he could see that. She carried herself like a lady in the truest sense of the word. Oh, she could talk shit with the best of them, but she had class. All the guys stood a bit taller when she was around and, while she was always as polite as could be around her superiors, he'd seen more than one occasion when she'd gone toe to toe with a superior officer over a medical decision that she believed would endanger her patient's life.

Wyatt and Sapphire gotten into it a few times as well when he thought she'd been pushing herself too hard. A human being could only go so long without sleep and Sapphire would stay up for days at a time tending to wounded if they let her. Damn stubborn woman. He'd switched her regular coffee with decaf one night in an effort to get her to sleep. She'd crashed earlier than usual, and he'd been tempted to do it again, but the other doctors informed him that if he ever switched around the coffee pots again he'd find himself on the wrong end of a scalpel.

She cleared her throat and shifted so she was looking at him instead of the road. "Callahan, I wanted to say thanks."

"For what, ma'am?"

He switched on his headlights as the sun dipped below the horizon and checked the time. Their trip had taken longer than expected due to the number of IEDs that had to be removed from the road before they could proceed. Right now, they were driving over a winding road that curved around a set of hills.

She smiled, more a curving of the corners of her lips than a true grin. "Do you think I didn't notice the upswing in men doing mountain climbers after you arrived?"

He stared at the road like it was suddenly infested with sharks. "I don't know what you're talking about, ma'am."

"Must have been my imagination when I saw you yelling at them to climb higher, to keep climbing until they remembered that the nurses inside that tent were superior officers, not some cute girl from their high school."

Heat filled his cheeks. "Must have been someone else. Us jarheads all look alike."

"Hmmm. Well, regardless, I appreciated it. It's nice knowing I have someone at my back I can trust."

He wasn't sure, but he could have sworn he heard a bit of heat in her voice. Then again, he was so obsessed with her it wasn't even funny. While he knew she was way out of his league, and completely hands off as not only a superior officer, but a superior officer in a war zone, that didn't stop him from thinking about what it could be like to hold her, to kiss her. The peach and vanilla scent of her shampoo haunted his sleep and he'd had more sexual dreams about Michelle than he'd had about any woman since he'd hit puberty.

She cracked her neck and sighed. "I can't fucking wait to be able to walk around without this heavy ass body armor."

"You have what, another six months?"

"Yep."

She leaned forward and looked out the windshield as the brake lights on the M-ATV in front of them flared red. The caravan slowed to a crawl and Wyatt hoped that whatever the fuck was holding them up would pass quickly so they could reach the other base. He really didn't like being out on the road at night.

"Any plans for after you get out, ma'am?"

"Not sure. I want to help those who can't get regular medical care - maybe volunteer at a free clinic or sign up with one of those doctors' organizations that treat the poor for free." She laughed. "I sure as shit don't want to return back to Chicago. Too fucking cold. What about you?"

"As soon as my time with Uncle Sam is up I'll be heading back to Austin."

She smiled. "I'm not surprised with the way you and Winters talked about Texas. You gonna go herd some cows, or whatever the hell it is cowboys do?"

Used to her good natured ribbing he shook his head. "No, ma'am. My dad is a master carpenter and I..."

Something hit the M-ATV in front of them from the left and his words vanished beneath a massive roar. Time slowed and he stared in disbelief as the vehicle in front of them blew up. He had a millisecond to register what had happened before shrapnel and larger metal fragments from the blast tore through their vehicle shattering the safety glass of the windshield.

Immense pain roared through his body and he blacked out.

When he came to Sapphire was leaning over him and yelling. "Wake the fuck up Callahan!"

"Doc?" His voice came out in a whisper and a shudder wracked his body from head to toe. He tried to remember what had happened. His senses started to come back and, as they did, he became aware of a terrible pain radiating from his lower abdomen. He reached down to his belly below his body armor. Before he could touch anything she smacked his hand away. "Don't fucking move, Callahan. Stay with me, okay?"

"What's wrong with me?" The pain began to register in his mind and he groaned, unable to form words.

"A mortar took out the vehicle in front of us. A piece of shrapnel sliced your gut open." She swallowed hard. "I'm holding your intestines in right now so don't fucking fight me and do not move."

Gunfire split the air somewhere ahead of them in a harsh chatter.

"Never...fight...you," he whispered. The world started to go soft and fuzzy and he gratefully began to slip back into unconsciousness. At least he would have if the woman holding his guts together hadn't started yelling at him again.

"Callahan, you wake the fuck up and stay with me. Look at me." Her voice had a demanding note mixed in with the command that scared him. He'd only heard her use that voice when she was ordering a patient on the OR table to stay alive, as if she could will them back from the edge.

He opened his eyes again and grimaced, or at least he thought he did. It felt as if he'd become strangely disconnected from his body. "Am I going to die?"

"Not on my watch, Marine. Trust me, Wyatt, I'm going to keep you alive even if I have to drag you back from the gates of Hell myself."

Screams filled the air around them and Wyatt wanted to tell her to go help the guys that needed her. A corpsman crouched down next to her with a first aid kit. They began to treat him as best they could, and he gave up trying to understand what they were saying, instead choking back his moans as they carefully touched places inside of him that should have never seen daylight. It really bugged the shit out of him that he couldn't remember what happened. The last thing he could recall was loading up the trucks this morning. He vaguely remembered that Sapphire was going to ride along with him, so that meant she must have been in the blast.

"L.T....you okay?" His lungs burned with the effort to speak, but he had to know.

"Some cuts and busies, no big deal."

Relieved, he stared at the sky overhead, bright pinpoints of light piercing the heavens where the first stars sparkled against the twilight. Wispy clouds took on a pink haze around the edges and he marveled at how something could be so beautiful while he lay dying on some god forsaken dirt road in the middle of hell.

"Callahan!"

"Wha...?"

"You stay with me you stubborn asshole. Look at me. Eyes on me Marine!" She grasped his chin in her hand and turned his face. When he looked into her eyes an electrical charge went through him at the emotion he saw there. An emotion so big it could only have one name but his rational mind refused to believe it.

"Never....leave...you."

"You're damn right you're never gonna leave. You are going to be okay. I'm not going to let you die. Just hold on, the choppers are on the way."

He tried to reply, but only a faint moan came out.

It hurt to breathe, and a sizzling pain tore a groan from him when she did something to him. "Sorry, Callahan. I'm being as gentle as I can but we have to get you stabilized. I think some of your intestines may have shrapnel wounds." Her voice trembled the slightest bit on her last word, probably not enough for anyone else but him to notice.

"S'kay if I die." He tried to take a deep breath and that ended in a moan. "Not...your fault."

The distant drone of choppers cutting through the air reached his ears and Sapphire let out a low breath. "They're almost here, Callahan. You keep fighting. That's an order, Marine. Don't you fucking pussy out on me now. You hear me, Wyatt? You must live."

He wanted to reply to her but doing anything other than dealing with the increasing agony was beyond him. From there everything blended into a haze of pain and movement. The last thing he remembered was her bluer than the bluest autumn sky eyes staring into his, filled with heartbreak and, he was sure now, love.

Chapter 2

Eight Months Later

Michelle Sapphire swallowed hard as Aaron Winters' oldest son, probably no more than thirteen, accepted the folded flag that had been draped over his father's coffin from the Marine honor guard. Next to him sat his mother, a small woman with mousy brown hair who looked shell shocked and fragile enough to shatter. Two weeks prior she'd filed for divorce from Aaron. Mrs. Winters stared at the coffin, her face totally devoid of emotion as she clutched a framed photograph of Aaron so hard her knuckles were white. Michelle's heart ached for her, and she wondered if someone was making sure she didn't follow her husband's lead and commit suicide. More family and friends filled the graveside and Michelle saw a few familiar faces from the Navy and Marines.

Michelle had been looking for one man in particular but so far she hadn't seen him. When she'd received the call from a friend about Winter's suicide she'd been absolutely floored. He'd been such a strong and vibrant man. He was the kind of guy that people would willingly follow not because he outranked them, but because he was a genuinely good leader. Never in a thousand years did she think that he'd eat his gun because of PTSD.

Before the image of his last moments could fully

form in her mind she forced herself to think about something else. Scanning the crowd on the other side of the coffin she caught a glimpse of weary hazel eyes staring in her direction her whole world froze.

Wyatt.

He looked away when he saw she'd noticed him and moved back into the crowd. That one glimpse of his face set off all the alarm bells in her head, and she had to keep herself from pushing through the mourners to find him. The priest droned on but she no longer heard the words, her thoughts too focused on Wyatt. Dark circles stood out beneath his eyes and his hair was a tad longer than she remembered. There was a gaunt look to his face that she'd never seen before. He must have returned from Walter Reed recently because she'd been keeping an eye out for him in Austin.

She wondered if he was shocked to see her but, then again, while he was recovering at Walter Reed she'd casually mentioned in a letter she'd written to him that she'd accepted a position at a free clinic in Austin. While she hadn't expected him to write back confessing his love for her, the fact that he hadn't written her back at all hurt. She'd thought they had a connection, something special, but it had apparently all been her imagination.

The service ended and people began to disperse to their cars. She spotted Wyatt by his dark hair and pinstriped grey suit as he walked between the gravestones to a big, dark green truck parked away from the rest of the mourners. After saying a few quick goodbyes she followed Wyatt, her attention focused on him with the precision of a laser. She tried to tell herself it was because she was worried about him, but she knew in her heart of hearts it was more.

A lot more.

He reached his truck and opened the passenger door before leaning inside. A second later, he straightened up and rested against the side of the truck. Something silver flashed in the sunlight and her stomach dropped when she realized he was chugging from a hip flask that probably wasn't filled with Kool-Aid. Anger mixed with her concern and she quickened her pace.

He glanced up right before she reached him and tried to hide the flask behind his back with a guilty look. His suit hung off of him and she was pretty sure he'd dropped at least twenty pounds. Sure, he could have lost muscle mass while recovering from his wounds, but she didn't think so. The lines around his mouth were deeper, and he hadn't even bothered to shave. She almost didn't recognize him as the strong, dependable man she'd known in Afghanistan. He studied her for a moment before his posture changed from a guilty slouch to an arrogant lean. Then he turned on the charm, giving her the smile that never failed to make her heart skip a beat

"Lieutenant, I'm surprised to see you here."

"Callahan, what the *fuck* are you doing?"

He flushed. "Same as you, attending the funeral. What're you doing in Austin?"

"I live here." She frowned at his surprised look. "Didn't you get my letter?"

"What letter?"

"The one I sent you at Walter Reed."

"No." He shoved the flask in his jacket pocket

and started to turn away. "I've gotta go. Maybe we can get together sometime."

She pushed at his shoulder, turning him to face her again. "If you think I'm going to let you drive, you're probably high as well as drunk."

"I'm not drunk," he snarled and jerked away before slamming the truck's passenger door.

Oh, so it was going to be like that was it? Fine. If he wanted to dance, she'd dance.

Refusing to be intimidated by his anger, knowing he would never hurt her, she got right up into his personal space. "You're going to get into my car and I'm going to drive you home. If you give me any bullshit about it, I *will* call the police. Fuck, Callahan, do you want to kill someone because you decided to drive drunk after your friend's funeral?"

He recoiled as if she'd slapped him. Michelle watched Wyatt try to regain control of himself – first anger, then fear followed quickly by indignation. "I would never do that. I can handle my shit. And just who the fuck do you think you are? We're not in the military anymore and I don't have to listen to your bitching."

"How many times have you driven drunk?"

He opened and closed his mouth, but didn't say anything, the guilt and shame evident on his face.

"That's what I thought." She held out her hand. "Give me your keys."

Scowling, he did as she asked. After making sure his truck was locked up, she looked over her shoulder at him.

"Come on, my rental's over this way."

Her heart hurt for him as she caught a hint of the immense sorrow burdening his heart. She held out her hand to him, wanting to give him comfort even if he wasn't ready for her brand of tough love. He stared at her outstretched hand and slowly lifted his. When his calloused fingers brushed hers electricity sparked through her entire body, starting a slow burn between her legs. She couldn't believe she was actually touching him, but fought to keep her emotions off her face. He needed her strength right now.

They walked hand in hand through the cemetery over to her gray sedan. She clicked the key fob to unlock it and reluctantly let go of his hand. "I swore after getting out of the Navy I'd never own anything gray again, but this was the last car the rental place had available."

He slid into the car without comment and she followed suit. After starting the engine and putting on a soft classical station she looked at him. "Mind putting your address into the GPS?"

The scent of liquor reached her nose as he leaned over and began keying in his information. His hair had grown long enough so it brushed his ears and she found she rather liked the streaks of silver that were coming in around his temples, giving him a distinguished, seductive look. Then again everything he did made her hot, so it was no wonder she found his gray hair sexy.

"Doc, I mean, Michelle, uh-sorry about yelling at you."

She didn't comment, just drove out of the cemetery and followed the directions given by the female voice from the GPS unit.

"So, you live here now?"

"Yes." She glanced at him then back at the road. "I bought some land outside of Austin."

"Where at?"

"Southwest of Lakeway. Where are you calling home?"

He fiddled with the door. "Right now, just an apartment down by Buda."

"Is that where your family is? I remember you mentioning something about your mother being a high school teacher in Buda."

Surprise crossed his weary, but still handsome features. "Yeah. I didn't realize you were paying attention."

"Wyatt, I've always paid attention to everything you said."

"Me too, Doc, me too." He shifted like he was going to touch her, then clenched his hands together in his lap. "So how're ya liking Austin?"

"It's nice."

She glanced over at him and her heartbeat picked up. From the moment she saw him she wanted him but, first, he needed to know some things about her. She wasn't going to change who she was but, at the same time, she really wanted to get to know Wyatt better. Something about him called to her heart, and to her soul, in a way she hadn't felt in years.

"I found a local club that I go to now and again."

"Really? What club? Maybe I could meet you there sometime." He cleared his throat and quickly added. "You know, to catch up and stuff."

"It's called Lila's." She waited for his reaction, half expecting him to say that yes he did, indeed, know of the BDSM club and went there often. It wouldn't surprise her one bit to find out that he was a Dom.

"Never heard of it."

She licked her lips and decided to go for broke. Life was too short to tip toe around shit. "It's a BDSM club."

His jaw dropped and he stared at her. It would have been comical if she hadn't been so unsure of his reaction. "No fucking way."

"Yes fucking way." She tried to keep her voice cool and measured even though she had a million butterflies dancing around in her belly. "I'm a Domme."

"A what?"

"A Mistress...a Dominatrix. Take your pick of titles but that's what I am and what I enjoy."

"No. Fucking. Way." He sat up straighter. "So...you like to beat the shit out of guys?"

"No!" She took a deep breath and tried to calm herself. "No, I do not beat the shit out of guys." His disbelieving stare made her shake her head. "Well, okay, I only beat them if they ask nicely."

"But isn't whipping some poor bastard's ass what Dominatrices do? I mean, at least that's what they do in pornos. Oh God, you don't want to pee on me do you?" She shot him a dirty look and he grinned. "What?"

"If you base your beliefs on how women behave on pornos, then I think I'm very wrong about what kind of man you are."

"Hey now, I was just kidding." He scrubbed his hand over his face. "I mean, fuck, I never would've thought you were into that kind of kinky shit."

She tapped her finger on the steering wheel as they waited for the light to change. "I am, and if any man wants to be with me, he'd better understand what he's in for. I'm not going to pretend to be someone I'm not for anyone."

That shut him up and he stared out the window as they drew closer to his apartment building. "I can understand that...but, I mean, I'm not trying to be outta line, and I could be totally misreading this, but I'm not the kind of guy that could let a woman boss him around."

She wanted to point out that she'd done just that while they were over in the sandbox, and that he'd been quite happy following her directions, but she didn't think that was the right approach. With all of her heart she wanted Wyatt, and was pretty damned sure he wanted her, but she also wanted more than meaningless sex.

She wanted a submissive.

"Why don't you research it a little bit. And no, I'm not talking about watching pornos."

He blew out a harsh breath, the scent of alcohol drifting through the air. "Doc, I don't know what to say."

"I understand."

An uncomfortable silence descended on them, but she wasn't going to break it by begging him to give being her sub a chance. So what if she still dreamt of him? So what if being this near to him set her body on fire? And, dammit all, so what if she thought there was something special between them? If bottoming for her didn't turn him on, if it wasn't something he could learn to appreciate and crave, then their hypothetical relationship would never work.

Maybe she was coming on too strong, too desperate. She'd been looking for him for months now and thinking about how good it would be to see him again. She hadn't taken into account that he might not be adapting to civilian life as well as she had. And his drinking worried her.

He leaned forward when they reached the entrance to his apartment complex. "I'm the third building on the left."

She pulled into a spot near the entrance to his unit and put the car into park before turning to him. "Well, here we are."

"Yeah." He made no move to open the door, but he also wouldn't look at her.

She reached into the back seat and dug around in her purse for a pen and one of her business cards. While writing on the back of it she said, "Here's my card. My home number and cell are on the back. If you ever need me, call me."

He took it from her, their fingers brushing. For a long moment he didn't say anything, then he leaned across the seat, his intent obvious. Everything inside of her clenched in anticipation, her need for his touch deep enough to drown in. At the first brush of his lips against hers she trembled.

The second pass of his lips was a little bolder, lingering against hers before slanting his head and giving her a kiss that sent a warm cascade of tingles through her body, awakening her senses to him in a decadent rush of lust. She opened her mouth and he groaned, taking advantage of the invitation and meeting her tongue with firm strokes of his own. Unable to help herself, she fisted her hand into his hair, holding him still. God, he was so big, so strong. Here in the confines of her car he seemed to take up most of the space. She thought about what it would be like to rub her body against his muscled frame, to orgasm merely from her flesh sliding against his.

Moving back just enough to break their kiss she whispered against his lips, "Hold still. I want to enjoy you."

He did as she asked and she began to slowly devour his mouth, tasting and sucking on his lips, paying attention to his every shift, to the changes in energy coming off his body. Her mind kept stumbling over the fact that this was Callahan, the same man she'd absolutely lusted after but who'd been totally off limits. He groaned when she nipped his lower lip and pulled her into his arms when she sucked on his tongue. Beneath the loose suit jacket his body was still firm, solid muscle, and she ran her hands over him trying to memorize the feel of his form.

When his hand went to her waist and began to travel towards her breast, she reluctantly broke their kiss.

"Come upstairs with me," Wyatt urged, his eyes fever-bright with need.

Oh, she was sorely tempted to go up there with him, to lose herself in fucking this amazing man, but she wanted more. As hard as it was, she somehow managed to shake her head. "No, Wyatt."

His face fell and he pulled back, reaching for the door. "Yeah, well it's been goo—"

"Wait. I'm not saying no, or that I don't want you. Right now I could fuck you up one side of the room and down the other, but I want more than that." She hesitated, then decided to tell him a little bit of the truth.

"Something happened a while ago that taught me to live everyday like it's my last and I... fuck, I'm explaining this badly."

He reached across and ran his knuckles down her cheek, his eyes becoming heavy lidded with desire. "Take your time."

"Look, I don't want just a fuck. I want more, but I don't know if we could work out long term." His hurt look cut at her heart and she tried again. "Being a Domme is part of who I am, it's as much a part of me as my hair or the color of my eyes. I was born this way, and I can't become something I'm not in order to please someone. I need someone who won't just be my partner, but will also be my submissive. And I don't want someone who will fake it. I want someone who craves my dominance."

He closed his eyes and thunked his head back against the seat. "Right now my cock wants me to say whatever I need to in order to get you into my bed, but that wouldn't be fair to either of us. I don't know if I can be, you know, like that with you."

"How about this? You do some research and call me if you have any questions."

"'Kay." The look he gave her let her know that phone call would probably never come. "I'll see you around, Doc."

"I really hope you call, Wyatt."

He shoved the card into his pocket and got out of the car without looking back. "Thanks for the ride."

Before she could say anything more he shut the door and left her alone with her thoughts, the scent of his cologne and the alcohol on his breath still hung in the air. As she watched him walk into the building she had to fight herself to keep from running after him. Every word she'd said had been true, and she told herself that if they were meant to be together he'd call. Still, as she pulled out of the parking lot and back onto the main road she didn't wipe away the tears that rolled down her cheek.

Chapter 3

Present Day

The darkness of deep night still reigned when Michelle pulled into the long, paved drive of her ranch. Callahan woke up when she called his name, blinking in confusion as he took in his surroundings. When his gaze turned to her his eyes widened and he rubbed his face, then looked again.

She waited for his brain to kick in while they drove past the empty paddocks and fenced in meadows that covered the front two acres of her property. Back in the fifties this had been a working ranch, but when she bought it last year, it had been a neglected mess. The main house came into view, a stately Spanish style home with a stacked river stones foundation, softened by the cream stucco walls leading up to the red tile roof and the exposed stone chimneys. Lights shown from the wrought iron chandelier hanging in the main foyer, visible through the vaulted windows.

Instead of pulling into the garage she pulled up to the front door. Thankfully her chef and grounds keeper as well as long time good friends, Yuki and James, were still asleep in their log cabin past the stables. The last thing she needed was them noticing her late arrival. In an odd way, she felt like a teenager coming home past curfew and trying to sneak in. Not that James and Yuki would have done anything except cheer that she'd finally broken her celibacy, but she had enough on her plate right now.

Putting the car in park, she raised the roof and secured it back in place.

Callahan finally broke the silence. "Nice place, Doc."

"Thank you. I've been remodeling it for months now; I'm almost done." She opened her door and stepped out with Callahan following suit. When they reached the front door he patiently waited for her to unlock it, then opened it for her. One of the things she'd always liked about him was his old world manners, even if his smart mouth usually ruined the effect.

Once they entered the foyer he wandered over to the fountain that sat in the middle of the large space, perfectly tucked beneath the winding staircase leading to the second level. A low, amber glow came from the chandelier above that gave the Mexican tile floors a mellow sheen. The fountain stood almost as high as Callahan was tall, a bronze sculpture of horses running through the surf. The water of the fountain flowed beneath the horses' hooves as they ran through the waves.

He didn't look at her, trailing his finger through the water. "I thought I heard a horse neigh outside. Do you ride?"

"Yes, we had horses when I was growing up. Right now I have two, an Arabian and a Tennessee Walker. Yuki and James, my chef and grounds keeper respectively as well as good friends, are thinking about getting horses, but they're not sure if they want to put down roots in Austin yet." She moved into his line of sight, resting her hip against the edge of the fountain. "Now tell me, Callahan, are you ready for my help?"

Need blazed across his weary features, but his stubborn pride was stronger...for now. "No, Doc. I don't need your help. I'm fine." She arched her brow and he flushed, looking down at the rolling waves around the horse's feet. "I mean we all have our problems, right? Everyone has a cross to bear."

"Callahan, right now you're not dragging that cross, you're nailed to it."

"I'm fine," he said in a low, dangerous tone.

Oh, she'd hit too close to home and he didn't like it. Well, now, it was time to find out how far she could push him, if she'd totally misread him and whether or not he'd try something physical. Her mind slipped one notch higher, taking her into a more aggressive headspace, a place where she was a Mistress and expected to be treated as such.

Plus, she was tired and she wanted to go to bed.

"You have a choice. Tonight you can sleep in your own guest room where everything you need will be provided for you. We'll have breakfast tomorrow morning and then you'll be off, back to your home, back to the punk ass excuses that your family lets you get away with."

"Fu—"

"I'm not done!" Her voice echoed in the large foyer, the same voice she'd used as a battlefield surgeon to get a bunch of shell-shocked, wounded Marines to listen to her. "Eyes on me."

His head whipped up and he swallowed hard. She ignored the urge to take him in her arms and comfort him. He closed his eyes and breathed out, "Yes ma'am."

"I'm assuming you did some research on BDSM

since we last spoke."

He nodded, but didn't volunteer any information. She was actually glad because she had enough mental gymnastics to perform with him already. They'd have a deep, philosophical discussion about the lifestyle later. Well, she hoped they would.

"As I said, you can stay in the lower level bedroom, sleep it off, and I'll have my groundskeeper drive you home in the morning. We part ways, never to speak again. Or, there is the second option..."

"That's a little harsh, don't you think?"

"Not at all. I'm being honest with you, Wyatt. Both you and I know that I want you as more than a guy to fuck when I have the urge. If you're really thinking about giving this a go with me, being my submissive in truth, I expect you to be aware from the start how things will work."

"Wait, I'd like to make something a hard limit or negotiate it or some shit."

Curious now, she nodded and he gave her a dangerous look that tightened things low in her belly. "When we're in the bedroom I'll bottom for you, but out in the real world I want to have an equal say in things. I don't want one of those relationships where I have to walk five paces behind you."

She snorted. "That is so not my thing. Tell you what, I will always consider you as an equal, a partner, but in the bedroom and sometimes at a club or friend's private party I may want you there as my submissive, not my vanilla boyfriend. And by bedroom I mean my whole house."

"Just don't make me get naked in front of your

gardener or groundskeeper or whatever." He closed his eyes, rolling his neck. "Fuck, I'm tired, Doc. Can we talk about this in the morning?"

"Yes. But I haven't given you your second option yet."

He grinned at her, the lines deepening around his mouth. "Okay, what's behind door number two?"

"That you come upstairs with me and sleep in my room."

Now his eyes flew wide open and she suppressed a smile. His shocked look was almost comical. Then, his male brain kicked in and she could almost smell the surge of testosterone flooding his body. Sure enough, his lips curved in that familiar smirk and his chin titled up at an arrogant angle, and he gave her a leering wink. "I'll take door number two, please."

"Don't get cheeky with me." She held him with her gaze and the force of her will alone. Her dominance wasn't a role she was playing in order to fulfill a kinky urge, this was who she was. And the sooner Wyatt recognized it the better it would be for both of them. "If you decide to come to bed with me tonight, we will sleep. You will not try to take advantage of the situation in any way. Understood?"

"Yes, ma'am."

He had a devilish glint in his eyes, the kind of spark that made things warm low in her body. She couldn't help but notice how big and strong his hands were, and she knew he could kiss. Lord, could that man kiss. What was it about bad boys, the man who could and would push her limits, who also had the strength necessary to submit himself to her will? She liked a man with some steel in his spine, a warrior who would bow to no one but her. But with that strength came a great deal of work for a Mistress to remind him who was on top.

"In the morning you will undoubtedly wake before I do. When you do you will open the top drawer of the table next to the bed. You'll find a sheet of paper in there, a proposal. You have until I wake to think about it. If you agree to my terms you will draw me a bath and wait for me. If you don't agree with the terms, go to the stables to the right of the house and let my groundskeeper know you need to borrow a car to get home." He gave her a questioning look. "And I'm not letting you drive the Corvette. I've ridden along with you on transport, Gunny, and you driving my 'Vette isn't happening in this lifetime."

"A man can dream."

"So where would you like to sleep, Wyatt?"

"Shit, you don't have to ask me twice."

"Eloquent as always." She held out her hand, a great deal of relief flooding her that he'd taken the first step towards becoming hers. Her man to heal and cherish. She had to remember that he came with some major baggage, and she had her own cross to bear, but right now she was almost giddy with relief that he was still here.

A ghost of guilt brushed her soul that she was bringing a man to her bed for the first time since her fiancé Owen's death, but it wasn't like she was breaking the promise she'd made on his grave. She was sure when Owen died that there was no chance she would ever love another man like she loved him. Now, she wasn't so sure; maybe it was possible to love again. Or, if not love again, maybe to truly care about someone else. Wyatt needed her help, needed her.

And in her own way, she needed him just as much.

Keeping all of those intense emotions off her face became even harder when he slipped his hand into hers, calluses still heavy on his palms. She wondered what he did that kept his hands in such rough shape. Even more, she wondered what they would feel like on her body. As she held his hand she did so at an angle that kept him a half step behind her, not the five that he'd feared.

While he hadn't agreed to anything yet, old habits die hard and, on a barely conscious level, she'd begun to coast through the lowest levels of her Domme space, a state of mind as natural to her as breathing. It also felt like a part of her soul that hadn't stirred since Owen's death was slowly waking again and that scared her. If she ever fell in love with someone again and lost them, she was sure she wouldn't make it.

They went up to the second floor together and headed left, to her wing of the house. Opening one of the cedar double doors she led Wyatt into her room and smiled when he stopped and stared.

"Not what you were expecting?"

He moved further into the room and turned in a slow circle, taking in the fifteen-foot ceiling consisting of exposed timbers and skylights. She flicked a switch next to the door and the gas logs in the fireplace came to life, creating twisting shadows on the sturdy mission style furniture draped with colorful Native American rugs. The warm colors complimented Wyatt's deeply tanned skin, giving it a bronze gleam that begged for her touch. Studying his face, she watched as his gaze went down the enormous river stone fireplace and to the polished floors.

He squatted down and ran his fingers over the boards near his feet conjuring an image of him doing that naked, with his hands behind his head and his testicles just begging for her touch. "What kind of wood is this?"

She had to swallow hard before she could speak. "It's actually a combination of the floors that we were able to salvage when we started rebuilding."

He stood and looked around the room again. "They're really nice. I've been working for my dad doing carpentry and carving, mostly handling the detailed inlays and delicate stuff. He'd love these floors."

His gaze flickered to her enormous canopy bed made of unfinished oak logs. She knew her bed was a bit excessive with its deep burgundy silk sheets, fluffy goose down quilt, and mountain of pillows, but she loved coming home to such a luxurious comfort. Anyone who'd ever spent months sleeping on a cot knew the decadent pleasure a good bed provided. Next to the bed on either side were thick cream sheepskin rugs, put there to keep the morning chill from her feet.

"Shoes off at the door."

He complied and hesitantly followed her. She sat on the edge of the bed and toed her own shoes off. "The bathroom is through that door. There are some unopened toothbrushes in the vanity. Feel free to brush up, shower, whatever."

He nodded and walked away with a dazed expression. How she would love to be able to be in his head right now. Once he closed the door behind himself she let out a breath and flopped back on her bed, her arms spread wide as she started at the ceiling.

She'd have to call the clinic and let them know she'd be taking a couple weeks off. She hadn't taken any vacation since she started volunteering and the full-time employees were always telling her to take a break. There were enough local doctors who volunteered as well, so they would be able to cover her absence.

God, she was planning this like he'd already said yes. With a groan she covered her eyes. He hadn't agreed to anything other than spending the night, and what she was going to ask from him was way out of his comfort zone. Most guys didn't do well with change, and she was going to try to get him to change the way he viewed the world, to get him to start living life instead of waiting to die. She needed to help him learn how to appreciate the simple joys in life again, to want to live another day, to have hope. He liked to be needed and she already needed him far more than she wanted to admit.

"Doc?"

She'd been so preoccupied with her thoughts she hadn't even heard him come out of the bathroom. As she sat up the strap of her tank top slid off her shoulder and she didn't bother to pull it back up, liking the way Wyatt focused on her now totally exposed shoulder.

She shifted and his gaze returned to her face. "Yes?"

"I feel bad for dragging you out of bed. I'd like to make it up to you."

She smiled and enjoyed the way his eyes widened. "You might want to wait to see where you're sleeping first."

To her surprise he nodded, then shrugged. "I guess it's your prerogative where I sleep tonight. Let me take care of you before you show me what you have in mind, and maybe I can persuade you to reconsider."

While her hormones danced around with glee, her mind stomped them down – hard. She leaned up on her elbows and looked at him. "What *do* you have in mind?"

"I was talking about giving you a foot rub." He gave her a cheesy grin. "But, if you want, I could do something else."

Her lips twitched as she fought a smile. "A foot rub? That I can do. Get on your knees next to the bed."

He immediately stiffened. "So you're into that crawling humiliation type stuff?"

Exasperated, she kicked her legs, her knees hanging off the side of the bed. "My feet are over here. I'm comfortable, so I'm not moving. That means if you want to offer a proper apology you'll do it on your knees next to my bed. And no, I'm not into humiliation, I'm into delayed gratification. I like to tease a man until he feels like his balls are going to explode, like he could tear through anyone and anything to get to me, then push him a little bit closer to the edge before I unleash him on my body. I want to own every ounce of his pleasure and keep it all for myself. This is merely an easier position for me to allow you to rub my feet."

He stared at her, then shook his head. "Man,

Doc, I never would have pegged you as being so kinky."

"Oh, honey, you have no idea."

With a contented sigh she reclined into the lush comfort of her bed. A moment later his big hand grasped her ankle and she smiled, knowing that he'd followed her directions by the angle of his touch. He carefully pulled off her sock, then ran his thumbs up the arch of her foot, unerringly finding the tense muscles and stroking them until they relaxed. His hands were so big that they almost enveloped her foot from her heel to her toes, and his grip was strong enough to make her groan in pleasure as he squeezed.

"Good God, Callahan. If I'd known you were this talented I would have invited you over sooner."

He gave some low reply that she barely heard. Not that it mattered, his hands were magic. As she'd anticipated, the roughness of his palms added a delicious friction over her skin. When he finished her first foot he moved onto the second. After removing her sock he paused.

"Cute toe ring, Doc."

She didn't bother to reply, only humming in pleasure when he began to firmly stroke her. Warmth pooled in her belly and spread outwards until she felt like her bones had turned to mush. He paused for a moment and she thought he was done, but then came the soft feel of his lips pressed against her toe, kissing the ring there. Her heart slammed into her ribs and her sex contracted, the warm rush of arousal making her pussy swell.

He took her by such surprise that she forgot to

protest when he licked the inside of the arch of her foot, his tongue tracing a searing path to her ankle.

She started to remove her leg from his grasp, but he tightened his grip. "Let me do this for you, Doc. I can make it so good for you, I swear. Let me take care of you." There was a desperate note to his voice that hadn't been there before, the sound of a true plea.

Of begging.

She loved it.

Hard, intense lust drew her muscles tight. How he tempted her with those rough, needy words that tugged at her both emotionally and physically. Her body was more than ready to accept him, to have that clever tongue licking at her. To ride his face while he was tied to her bed, to cover him with her scent, marking him as hers.

Whoa, Nelly.

No, she couldn't let that happen yet.

With a firmer jerk she pulled her foot from his hands and sat up. He looked up at her with hurt, anger, and something more mixing all together.

Trying to ignore her hormones' outraged screams, she tilted her head and looked up at him through her eyelashes. "Open the bottom drawer next to the bed."

She scooted closer and pulled her pajama pants off, leaving her clad in her t-shirt and white cotton panties with lace around the edges. The low light from the fire threw interesting patterns on the room, shapes that invited the mind to relax and wander. It certainly brought out Wyatt's rough beauty as he stared at her side table, a hint of trepidation tightening his lips. He opened it and found two sets of wrist and ankle restraints, one metal and one soft leather padded with fleece.

He cleared his throat before looking up at her. "What do you want me to do with these?" His need was evident and a shiver of desire went through her whole body, making her hyper-aware of the throbbing between her legs.

"Take out one of the leather ankle restraints. They're the ones that are a little bit thicker."

He slowly reached into the drawer as if a poisonous snake might jump out and bite him. His hand hovered over the leather and she held her breath. He looked up, rage in his gaze that she was making him do this. Oh, he was alpha to the core, but if she couldn't establish dominance over him this would never work. They'd be constantly battling each other over who got to be on top. She'd been there, done that, and would not do it again. It had been exhausting.

"What's the matter, Callahan?" She consciously put a purr in her voice and watched as his hands began to shake. "Are you afraid you can't take what I'm going to dish out?" She leaned up and arched her back, allowing him a glimpse of her panties. "Do you see how hard my nipples are right now? If you touched them just slightly with your tongue it would feel so damn good."

"Then stop playing your mind games with me and let me fuck you." The snarl in his voice made her even wetter.

"No. Now, either bring out that ankle restraint or get out of my room. I don't have time for cowards."

Quicker than a flash he snatched the cuff out of the drawer, a defiant look on his face. She smiled and ran her hand down her thighs, drawing his gaze lower, making him burn hotter. "Now put it on and fasten yourself to the chain attached to the bedpost."

She didn't mention that the chain had never actually been used, and that her handyman James had installed it without her knowledge. Both James and Yuki thought it was well past time that Michelle found a man of her own, and the chains at the end of the bed had to be Yuki's idea. That bitch knew Michelle would look at those chains every night before she went to sleep and think about what it would be like to have a man restrained at the foot of her lonely bed. The idea of Wyatt being the first man to use her equipment gave her a primal satisfaction. Plus, the shock on his face was enough to make her fight a giggle.

"Are you fucking for real?"

"Shut your mouth, Callahan, before I make you do mountain climbers for me. Do you want to sweat your rage out or have me suck it out?"

"If you're going to do that, beautiful, I'll need to take my pants off first."

"Leave them on. If I see you naked right now I'll lose my control and what should have been a long, slow seven-course banquet of desire will become a drive-through cheeseburger orgasm."

His startled laugh made her smile. "I can't argue with that logic."

She smiled and made a motion pointing towards the bedpost.

He began to fasten the restraint onto his ankle, then reached for the chain. "Goddamn it, I must be a fucking idiot." Defiance and desire mixed in his gaze as he stared up at her and snapped the hook on the chain to the ring on the ankle cuff. Holding her gaze, he licked his lower lip in an all too tempting way, reminding her of how soft that sensitive flesh would feel between her teeth as she bit him while they kissed. "Now, come down here."

"Oh no, I'm sleeping up here tonight." She was proud that her voice came out steady despite the nearly volcanic amount of lust burning through her blood. Without breaking their stare, she reached back and grabbed at her pillows. She tossed a couple down to him and he looked away first. Hiding her smirk, she turned and tossed down a blanket from the end of the bed. "You're sleeping down there."

"Seriously?"

"Did you really think I would allow our first time to be when you reek of alcohol and jail sweat? Come on, Callahan, you can court a girl better than that."

"Is that what I'm doing, ma'am?" Some of the tension drained out of him, his shoulders relaxing, and he grabbed the pillows. Fluffing the pillow he put it behind his head and lay down, looking up at her with the shadows of the fire creating deep hollows beneath his cheekbones. "Courting you?"

"Of course you are. I'm not a sure thing, Callahan. You're going to have to earn this pussy." She grinned as he laughed again. "But, I am serious when I say that I expect you to earn my affection. You won't have to guess what I want, I'll tell you. I will keep you informed of everything I expect from you."

"Sounds like I'm gonna be doing a lot of work. What do I get out of the deal?"

Warmth flowed through her body as she began to imagine all the things she'd do to him – and hoped he'd do to her. "You get me, taking care of you, fully trusting you, and bringing you pleasure like you can't imagine. But you have to earn it."

He pursed his lips and stared at the ceiling, his gaze a thousand miles away. "Do you enjoy teasing men? Is that what gets you wet?"

"Not all men. But with you, yes, I do."

"Huh." A few more minutes passed. "It makes you hot?"

"It does."

"So, you like me?"

"I do."

"Huh."

"Wyatt."

"Yeah?"

"I need an orgasm before I can fall asleep. Being around you has made my body ache with need." The chain on the bed jerked and she smiled. "No, I'm going to take care of myself tonight. And while I do, while you listen to me make myself come all over my fingers, you are not to orgasm. I don't want to hear one sound of movement from you. Your pleasure, all of it belongs to me. I say when you come. I say when you can touch yourself. And, right now, I'm telling you that you will not put one finger on that big cock of yours."

"You're fucking killing me! How the hell am I supposed to resist that temptation?"

"If you do as I ask I will come down to you afterwards and rub my wet, still swollen pussy on your palm and allow you to lick my essence off your skin."

"I swear to God you're going to kill me. Okay, you got a deal, but, fuck, can I at least adjust my cock first?"

A smug smile curved her lips as she lay back in her bed, arms outstretched as she gloried in the feel of the silk sheets against her skin. When she began to rise into Top space the world somehow expanded. Her senses became heightened and, if she concentrated, she could feel every inch of skin on her body. This was the feeling she craved like a drug, this insane pleasure. Knowing that Wyatt was close enough to hear her, while bound to the floor by her will sent a flood of moisture to her sex.

She slid her hand beneath her panties and gasped at the first brush of her swollen clit. "Oh God, Callahan, I'm already so wet."

He groaned in frustration and she closed her eyes, imaging what he looked like right now as she continued to stroke herself. Would he be straining to hear her, or trying to pretend she wasn't there? His breath came out in tight bursts, but she didn't hear the rattling of his chain, yet.

Time to drive him crazy. To see how far she could push him until he snapped.

"Wyatt, I'm circling the entrance to my sheath with the tip of my finger, imagining what it would be like to have the head of your cock almost pushing into me. As soon as you did my cunt would clamp down like a fist on you."

"Doc, you're killing me."

"I know, and it makes me wet."

He gave a strangled laugh. "What am I going to do with you?"

"What you should be asking is what *I* am going to do with you. I'd spend entire days tormenting you, driving you to one sweaty orgasm after another before I finally stopped. You'd feel like you had just run a marathon, but you would be so very relaxed and satisfied. Then, when I am certain that I've wrung every drop of pleasure from your body that I can, I'd bathe you, then take you into my bed. You'd fall asleep with your head pillowed on my breasts, listening to the beat of my heart, knowing that you'd pleased me."

He moaned and then cursed. She slid her finger inside of her pussy and began to circle her clit with her other hand. Oh, how she wished he was already hers. She wanted to order him up here to lick her to an orgasm without worrying that he'd push for more than she was ready to offer. She wanted it all, the total package. She wanted every inch of his mind and body to belong to her as surely as hers belonged to him.

"Mmmm...I'd love to feel your tongue on me right now, Wyatt. I imagine you flicking my clit, making me hot, making me ride your face. I love doing that, my hands braced against the headboard while you eat my pussy. What would that talented tongue of yours feel like....fuck I'm getting close...feels so good...." The chain jerked against the bedpost and Wyatt swore when it wouldn't let him move and jerked again. She'd done it, she'd driven him to the point where her will could no longer hold him.

All the muscles of her body clenched and then the first glorious release came, throwing her mind and soul from her body and filling her with pleasure. She came hard, arching up into her fingers, giving her sensitive clit another slow rub to draw her orgasm out. When the last contraction faded she withdrew her fingers from her pussy.

"You moved, Wyatt."

"How could I not move!" His voice came out in

a furious whisper. "You talk about me eating your cunt like that and expect me not to react?"

She wiggled beneath the covers with a low sigh. "Goodnight, Wyatt. I do hope you're strong enough to resist wanking off like a horny teenager. I need a man strong enough to overcome his selfish need to come in order to put my pleasure first. You have no idea how arousing it is for me to know that you're so hard it hurts, but are waiting for my command in order to have your release."

For a few minutes the only sounds that came from her floor were swear words. Then he took a deep breath and slowly let it out. "Goodnight, Michelle."

The tight anger, the controlled aggression in his tone sent a warm wave of lust through her. He was such a big, bad alpha male. Chained to the foot of her bed, yes, but nowhere near tamed, the kind of challenge that would tempt any Domme.

In other words, he was the perfect sub for her. She didn't want a doormat of a man, she wanted someone who was just as strong as she was. It had been so long since she'd had a submissive, five long years since the death of her submissive fiancé, Owen. Shaking off the instant sorrow that thought brought, along with a brush of guilt, she returned to watching Callahan's shadow on the floor out of the corner of her eye.

He needed her. She wanted the submission of the alpha male and, oh boy, Callahan was all that and more. Texas born and bred, he had that kind of swagger that made any woman's heart beat faster. At least he used to. At the moment his swagger was more of a shuffle. Right now, she'd settle for him not courting death.

By his frustrated mutters, she knew he was finding it hard to get comfortable. She was also pretty sure he would jerk off once he was sure she was asleep. They hadn't entered into any formal agreement yet, and tonight was more about showing him what it would be like to be her submissive than actually making him her submissive. And truth be told, she loved a bit of occasional defiance from her sub. It gave her an excuse to punish him in the most marvelous ways. Then again, he might keep his hands off himself just to prove to her that he could. As she drifted off, her last conscious thought was of Wyatt pleasuring himself while chained to her bed.

Chapter 4

Wyatt didn't want to open his eyes yet. He didn't want the first peaceful night's sleep he'd had in months to end. It had been so long since he'd slept more than a few hours at a time and he'd forgotten how good it felt to be rested. His body certainly thanked him and he wanted to thank the woman who'd made it possible. A hint of her delicious peach and vanilla scent teased his senses and his cock started to get hard.

It was the memory of the woman sleeping above him that pulled him fully awake. Her even breathing was the only sound in the room. And what a room it was. The skylights overhead were shuttered with screens and blackout curtains covered the windows, leaving the room in darkness. He could tell from the faintest gleam of light coming around the edges of the curtains that the sun was up.

The thick sheepskin rug had proven surprisingly comfortable to sleep on and the pillow Michelle had tossed him smelled like her. He'd felt like an idiot, but had fallen asleep taking in deep breaths of the mixture of her shampoo, perfume, and natural scent. The soft whisper of her breathing had soothed him, and he'd found himself breathing with her, easily drifting off.

Moving very slowly, he unhooked the ankle cuff as quietly as possible, cursing when the links rattled. Rubbing the stiffness out of his muscles, he stood and looked down at her. She didn't stir so he took a moment to stare at her, to examine the woman who'd fascinated him from the moment he first laid eyes on her. Her long, sun streaked blonde hair lay around her head in a halo and he touched the curl nearest to him. He'd never seen her with her hair down before. Even at Aaron's funeral her hair had been swept back in an elegant twist.

No, he didn't want to think about that funeral right now, not when he'd just found a port in the storm. Murky memories of sitting at Aaron's grave spun through his mind like razor wire. He'd found the perfect piece of wood earlier in the day for making a cross, he could see the shape in the wood, waiting to be coaxed out by his hand. So, late that afternoon, he'd gone to Aaron's grave with the wood, his knife, and a bottle whiskey. Fuck, he was lucky he hadn't sliced his damn hand off. If that caretaker hadn't stumbled across him when he did...well he didn't want to think about that right now, either.

Instead, he focused on Michelle. She had refined features and an elegance about her he found hard to put into words. He'd watched a movie a while he was in Walter Reed, some cowboy movie from the nineties on cable, and the moment Sharon Stone appeared on the screen he'd had to rub his eyes because she looked so much like Michelle. There were slight differences in their features, but they could have been sisters.

Either way, that exquisite woman now lay before him in a pair of sexy white cotton panties with a rumpled silk sheet covering everything but her lower back and ass. His Marine buddies would never believe he'd made it into the Ice Queen's bedroom. Well, it was on her floor but, fuck, it was still her bedroom. Hell, he hardly believed it himself. Her lips, soft in sleep, parted and she mumbled something before turning onto her stomach. When her even breathing resumed he moved quickly to the bathroom, the call of nature pulling him away from his obsession.

After taking care of business, he brushed his teeth, avoiding his reflection in the mirror. He knew he'd been treading in dangerous waters lately, but it had been hard to make himself care. He was drifting, having no purpose really and nothing to be excited about anymore. While he didn't miss the war, or the bullshit everyday stuff of the military, he missed having a goal, something to strive for. He'd tried working at his dad's company, thought about going back to school, and had basically done nothing as far as socializing other than drink and avail himself of the occasional one night stand.

What shamed him even more was that Michelle recognized his downward spiral when they'd met at Aaron's funeral. After the service she'd found him taking his first drink of the day at his truck, too emotionally fucked up to hold out any longer. She'd looked like a cool dream in an ice blue suit that made her dark blue eyes seem all the more striking. It was also the first time he'd ever seen her wearing makeup, and he'd been knocked on his ass by how fucking kissable her lips looked with a sheen of pink lip-gloss. Then she'd laid the smack-down on him and, before he knew it, he was in her car on their way to his apartment.

The conversation they'd had about her being a

Dominatrix had been one of the most surreal moments in his life. He'd never, ever imagined getting off on a woman tying him up the way he sometimes liked to tie his lovers up. But, even then, his dick had almost instantly swelled rock hard as soon as she started talking about it. After that, he'd done a bunch of research that left him more confused and aroused than before. He'd vowed that he could never do that stuff for her, and yet here he stood with an aching erection and the marks of a cuff on his ankle.

If it had been anyone but her he would have thrown away the card she gave him after the funeral, but he'd kept it, tucked it away in his wallet. Over the ensuing weeks, he'd pulled it out dozens of times, looking at the elegant scrawl of her handwriting. The paper retained a trace of her perfume, an elusive hint of the woman who'd once touched it. When his brother-in-law had asked him who to call Wyatt told him to grab Doc's card and call her. Sure, he'd been really drunk at the time, but hadn't he been waiting for an opportunity to call her? A time when it wouldn't have to be him doing the talking, but someone else? A random third party who could say the words he'd been choking on, that he needed help...that he needed her with a desperation that scared him.

Splashing his face with hot water he tried to wash away the invisible grime that always seemed to coat his skin after drinking. As he dried his neck, he wondered what was on the paper she'd said waited for him in her drawer. She must have written it before she came to pick him up, and that made him curious as to how she'd been so sure he would stay the night. Then again, he'd always been a complete fool when it came to Doc, and he was pretty sure she knew it.

With a sigh he tossed the wet washcloth into the hamper and slowly opened the door to the bedroom. She was still deep asleep and he envied her the ability to relax like that. Moving as quickly and quietly as he could, he grabbed the envelope with his name on it from the side table. The room was too dark to read, so he went out into the hallway and closed the door after himself.

Not sure where to go, he wandered down the hall following the bright light coming from a glass door. Gauzy curtains hung down over the other side of the doorway and he wondered what they concealed. Curious, he opened the door and parted the curtains. Humid warmth bathed him and he stepped forward, grinning as soon as he got on the other side. He'd never seen a room like this in person before.

It was a conservatory, a greenhouse with high, vaulted ceilings. Easily twice the size of his living room, the smooth stone floors were warm beneath his feet as he wandered to the center of the room. Tall palm trees almost touched the glass roof, and exotic flowers grew everywhere in raised beds that somehow looked like natural rock formations. A small pond bubbled over in the corner and the glass window-walls looked out onto a vast field enclosed by a wooden fence.

A trough sat near the house and he figured that this must be one of the grazing pastures for her horses. In the center of the room stood a collection of wrought iron furniture covered with overstuffed cushions done in a delicate and utterly feminine floral pattern. Movement out of the corner of his eye caught his attention and he realized that the gauzy curtains at the entrance to the room served a purpose.

Not only was this a greenhouse, it also appeared to be a butterfly habitat. Now that he was paying attention, he noticed dozens of different butterflies either flitting about or sitting on leaves and flowers, their elegant wings slowly opening and closing. He made his way over to one of the chairs and sat down, awed by the sheer beauty of this place and the kind of mind that could have imagined it in the first place.

He blew out a low breath and fingered the envelope, turning it over and over, wondering what it contained. A butterfly landed on the black wrought iron table in front of him, a beautiful specimen with wings like black velvet, spattered with bright blues and golds. When he opened the envelope it took off, leaving him alone with her words.

Dear Wyatt,

I have a proposition for you, one that I think will be mutually beneficial. For the next month I want you to become my submissive, to serve me as I desire, to give over all the control to me and trust me to take care of you. If, after that month, we decide to maintain our D/s relationship we will discuss a new contract and set of terms.

His cock certainly seemed to enjoy the thought. Blood rushed to his groin as he imagined different scenarios with her, each more erotic than the last. But wait, he was getting ahead of himself, there was still more to read.

During our first days together your role will be

as my service submissive. I don't know how much you know about the lifestyle, so I'll explain it. When you act as my service submissive you will assist me and perform tasks I set for you as directed. These tasks will include but are not limited to drawing my bath, turning down my bed, helping care for my horses and any other chores I deem appropriate.

Fuck, that wasn't quite what he was thinking, though he liked the bath idea.

From there, depending upon your behavior, I will either continue to train you as my submissive or I will send you, at my expense, to the best program in the country for dealing with PTSD and substance abuse. And wipe that fucking scowl off your face; you and I both know you're not handling your shit right now. You're using alcohol to make the pain go away, and that sad story always ends in tragedy.

He rubbed his eyes, wondering what the hell he was getting himself into with a woman who knew him well enough to know what his reaction would be to her words. He'd only recently admitted to himself that maybe he wasn't doing as well out in the civilian world as he could be, that maybe the shit that had happened over in the sandbox was affecting him more than he first thought. A cold wind blew across his soul as he thought about how tempting the idea of ending it all had been last night deep in his alcoholic haze.

There, in that peaceful graveyard, he'd envied the dead.

Another butterfly danced through the air in front of him before finding its way to a flowering vine that twined up the trunk of one of the trees.

There was a flow to the room, a design that made everything work together in harmony. The warm, moist air felt good against his skin and he briefly considered going to sleep out here, but time was running out.

So this is where we stand, Wyatt. You can either agree to become my submissive for a month and see where this takes us, or you can go home. I won't say that I wouldn't be disappointed if you left, but I understand that my lifestyle is not for everyone. I see something in you Wyatt, something special. I'd like to help remind you of the joys life has to offer. If you agree I want you to take off your shirt and go draw a bath for me. When you're in my presence I want you barefoot and shirtless, always. If you decide this is not for you, wait for me downstairs and I'll make sure you get home okay.

That was it, nothing more. He tossed the letter onto the table and stood, cracking his knuckles before he began pacing. Why the fuck was he even considering this? He didn't have a submissive bone in his body. He'd always been the one who called the shots in bed, who swept women off their feet, not the other way around. Then again, men spent their entire lives trying to find a woman like Sapphire. He'd be a fool to let this opportunity slip away.

He needed to think about this in a logical manner, not with his cock. What did he have to lose? Not his self-respect, he'd already lost that last month when he'd been busted for drunk driving by his brother-in-law. Not his freedom, he didn't even know what to do with it now that he had it. And his sanity was questionable at best.

What did he have to gain? At the very least it would be a much needed distraction from the endless memories of battle. Out here, in the middle of all this land, he didn't have to worry about the sound of an engine backfiring making him want to hit the deck, or when someone drove to close to him worrying if they were a suicide bomber. Then again, he couldn't stay here forever. He'd have to return to the real world eventually, and he worried that he'd be even more broken than before he came here.

Yeah, Sapphire didn't seem vicious, but what did he really know about her?

He fingered the scar tissue on his lower abdomen, the physical reminder of how she'd saved his life.

Before he could change his mind he turned on his heel and left the butterfly room. His feet were already bare so when he opened the door to her bedroom his footsteps were hushed. She appeared to still be asleep so he went into the bathroom.

Warm sunlight spilled over the marble floor, bringing out the veins of bronze and peach in the creamy stone's surface. Her enormous bathtub took up the far wall of the bathroom and he grabbed a couple towels before heading over there. Shit, he'd seen smaller hotel Jacuzzis. Along the side on a small built-in shelf there was a variety of different soaps. He grabbed a bottle of some orange stuff and turned on the water. Opening the cap he took a hesitant sniff and was pleased to find it smelled like vanilla and peaches.

After pouring the bubble bath into the slowly filling tub he noticed some buttons on the side of the wall. One button turned on lights in the water, and another started the jets. The third button made a TV rise up from the other edge of the tub. It would be nice to sit in a hot bath with a cold beer and watch football. Even better if Michelle was cuddled against his chest watching the game with him. Damn, he could get used to this place.

Unsure what to do now, he refolded the towels and fidgeted, testing the water now and again. When the tub was finally full he turned the water off and glanced towards the bedroom door. Sapphire stood there with an unreadable look in her eyes. She still wore the t-shirt she'd slept in and her white cotton panties, which made her smooth, slender legs look a mile long.

His mouth went dry and he swallowed hard. "I-uh, ran your bath."

"I see."

When she didn't say anything else he stood and gestured to the water. "Let me know if you need anything."

"Sit down."

Raising his eyebrows he did as she asked, sitting on the wide tile edge around the tub, and tried not to groan out loud as she crossed the room. Even in bright sunlight she was flawless, all creamy skin and golden hair. When she stopped before him he reached out to touch her, but she shook her head. "No, Callahan, touching me is a privilege you haven't earned yet. Now close your eyes, and don't peek. I'm trusting you not to."

Damn, if she'd ordered him to close his eyes he might have been able to sneak a look, but when she said she was trusting him all the fight went out of him. Cloth slipped over skin, barely audible over the fizz of the bubbles.

Her delicate hand touched his shoulder and he almost looked but caught himself. She shifted and he imagined her slipping her underwear off, naked and inches away from him. Fuck, he wanted to look, wanted to see if the curls guarding her sex were the same color as the hair on her head, wanted to see if she was as wet for him as he was hard for her. His cock ached but he didn't dare move to adjust himself.

A moment later her touch left his shoulder and water sloshed as she slid into the tub.

"You can open your eyes now."

To his dismay the bubbles fully covered her, leaving nothing but her head exposed. She grinned at him and he smiled back, thankful for a break in the tension between them. "Do you want me to leave?"

"No. I want to talk with you. I'm assuming that since you're here you wish to become my submissive for a month's time?"

"Yeah. I-uh, yeah. I guess. But that stuff we talked about last night still applies. I don't want you treating me like your bitch in front of other people."

"Eloquent as always, Callahan." She pointed to the sink. "Open the first drawer and you'll find my hairbrush. Bring it to me."

He did as she asked, conscious of her eyes on him, teasing his skin almost like a physical touch. When he returned with her hairbrush the heat in her gaze seared him. He went to hand her the hairbrush but she shook her head. "No, I want you to do it. Put a towel down on the floor and kneel behind me."

After kneeling behind her he hesitated. "I don't

really know how to brush long hair."

"Just do small, gentle strokes. Work out any tangles with your fingers."

"Okay."

She leaned her head back on the curved edge of the tub and let out a contented sigh as he began to slowly work the brush through her hair, small tugs that moved her slightly. "Have you ever been in a relationship with BDSM elements before?"

"No." He put the brush over to the side and concentrated on untangling a snarl. "I mean I've thought about it, but I always pictured myself being in charge."

"Hmmm." She lazily drifted her hand through the water, swirling the bubbles.

"What about you?"

"Yes. I've been into the lifestyle pretty much as soon as I learned about it."

He paused in his brushing. "Why do you like it?"

Her hand in the water stilled, then resumed its slow swirls. "It's complicated and hard to put into words."

"Nice evasion, Doc."

She snorted. "It helps me to clear away everything from my mind, all the garbage that clutters our thoughts every moment of the day. When I'm deep into a scene with my submissive we are the only things in the universe. Two bright candles burning through the darkness." She gave a wistful sigh. "I can't explain the feeling of connection that I get from Dominance and submission any more than I could try to explain color to a blind person. It is one of those things you have to experience for yourself. I can say I believe it is one of the most profound connections that two human beings can make."

"And you want to experience it with me? Why me? I mean look at you, you could have pretty much any man you wanted. Why me?"

"Because I trust you, Wyatt. You are a good man down to your bones and that is something hard to find in these modern times. If we had lived in the Middle Ages you would have been a knight. I can trust you to keep me safe."

Pride, something he hadn't felt in a long time, filled his chest. "You know I'd never hurt you, Doc."

"I do." She winced when the brush got caught in a tangle. "At least not on purpose."

Something about her tone caught his attention, a hint of pain that pinged off his radar. "Has someone hurt you before?"

"Callahan, no one gets through this world without a little pain. It is part of what shapes us, what makes us appreciate what we have, makes us fight for the good things in this life."

An eloquent answer, but not the full truth. He let it go, for now, still glowing from the knowledge that this extraordinary woman wanted him. "So you've had submissives before? I mean, like guys you dated."

"Yes."

The sorrow in that one word made him pause.

"Don't stop, Callahan." She rested her head against the back of the tub and from this angle he could see her eyes were closed.

Unexpected jealousy twisted his stomach at the thought of her being intimate with other men. He knew it was stupid, fuck he'd been with more than his fair share of willing females, but an unexpected possessive streak made him want to erase the thought of any other man except him from her mind.

He needed to get a grip.

And, motherfucker, he could use about a dozen cold beers right now. His mouth was suddenly parched and he ran his fingers through the softness of her hair, searching for tangles while battling his craving. He wanted her more than he'd ever wanted anyone, and the fact that she already had that kind of control over him was unsettling. He could all too easily see himself falling in love with Sapphire, and he didn't know if he could take the inevitable rejection when she found out how fucked up he was. Not many women could deal with men who had flashbacks in the middle of the mall, scaring the crap out of a bunch of kids and embarrassing himself and his sister.

"Doc, can you lift your neck up so I can get the hair at the bottom?"

She did as he asked and he was treated to the sight of her smooth shoulders. "Domina."

"What?"

"You will address me as Domina, or Ma'am, or Mistress."

"Seriously?" He rubbed the bridge of his nose, trying to stave off the hangover headache. "I'll go with Domina, if that's okay with you."

"I rather like the way you say that."

"What am I called?"

"Mine."

He grinned and gave her hair a brisk brush, the slight curls now a soft fuzz. "That goes both ways, you know. If we're gonna do this, I don't want to have to worry about some other sub being kept chained to the basement floor."

"Trust me when I say that even though I would never do that for moral and ethical reasons, I seriously do not have the energy to cope with two subs. You're more than enough for a dozen Dominas to try to handle."

His cock twitched at the thought of more than one woman commanding him and then swelled as he imagined Michelle kissing some vague female while he ate his Domina's pussy. "You aren't going to share me with other Doms, are you?"

"Of course not." She raised her hand, water running down her skin and giving it an almost pearlescent sheen. "Now take off your shirt."

He froze, not wanting to show her what he'd done, how he'd marked himself in her memory. It was something she'd said in passing once, a comment that could have been taken as a joke, but he'd sensed a sincerity to her words. More than that, he'd seen the flush of desire as she'd talked with one of the nurses about a man with pierced nipples, how it was one of the sexiest things on earth. If she saw the hoops going through his nipples she would know instantly why he had them.

"I'm, um, I'm cold."

She stilled, then turned her head and motioned to him. "Come here."

"What?"

"Come here. In the water. I want you kneeling in front of me."

He hesitated, torn between wanting to dive in and run away. Why the fuck was he afraid of showing her? It was no big deal, really. He'd just play it off.

"Callahan, come here."

The authority in her tone had him moving before he knew it. The warm water swirled around his pant leg, making the wet, worn denim cling to his skin. He knelt before her, willing himself to keep his gaze on her face. Considering how absolutely amazing she looked right now he didn't think that would be a problem.

The warm water had leant a flush to her cheeks and her hair hung down her shoulders, smooth and silken, if a bit frizzy. But he kinda liked the frizz. It turned her from an unapproachable goddess into something warmer, more inviting. The water sloshed against his waist as she moved forward, sleek hints of her form showing through the bubbles, tantalizing glimpses of a body more beautiful than a Texas sunset.

When she rose to her knees, he immediately looked away, not wanting to give her any reason to stop. Just being close to her had always made his dick hard. To be close enough to smell her warm skin was the most exquisite torture. Her slender fingers curled beneath the edge of his shirt. Ever so slowly, she lifted the fabric from him, pausing to run a nail over his torso, to trace the line of hair leading from his navel to his chest. Before she got to his nipples he moved, jerking the shirt out of her hands and removing it himself with a violent motion.

Instead of recoiling from him she remained perfectly still. When he looked at her out of the corner of his eye he found her gaze riveted on his chest, her heat-softened lips parted in a silent gasp. A trail of bubbles slowly coasted down the delicate slope of her upper chest, his gaze riveted on her as the foam slowly inched down the plump curve of her full breast, stopping before it slid off completely and revealed her to him.

She reached out and ran her fingertip over each gold ring piercing his nipples. "When did you get them done?"

"After I got back."

She made a little humming sound and played with the small stones at the center of each ring. "Are those star sapphires?"

He cleared his throat, and shifted, wanting to touch her, to taste her to have her do something, anything besides that light touch that aroused him more than most women's kisses. Still, he hesitated at telling her the truth, of opening himself to ridicule or even worse, understanding. It would be even more embarrassing if she knew he got them pierced two days after she'd told him about her kink.

"No idea. Just liked the color." His words sounded lame even to himself.

She leaned forward and he tensed with anticipation, every nerve in his body on fire. When her full lips wrapped around his right nipple he groaned. He went to touch her and she nipped at his chest. "Hands behind your back."

Struggling against himself, against his urge to fuck this woman who so obviously wanted him, he clasped his hands and endured the delicate flick of her tongue against first one nipple, and then the other. Her slow torment of his sensitive flesh coupled with the ball-tightening feeling of her breasts rubbing his ribs as she leaned closer. She rested her face against his chest and made a happy sound that was almost like a purr.

"Wyatt, you remembered my favorite thing on a man. Now, you can pretend that this was just a random action, that you just happened to pick blue star sapphires to adorn yourself, or you could tell me the truth." She nipped him again and her voice took on a wicked edge. "As they say, 'the truth shall set you free'."

He clenched his hands together behind his back, every nerve in his body yelling at him to grab her, take her, show her how much he could please her, how he could eat her little pussy better than any man she'd ever had. He wanted to fuck her, to taste her, to surround himself with her presence, to let her body be a balm to heal his wounds.

Thrown off stride, he shrugged his shoulders. "Don't know what you're talking about. These were on sale so I got 'em."

She pulled back and captured his chin in her grip, turning his face to hers. "Don't lie to me, Wyatt. You can tell me you don't want to talk about it, and I may or may not honor that request, but don't lie to me."

He jerked his chin out of her hand. "I don't want to talk about it."

"All right." She turned around and moved to the other side of the tub and lifted a bottle. "Wash my hair."

He groaned, entranced by the sight of her slender back and wishing all the bubbles would burst at once so he could see that perfect heart shaped ass. "Yes, Domina."

She grinned, a bright flash of teeth that made her look much younger. "Much better."

He sloshed through the tub and held out his

hand, letting her pour the amount of shampoo that she desired into it. Then he worked it into a lather and massaged it into her scalp, loving the soft moan of appreciation as he worked. His cock throbbed, ached with the need to come. He couldn't remember the last time he'd been this turned on. It was something about her, some intangible energy she put off pulling him like a moth to the flame.

The motions of caring for her were strangely soothing. The happier he made her, the happier he felt. But hadn't it always been that way between them? When they'd been stationed together in Afghanistan he'd always made sure that she was taken care of, that she had everything and anything she needed.

Yeah, she was an officer and his superior, but he'd been in the service longer and knew how to get things done. It got to the point where his buddies started to call him her guard dog, but he'd laughed it off, knowing any of them would have given their left nut to be the one Sapphire turned to when she needed help. Not only was she beautiful, but she was something of a legend among the troops for how hard she fought to keep her patients, their brothers and sisters at arms, alive. Yeah, she could freeze your dick off when she was in Ice Queen mode, but when it really mattered, she could be depended on to do everything humanly possible to save someone's life.

Shit, she'd surely pulled him back from the gates of Hell on the fateful day that ended his military career. After the mortar round shredded the transport vehicle in front of them he knew he was going to die. The pain had been terrible, something he still experienced in nightmares.

"Wyatt, come back to me."

"Huh?" He blinked, realizing he'd frozen behind her. "Sorry."

"What were you thinking about?"

He swallowed hard, the lie tripping about on his tongue, but he'd promised not to lie to her. "I don't want to talk about it."

She stiffened and he prayed she wouldn't push him, wouldn't make him go back there, wouldn't send him off into another panic attack that could leave one or both of them hurt as he reverted to an animalistic state of fear. The memory of his sister's fright when he'd had a flashback while shopping with her at the mall still haunted him. What scared him the most was that he didn't remember exactly what had happened, only that one minute he was feeling claustrophobic and the next his sister was screaming at him to stop while some teenage kid backed away with his hands up and terror in his eyes.

Hurting Michelle would kill him as surely as a bullet to the head, so he needed to remain calm and not fight the small shit.

She took a good, long look at him, her gaze traveling over his face then down his body and nodded. "Okay. But I will ask again, Wyatt, and I will expect an answer. Just not today."

His relief made his knees weak as she dunked her head beneath the water, rinsing her hair out without giving him more than a glimpse of the side of her perfect breast. When she surfaced she slicked her hair back and stood up, rendering him speechless.

She had the legs of a pinup girl, long and shapely, topped off with an ass that he wanted to sink his teeth into. Before he could move, she'd stepped out of the tub and grabbed a towel, seemingly unconcerned about her nudity. After wrapping it around her body, she grabbed another one and wrapped it around her head.

"I'm going to get dressed. Feel free to wash up. And that is not a suggestion, that is a command. When you're done, meet me downstairs in the kitchen. You'll be able to follow your nose." She used the edge of the towel to wipe her neck. "Yuki makes breakfast for me. It usually includes some type of bacon because her husband is a bacon fiend."

He sat up on his knees in the water, the warmth a disconcerting sensation against his hard-enough-to-pound-nails cock. "Is she your housekeeper?"

Michelle laughed and wrapped the towel more securely, much to his dismay. "Yuki is many things, my housekeeper is not one of them. She only cooks for me because she loves to do it and I can't make anything more advanced than mac'n cheese. I have a woman who comes in twice a week to tidy up. I like my privacy too much to have someone in the house with me 24/7."

"But Yuki lives here with her husband? I'm guessing he's the handyman?"

"Yes, his name is James and I've been friends with them for years. They've made the old ranch hands' cabin into a more traditional home. James did most of the work."

"Huh." He noticed that her eyes kept flitting down to his cock, pressed against the denim of his jeans. "Do you think you could find another pair of pants for me somewhere?"

He played with the fly of his jeans, lust surging through him as her eyes darkened and her lips went soft. It seemed like the only time she truly relaxed was when she was aroused. Her whole posture changed, a slight shift of the hip making her stand a bit taller, thrusting her breasts out and drawing attention to the lean line of her calf.

"I believe James might be about your size." The pink tip of her tongue swept her lower lip as he adjusted his dick, giving it an extra squeeze to show her what could be hers if she just asked for it. Hell, as turned on as he was right now he'd be jerking off before the door finished closing behind her.

Fuck, why wait.

He moved his hand over his cock, squeezing at the base and slowly dragging his fist up. She watched him, as still and poised as a lioness contemplating her prey. With his other hand he flicked open the top button of his jeans and she took in a sharp breath. When her gaze met his the intensity of her desire made his balls draw up tight and drew a groan from the pit of his stomach.

"Wyatt, if you can keep from jerking off I will reward you for being a good boy later today."

He ran the tip of his thumb over his still covered erection. "Why wait? Come on, Mich-uh-Domina, I know you want me and I want you. Fuck, I want you more than I've ever wanted anyone in my life."

Her lips curved into an almost feline smile and a bolt of apprehension went through him. He knew that smile. It was the same one she used to give him back in Afghanistan when he'd pushed her too far. But he didn't think she'd have him doing 100 mountain climbers as punishment this time.

Her voice changed, becoming a seductive whisper that drove him crazy. "Because I want to know that you're as needy as I am. Because I do want you, Wyatt, but I will have you on my terms. I like the long, slow tease. I love making you so fucking hard I could make you come just by gripping you in my fist. But I won't rush things, not with you. We both deserve better and like I said earlier, your orgasms, your pleasure, all of it belongs to me now."

With that she turned on her heel, leaving him with a handful of aching prick and no intention of doing anything to relieve his discomfort.

Chapter 5

Michelle gratefully took a steaming mug of coffee from her best friend, Yuki. "Did I ever tell you how much I love you?"

Laughing softly, Yuki turned back to whipping up another omelet. Today she wore an almost sheer peach and gold silk sundress that flattered her lean frame, and her long black hair was tied back in an intricate braid Michelle knew Yuki had made her husband do. She added some chopped onions and ham to the bowl. "Rough night?"

"You could say that."

Yuki turned and raised one perfectly arched eyebrow, a skill Michelle wished she had. "James said you pulled in late last night...what's going on? Why are you blushing?"

"I'm not blushing." She took another long drink and moved her stool away a bit from the breakfast counter so she could keep an eye on the stairs. "I...well...we have a houseguest."

Abandoning the egg mixture Yuki slunk across the kitchen and asked in a purring voice, "Really? Immaculate Sister Michelle has decided to break her celibacy streak?"

"It's not what you think." Yuki did that eyebrow thing again and Michelle sighed in defeat. Lying to her best friend of fifteen years wasn't going to happen. "Well, it is what you think, but not like before. I've asked him to stay for me with a month.

Wyatt—"

"Wait...did you say Wyatt?" Yuki leaned on the counter, her excitement visible. "Is this the same Wyatt that you had that major crush on over in Afghanistan? Mr. Sergeant Callahan Hot Pants? The one you talked about in every one of your letters to me?"

"Shhh!" She couldn't see Wyatt but he should be coming down soon. "Yeah, him. But it's not like what you're thinking. He's in a dark place, Yuki. He needs me."

"How dark?"

Turning the mug in her hands, she tried to figure out how much to tell Yuki. On one hand, she and her husband had a right to know about a potential danger in their lives, but Michelle didn't want to betray Wyatt. Then again, if she didn't prepare her friends and something terrible happened because of a misunderstanding, she didn't think she could live with herself.

"He's having issues with PTSD.....and drinking more than he should."

Yuki took a deep breath and let it out slowly. "Michelle, you need to be careful."

"It's okay. He would never hurt me."

"Maybe not when he's himself, but what about when he's in the middle of an attack or whatever? Do you know what he's like then? Maybe he won't even see you when he looks at you. Maybe his mind will tell him you're the Taliban."

"No, Wyatt would never hurt me. He'd hurt himself before he ever harmed a female."

Yuki leaned against the counter and rearranged the green apples in the wooden bowl next to her. She glanced up, her gaze intent despite her relaxed pose, the sharp look of a Mistress concerned about the safety of her submissive, in this case, her husband "Do I need to warn James to walk lightly around him?"

Michelle wanted to say no, but since she didn't know for sure she nodded. "I don't think there will be any issues like that, but tell him not to push Wyatt." She fingered the edge of her low-cut shirt and grinned. "That's my job."

Some of the tension left Yuki's frame and she gave Michelle a grin. "Does he know about your lifestyle?"

"Yeah." She smirked, then gave Yuki a full out smile. "In fact, right now he is upstairs probably wondering why the fuck I didn't leave him any new pants to wear."

"Really?" Yuki laughed. "So can I expect some extra sausage with this morning's breakfast?"

A man's deep voice came from the mudroom off the kitchen. "Extra sausage?"

James strolled in wearing nothing but a worn pair of jeans, just how Yuki liked it. To be honest, Michelle didn't mind it either. James was a good looking man in or out of clothes. He had the lean build of a long distance runner, all sinewy muscles and blond hair. He went to his wife's side and knelt before her, wrapping his arms around her waist and resting his head against her flat stomach. "Good morning, Mistress." He nuzzled his nose against her, eliciting a soft laugh. "Did you say you needed extra sausage?"

"Easy there, killer." Yuki smoothed his hair back with a smile and a pang of yearning went through Michelle at their obvious love for each other. "Michelle brought a man home last night.

Not just any man, but the hunky Marine she was all wet for over in Afghanistan."

"Yuki!" Michelle grabbed an oven mitt off the counter and chucked it at her. "Not so fucking loud!"

James stood to shield his wife, a wide grin splitting his tan face. "Thank you, sweet baby Jesus. You two evil Dommes will have some other poor fool to torment."

Yuki pinched his butt hard enough to earn a yelp then gently pushed him the direction of the wide oak kitchen table. "I'll have to try twice as hard to make sure you feel equally tormented."

James' smile slipped a fraction. "Whatever your pleasure, Mistress."

"Damn, Skippy," Yuki said as she turned back to her work. "Is Wyatt going to be down soon?"

"Maybe. He'll either come down in his wet jeans or nude. I'm waiting to see which one."

Wyatt's voice echoed through the foyer and down the short hallway to the kitchen. "Neither."

Inwardly cursing she turned to watch Wyatt stride into the room with a towel wrapped around his waist. Water still beaded his shoulders and she watched with great interest as a drop ran down into the soft hair covering his chest. There was just something so insanely masculine about his hard muscles covered by the dusting of hair. And those nipple rings. God, she wanted him.

Yuki's eyes went wide and she mouthed a silent 'Wow' at her then turned to Wyatt. "Hi, I'm Yuki."

Wyatt cleared his throat. "Nice to meet you, ma'am."

"Ohhh, listen to that Texas twang." She grinned and openly inspected him. "That man sitting at the table glowering at me is my husband, James. He's also my submissive."

Red streaked across Wyatt's cheeks and he gave Michelle an unsure look. "Okay."

James stood up and came over, his hand outstretched. "Feel like you're in an episode of the Twilight Zone yet?"

Wyatt gripped the other man's hand and shook it, his relief apparent. "The second I stepped through the front door."

James clapped him on the shoulder. "If your Mistress doesn't object, I have some sweats that'll fit you."

Michelle nodded. "Go ahead, James."

He blew a kiss to his wife and went out the backdoor, leaving Wyatt alone with Michelle and Yuki. They both smiled at each other then looked at Wyatt. He almost took a step back, but held his place and firmed his spine. "Any reason you wanted me to come down here in a towel?"

The slight growl in his voice warmed things low in her body. "Yes, because of that little stunt you pulled upstairs."

He flushed and his gaze darted to Yuki and back to her. "Can we talk about this in private?"

"Wyatt, Yuki is a Mistress. James is her full-time submissive. They've been in the lifestyle for over eight years. Trust me when I say you appearing in a towel, or you attempting to seduce me while naked with that big horse cock of yours won't offend her in the least. In fact, she might end up dragging James over to eat her pussy while they watch us."

Wyatt made a choking sound and backed up another step, the whites showing all the way around his eyes.

Yuki laughed. "If you're going to be with us for a bit you might as well get used to it now. James and I live out here with Michelle so that we can indulge in our lifestyle without fear of ridicule or prejudice. In addition to being in a D/s relationship, James and I are also exhibitionists. Public displays of affection are not out of the norm for us. I'm not saying you have to worry about us screwing while you're trying to eat dinner, but if you stop by the barn or our house unannounced you may get an eyeful, and instead of telling you to leave, we'll invite you to pull up a chair and watch. Can you deal with that?"

He tightened his hold on the towel encircling his waist and nodded. "Yes, ma'am." He looked to Michelle and she caught the hint of desire widening his pupils. "But I don't want to do anything to piss Doc, I mean my Domina off so I guess you'll have to ask her before I do stuff like that."

Pleased, Michelle motioned to him. "Come here."

He did as she asked, then tried to pull away when she grabbed onto the edge of his towel. She tugged him closer until he stood between the cradle of her thighs. Due to the height of the stool her head reached just below his chin. She looked up and studied his face. In the morning sunlight his various scars stood out slightly paler than his deeply tanned skin. He must have a bit of Spanish in his ancestry because that dark tone didn't come from British roots. A line of stubble shadowed his jaw, leaving his firm lips looking softer than normal. She reached up and traced those lips, enjoying the slight puff of air over the tip of her finger.

He opened his mouth and the swipe of his tongue caressed her skin. Liquid heat pooled in her abdomen as she remembered all of his bragging about how well he could eat pussy. He'd never said it to her, but trash talking among the Marines was as second nature to them as breathing. She'd played it off like she wasn't listening, but she'd heard the promise, the certainty, beneath his words. What would it be like to have those rough whiskers between her legs? The thought had her nipples hard enough to cut glass and she had to resist the urge to pull Wyatt's mouth down to her.

Taking a quick breath to steady herself, she rubbed his hip with her thumb in a gentle caress. "I would like to show you off as well. I love knowing that someone is watching us, appreciating the beauty of your submission, the rugged strength of your body. There is an amazing synergistic energy that can develop between a voyeur and an exhibitionist." She closed her eyes and pulled his face down to hers, but kept his lips from touching her by the slightest bit. Oh how she wanted to kiss him, but not now. "But you are mine, only mine, Wyatt. I will never let another have the pleasure of your tongue or your cock. Only me."

"Let me kiss you," he whispered, the hesitant brush of his lips over hers sending a fire raging through her blood.

"No making out in my kitchen," Yuki said in a loud voice. "I don't want pubes on the counter."

Michelle jerked back, startled by how close

she'd come to giving in. Wyatt coughed and turned his back on her, laughing deep in his chest. Curious as to his reaction, using it as something to distract herself, she ran a fingernail down his spine, hard enough to leave a faint red line.

"Something wrong, Callahan?"

Yuki giggled and poured the eggs into a skillet. "I think he's afraid of offending my delicate sensibilities."

"What?"

Yuki held her arm up in the universal signal for a hard cock.

"Ohhhhh…" She loved how the muscles in his back stood out in such sharp relief as he no doubt fought the urge to flee. "Wyatt, darling, turn around."

The door to the mudroom slammed and a second later James came into the kitchen. He took one look at Michelle and his wife and began to laugh. "I don't know what you two are up to, but leave the poor bastard alone."

Ignoring Yuki's glare, he walked over to Wyatt and handed him a couple pairs of sweats and some folded t-shirts. "Here, I doubt Michelle will let you wear a shirt in the house, especially with those pierced nipples of yours, but if she lets you outside you might need this. Bathroom is right down the hall, first door on the left."

"Thanks." Without saying another word Wyatt fled to the hallway.

Yuki took a mound of bacon out of the oven where it'd been staying warm and set it on the counter. "Don't think you can protect him from us, James."

He snagged a piece of bacon and gave his wife

an insolent smile. "I have no idea what you're talking about, oh beautiful Mistress of mine."

"Brat," Yuki muttered as she smacked his hand away with her spatula. "Unless you want Wyatt coming back to find you serving as our new center piece I suggest you behave."

James coughed and backed away. "I'm pretty sure it's an unspoken guy rule that you shouldn't be naked while you eat breakfast with each other for the first time."

Michelle helped Yuki set the table, grinning at their banter. In their relationship, Yuki enjoyed his antics, and let him get away with a great deal before taking her husband firmly in hand and giving him what he craved - discipline followed by amazing sex.

Speaking of amazing sex, Wyatt strolled back into the kitchen, his swagger now back in perfect form. Michelle allowed him to see her desire, to see how much she appreciated his body. He grinned at her and nodded at Yuki. "Anything I can help you with, ma'am?"

"No thanks. I enjoy feeding big guys with hearty appetites. If your plate is clean it makes me happy to know that I've filled the hole in your belly." She heaped two omelets and a mess of bacon onto his plate.

As she put food on Michelle's plate the two women exchanged a look. Yuki had noticed how thin Wyatt was as well, and Michelle appreciated her subtle way of making sure Wyatt ate everything on his plate. Sometimes honey worked better than vinegar and, by phrasing it in a way that made Wyatt think of it as pleasing her, Yuki had ensured he would clean his plate. With Yuki's willowy and almost ethereal exotic looks it was easy to forget how bloody good she was at being a Mistress.

James and Wyatt ate in silence for a bit, each of them making incoherent noises of appreciation, while the women chatted.

"Ma'am, this is amazing," Wyatt said around a mouthful of omelet. "Did you go to school for this?"

"No, cooking is my hobby. In exchange for using the old barn as my studio I cook and keep Michelle from trying to kill us with her attempts at anything culinary."

"Hey now! I make a mean batch of chocolate chip cookies and I can order out with the best of them. Besides, who else is going to let you create gigantic statues of nude men in bondage in their barn?"

Wyatt gave Michelle a confused look but James spoke up, "Yuki is a sculptor, mostly in metal but she does some stonework now and again. We moved down here from Chicago so she could have enough room to do some really big pieces."

"And not freeze my tits off," Yuki added with a smile.

Wyatt chewed in silence then looked towards the direction of the foyer. "Did you do that fountain?"

Looking pleased, Yuki nodded. "Yep. It was my welcome home present to Michelle after she got back from overseas." She glanced at Michelle then back at Wyatt. "She always loved horses growing up. We actually met when we were thirteen at a stables where we boarded our horses."

"Really?" Wyatt's obvious interest in Michelle's

past both pleased and irritated her. There were some things she wasn't ready to share with him yet. While she was sure he knew that her father was a Senator and her mother a well-known actress she wanted to know that he liked her for who she was, not just because she was some celeb's daughter.

Michelle kicked Yuki beneath the table. "I'm going to take him on a tour of the grounds as soon as we're done with breakfast. Callahan, can you ride?"

"Yes, Ma'am."

"Good. Then you can take Fancy Pants. "

"You have a horse named Fancy Pants?"

James laughed. "Don't let the name fool you. That horse will throw you the second he smells weakness. Kinda like some women I know."

Yuki slowly shook her head. "You just earned yourself some time in the cradle, my dear."

Her husband swallowed hard and plastered a smile on his face that wasn't fooling anyone. "I live to serve."

Wyatt looked over at Michelle and she saw a thousand questions in his gaze, along with speculation, anger, pain, desire, and a tiny trace of hope. He had the most expressive eyes she'd ever seen and their power hadn't dimmed over the past year. If anything, she was more attuned to him now than ever before. Was it because there were no longer any restrictions between them? There were no superior officers watching them now, no boots that would run their mouths. Now it was just Michelle and Wyatt and she marveled at how natural it felt to be with him.

Having the right to touch him as she wished,

she leaned over and slipped her hand into Wyatt's. As their fingers curled together, something deep inside of her soul shifted, a hidden pain roaring momentarily to the surface before she ruthlessly pushed it down. No, she would not think of the last man she'd loved and lost.

Wyatt turned his hand so that their fingers laced tighter together. He gave her a gentle squeeze, bringing her back to the warmth of the breakfast table on a beautiful, sunny morning and away from the ice of her memories. She could see his concern and smiled. Out of the corner of her eye she noticed both Yuki and James observing them.

She straightened, but didn't release Wyatt's hand. "If you want you can ride my horse, Bitch Goddess."

He laughed, a surprised and deep bass rumble. "No, I think one bitch goddess is enou...er...um... Aw, shit."

Michelle had to press her lips together to keep from laughing. Thankfully, Yuki stepped in and saved him by suggesting, "Stop by my studio. I'd love to get some sketches of Wyatt, if that's okay with him. He has a very interesting face. Not pretty boy handsome, but a face you'd remember nonetheless."

"By the way, my wife likes to sculpt nude men." James grinned. "So don't worry if she asks you to strip. Once she's in her artistic mindset you cease to be male and become a set of interesting angles and planes to shape."

Yuki smiled and sat back with a sigh. "That's why James doesn't have a problem with me staring at naked men for hours at a time."

Wyatt toyed with his last piece of bacon. "Can I ask you a question? And I'm not being offensive or anything, I'm just curious."

Yuki and James exchanged a look. "Sure."

"Since James is your submissive, would you really not do something if he asked you not to? Like, what if he didn't want you to sketch nude men. I mean you're a Mistress, shouldn't you do whatever you want?"

James shook his head. "She might be my Mistress, but she is also my wife. Man, you really are new to this, aren't you?"

Wyatt shrugged uncomfortably and Yuki gave him an understanding look. "I would never hurt James by doing something that we've both agreed is a hard limit."

James gave his wife a fond smile which she returned. "Just like I would never betray Yuki's trust."

Yuki stood and James followed suit, each clearing their plates. "You guys have fun today. If you need me give me a ring."

After pulling her hand away from Wyatt's delicious grip she stood as well. Stretching her arms overhead, liking the way Wyatt's gaze fastened onto her breasts, Michelle nodded. "We should be by the studio in a couple hours."

The door shut behind the departing couple, leaving her alone with a very sexy man who smelled wonderful, like her soap cut with a trace of his natural masculine scent.

Wyatt glanced down at his feet. "Can I go upstairs and grab my boots?"

"Sure."

He turned to leave and she suddenly didn't

want to be alone. Unable to help herself, she moved quickly to stand in front of him, her breasts pressing into his chest. Despite having used the local BDSM club three months ago to relieve some tension, and only oral sex at that, she craved his touch, yearned for the feeling of a strong man wrapping his arms around her. "Wyatt, please hold me."

He made a low sound deep in his chest and gently drew her to him as if she were made of glass. Instantly her whole body relaxed and woke up, the need that never seemed to sleep roaring back to life. She felt his cock stir against her belly but she only snuggled closer, loving the smell of her soap on his skin. He began to slowly stroke her hair and she smiled against him.

"Doc, what made you so sad back at the table?"

Tears stung her eyes and she shoved away from him. "I don't want to talk about it."

He tilted his head, calling her on her bullshit without saying a word. Unable to face the understanding in his expression she spun on her heel and walked to the mudroom. "Meet me out in the stables. I have a bunch of sports team t-shirts I sleep in. There should be one big enough for you to wear if the shirts James gave you don't fit."

Yeah, it felt like running, but she didn't care. She needed to get her shit together. This wasn't about her, it was about him. He needed her to be strong, he needed her. So, while she couldn't seem to manage to let go of her grief for herself, she would let it go for him. Or at the very least, hold it at bay.

When she walked into the barn both horses trilled a greeting, their feet stamping on the earth.

Goddess popped her head out first, a beautiful cream colored Arabian mare with a rather bitchy temperament. Michelle got her as a gift from her father for her twenty-first birthday, and she loved that horse more than just about anything in the world. One of the few things that had helped her wash away the horrors she'd seen overseas had been taking long rides on Goddess.

In the stall across the way she could see the white and black nose of Pants, her four year old pinto Tennessee Walker gelding. She'd named him Fancy Pants because his black and white pattern left his hind legs and rear end solid black, as if he'd been dipped in black ink while the rest of him resembled a Dalmatian's coat. Sweet as the day was long, he lifted his lip in greeting to her.

Both horses were eager to get out of the barn and she had to laugh at their high spirited antics. One of the barn cats, an orange marmalade tabby named Butter, watched them from her perch in the rafters. Growing up, Michelle had never been allowed to have a pet other than her horse which was kept at a separate location from her parents' penthouse condo in the heart of Chicago. So when she'd moved here and finally had the space for animals, she'd become a bit of a crazy cat lady. Right now, there were four cats on the property who kept it clear of rodents and kept the horses company. It wasn't unusual to come into the barn and see one of the cats sleeping contentedly on one of the horses' backs. Cats only had respect for themselves, so if they chose to gift you with their presence they expected you to worship them accordingly. This included horses. A few stalls down, sitting on a bale of hay, Murphy, her former tom-now-eunuch cat, sat regarding her with profound disdain for interrupting his nap.

She was coming back from the tack room with her saddle when Wyatt wandered in, a huge smile filling his face when he saw her and then looked at the horses.

"Doc, you have some beautiful horseflesh."

Pleasure warmed her heart and she smiled back. It almost felt like he'd complimented her children, as sad as that was. "Fancy Pants, or Pants for short, is the big pinto. He'll be your mount so why don't you say hello."

He pulled two carrots out from the waistband of his pants. "Am I allowed to bribe?"

She swung her saddle up, moving with Goddess as she shifted. "Sure. Just don't be offended if Goddess plays hard to get. She's a high maintenance bitch."

Wyatt's lips turned white as he pressed them together and turned his back at her narrow-eyed look, speaking softly to Pants. Of course, the horse turned on the charm as soon as he saw the carrot, arching his neck and nibbling at the edge of Wyatt's shirt. Actually it was her Chicago Bears shirt, but damn, it did look good on him. He had such broad shoulders and the light dusting of dark hair on his arms practically begged to be touched. Her gaze fastened on his wrists and she imagined what he'd look like in leather cuffs. Not the shiny black leather that most people preferred, but rather a rugged brown set of cuffs with bronze metal rings instead of silver. She'd have to contact one of her old friends in Chicago to see if she could have a pair custom made.

Keeping her mind on task was harder than she

thought, but they were soon saddled up and headed off to tour her property. They followed the trail she'd made over the past couple months, one that would eventually take them to the edge of the good sized lake that sat to the west of the house. Overhead the sun blazed down, but the trees on either side of the trail kept them shaded.

She tugged the brim of her cream-colored cowboy hat down a bit lower and felt a twinge of guilt that she hadn't gotten a hat for Wyatt. After they got back she'd find a men's store in Austin that would deliver and order him some clothes. He might bitch about it, but if he threw too big a fit she'd take away his privilege to wear clothing altogether. Part of her hoped he would throw a fit just for the excuse to see him naked.

A bolt of excitement lit her nervous system and she amended her plans for the afternoon. She was initially going to talk to him about why he was so despondent, but maybe it would be better to give him some good memories. Something to hold onto when the going got tough, when he hated her for pulling the scabs off his emotional wounds.

Clicking, she urged Goddess forward and they moved at a brisk trot. Behind her Wyatt swore softly and she wondered if it was because of her ass rising up and down in the saddle, or if he had an erection, making trotting a most comfortable experience. A hint of mineral tang in the air from the lake reached her nose and she smiled as they broke through the tree line on the shore of the lake.

Thanks to the previous owners, there was a large sandy beach adjacent to the water and a pontoon floated farther out. There was even a pier, but she had no interest in fishing or boating right now.

Wyatt rode up next to her. "Wow, big lake. How much property do you have?"

"Around a hundred acres." She dismounted and pulled a large folded blanket down from behind her saddle. She left the reins loose so Goddess could wander around at will. "This lake is pretty deep. It's mineral-fed so we can swim in it without worrying about splashing around in toxic waste from some factory upstream."

Wyatt followed suit, dismounting and giving Pants' neck a good scrub before sending him off to graze. "We going skinny dipping?"

"No."

He pursed his lips and helped her stretch the blanket out onto the sand. The red and gold patterns woven into the fabric blazed in the bright sunlight and she sighed, turning her face to the sky. "Strip."

"What?"

"I said strip. Take off your clothes and lie down on the blanket on your stomach."

"Why?"

There was so much suspicion in that word that she snorted and tossed off her hat. "Either do as I say or stop wasting my time."

He stiffened, then whipped his shirt off with a defiant tilt to his chin. She pretended indifference and turned her face back to the sun while closing her eyes. In reality, she was afraid of her own actions if she saw him fully nude, waiting in the sunlight for her like one of Yuki's most erotic bronze statues come to life.

Settling sounds came from the area of the

blanket before he said, "I'm on my stomach on the blanket, Domina."

Opening her eyes, she turned and slowly took in the visual feast of Wyatt's perfect ass. Round and muscular, a shade lighter than his tanned back, her hands flexed with the need to grab it and sink her teeth into it. He looked up at her with hazel eyes gone dark with desire.

"Close your eyes."

He frowned, but complied. She moved around to his side so he couldn't peek and began to take off her own clothes. After folding them in a neat pile she straddled Wyatt's back, tracing the muscles stiff with tension with her gaze. He kept twitching like he was going to look over his shoulder, but so far his eyes stayed closed.

"Callahan, you're wound up tighter than an eighty-year-old virgin's cooch."

He laughed, his voice rough as he replied, "Domina, you have no idea how hard it is to keep from looking at you. To see your beautiful body, to brush my knuckle between your legs to find out how wet you are for me."

She swallowed hard, her knees threatening to give out. "Do you want to know how wet I am?"

"Fuck yes."

She slowly knelt down onto his back until she straddled his hips. Tilting her pelvis, she leisurely rubbed her pussy in tight circles on his lower spine. She was wet enough that she slid easily, his muscles bunching and shifting beneath her aching sex. Unable to help herself, she lay full on his back, her breasts crushed against him as she pressed her clit into this tailbone.

"I'm going to give you a back rub, Wyatt. Do you

think you can stay still for me?"

"I don't know." His shoulders flexed, a delicious display of male power. "If I do, will you let me taste you? Please?"

"No." She leaned forward, breathing in his ear. "But if you hold very still I may orgasm while I'm touching you. Do you think you can do that for me? I'll need you very, very still."

He froze, then a full body shiver vibrated his frame against hers. "I'll try."

"Don't try. Do."

Beginning with his shoulders she pressed her thumbs into the rock-hard mass of muscle, working him until his breathing became more even. She placed a soft kiss where his spine met his neck, rubbing her lips back and forth on the soft hair there. He had a variety of tattoos and she admired them while she worked, tracing the patterns with her finger. She dragged her nipples over him, relishing the pleasurable ache radiating through her body, unwilling to do anything to assuage it yet.

She continued to work on him, moving down his ribs, pausing now and again to place a kiss on different sections, or a sharp nip if the mood hit her. Wyatt would tense, then relax, then tense again. Spinning around, she began to work on his tight buttocks, tracing her finger down the seam and smiling when he clenched up.

"Have you ever let a woman play back here?"

"Hell no." His voice was tight. "Domina."

"Hmmm." She mentally added taking him with a strap-on to her bucket list.

Soon the warmth of the sun did the work of her hands, soothing him and helping him relax beneath her. The scent of his heated skin mixed with her own, creating an intoxicating and very unique perfume that added to her arousal. God, she wanted to flip him over and look at what he was packing, see if the reality matched the glimpses she'd seen through his jeans, but she didn't dare. Giving herself to him too quickly would spoil his full appreciation of the pleasures his body had to offer them both. She needed him fully committed to the moment, every ounce of his concentration on her. She needed him to embrace life, to look forward to the pleasures that far outweighed the pains.

He'd been amazingly well-behaved today and she wondered what his triggers were for his panic attacks. Being exposed outdoors didn't seem to stress him out too much, but being out for a ride might have helped. There was just something about a horse's rocking gait that seemed to sooth the soul. She'd have to push him a little bit later today. Right now it was all about pleasure and he'd been such a good boy.

She turned around again and began to rock her hips back and forth, as if his hard cock was inside of her, her movements fluid and unhurried. Bracing her hands on his shoulders she moved a little faster, her throbbing clit dragging deliciously over his smooth skin covering taut muscle. His breathing picked up and he began to make rough sounds deep in his throat as she moved back and forth. With each drag of her hips she drifted closer to her orgasm, a tightening in her stomach making her moan aloud.

"Fuck, Doc...uh...Domina, please let me make you come. I swear I won't do anything you don't want. Please let me touch you." She'd bet her 'Vette that right now his cock was close to bursting, blood filling him until he wanted to rut into the ground beneath him. The pain from his denied orgasm must be exquisite and a deep wave of satisfaction moved through her. All that power, all that need, contained and controlled by her will. It made her feel like she held a tiger captive on a leash made of cobwebs.

"No." She smiled as he cursed and his hips rose just the slightest bit beneath her.

She didn't know what it was about teasing a man that got her off so intensely, but knowing that Wyatt wanted her so badly and couldn't have her because he'd chosen to submit to her wishes drove her crazy. Desire burned through her, hotter than the sun beating down on her shoulders, and she began to play with her nipples, squeezing and pinching them, imagining they were in his mouth. Her whole body became sensitized and she opened herself to the feeling, inhaling Wyatt's scent mixed with her musk deep into her lungs, mentally straining for a connection to him.

Each roll of her hips increased his agitation until he practically bucked under her, as if he was fucking a willing woman beneath him.

"Mmmm, I'm going to come, Wyatt. My pussy is so wet and swollen. Imagine what it would feel like to plunge your cock into me right now, to fuck the orgasm out of me."

"God dammit!" Wyatt started to get up, then settled back down. "I'm losing my fucking mind, Domina. Please come, please use me. Fucking hell, I can feel how hot and wet you are. Come for me, please come for me." His voice had a deep, guttural quality and yet still somehow managed to sound like begging. A rough and sweet pleading that moved her heart and brushed against her soul.

She rode him hard, all pretenses of seduction gone. Grinding her pelvis in tight circles on his back she gasped at the first tightening sensation deep in her belly, a delicious precursor of the pleasure waiting a breath away. She lay fully against him, her breathing ragged as she wrapped her arms around him the best she could, wanting this connection, needing it. This was Wyatt beneath her, the man who'd risked his life time and time again to save hers, the man who trusted her enough to give himself to her for a month's time.

"You feel so good," she breathed into his ear. "I'm about to come. Everything is getting tight, needy. I...oh God...Wyatt."

He rolled his hips beneath her, the muscles of his back contracting and flexing as he moved with her, giving her what she needed, what she craved. She pressed herself as close to him as she could and bit the swell of muscle where his shoulder connected to his neck, muffling her cries. Then her body broke with pleasure and she writhed atop him, her empty pussy clenching and releasing, a welcome rush of intense sensation that had her moaning incoherently. Through it all Wyatt kept whispering deliciously naughty things to her, a litany of how he was going to take her, fuck her, taste her when she finally gave him permission.

When the last shudder was wrung from her pleasure-saturated body she collapsed on top of him, her rapid breathing slowing while he continued to move beneath her, little involuntary twitches that made her smile. Oh, he was feeling it now, that raw hunger that could only come from fierce, unsated sexual need. She rubbed her face back and forth over him before lifting herself off and standing on unsteady legs. She'd left a slick spot on his back, evidence of her release.

It would be wonderful to make him flip over and ride either his amazing tongue or big cock, but with the edge taken off of her own need, she found herself more solidly in control of her own desire, allowing her to see to his. With his eyes tightly closed, Wyatt practically trembled from the strain of obeying her wishes. She ran her finger through the moist folds of her labia, gathering her arousal.

Kneeling on the side he wasn't facing, she traced her finger over his lips, gasping as he opened his mouth and sucked at her with an almost frantic need. Each flick of his tongue seemed to stroke between her legs, as if her finger had a direct connection to her clit. Her desire began to slowly build again and she reluctantly pulled away from him.

He started to turn, but she stood and placed her foot lightly on the back of his neck. "Don't move."

It took her longer than usual to put on her clothes due to her shaking hands, but she finally managed to get everything into place and nudged his hip with her foot. "Get dressed. Yuki is expecting us in the studio."

He leaned up on his elbows and gave her a dirty look that made her giggle. His brows drew lower, but the edge of his mouth twitched with a suppressed smile. "How cold is the water in the lake?"

"Not too bad at the shore, but if you swim out deeper it gets chilly."

"Excellent."

He leapt from the blanket and she had a brief glimpse of a very impressive erection before he sprinted away and surged into the water, his broad shoulders flexing as he dove beneath the surface. Feeling wonderfully alive and satisfied, she watched him swim out to the pontoon and back, splashing through the water with long, aggressive strokes while she went to gather up their horses.

*****

Yuki looked up with they entered the small living room off the barn, a wide smile lighting her face. She had on her welder's apron and James sat on the couch pushed against the far wall, his laptop open as he checked his investments and did some day trading. In the real world James was a very successful investment banker, so successful that he had been able to retire at the age of thirty-five, though he still played the market.

"Hi guys," Yuki said as she examined Wyatt's still damp hair. "Did you go down to the lake?"

"We did." Michelle glanced over at Wyatt with a grin. "It was most refreshing."

James closed his laptop and shook his head in mock pity. "Looks like one of you had fun."

"I don't know if fun is the word I'd be using," Wyatt muttered.

The combined laughter of Yuki and James filled the room. Yuki shrugged out of her apron and pointed her chin to the coffee pot. "Would you like a cup, Michelle?"

James stood and gestured to Wyatt. "Come on, I'll show you around while these two gossip. You have no idea how nice it is to have another guy here."

Wyatt shot Michelle a heated glance, but allowed James to lead him out the door.

As soon as he was out of sight Michelle let out a harsh sigh and collapsed back on the overstuffed pale blue couch against the wall. "Motherfucker."

"I was going to ask if he was any good, but the way you're all relaxed now speaks for itself."

She sat up and fidgeted with the edge of the couch that had begun to fray. "Well, we didn't exactly do that."

"Huh. Oral?"

"Um, nope."

"Fingers?"

"Uh uh."

"For fuck's sake woman, did you come from a kiss?"

"Actually we haven't kissed yet either." She dared a glance at Yuki and winced at the disapproval radiating from her best friend. "I don't want to rush things."

"Okay, so how is somehow having an orgasm with him not rushing things? You're putting the cart before the horse, my dear."

"Don't push me. I-I'm not ready."

Yuki crossed the room with a brisk stride before squatting down in front of Michelle, getting in her personal space. Typical Domme, always poking where she wasn't invited. "Honey, Owen would be super pissed if he saw you doing this."

Pain sliced through her soul, but it wasn't quite as sharp as usual. "Don't talk about him to me! I knew him better than anyone."

"Don't be stupid. You may have known him better than I did, but I also know that you're only hurting yourself by refusing to move on. It's been almost five years, Michelle. I believe that if there is such a thing as heaven, he is looking down on you and doing everything he can to make sure you don't close yourself off from a great guy."

Tears burned behind her eyes and she blinked them back, willing them not to fall. "I don't know if I can do it. I don't know if I could live through losing someone again." Her voice choked off and she swallowed hard. "I can't help but feel like I'm cheating on Owen with Wyatt."

"Oh, Michelle." Yuki gathered her in a hug, moving to sit next to her on the couch. "You ever hear that saying about life being like looking into a mirror and death looking through a window? It's true. I know wherever he is he wants you to move on, fall in love, get married, and have beautiful blue-eyed babies. Shoot, for all you know Owen pulled some strings up in Heaven and sent Wyatt to you."

Though it would have felt so good to let go, to let Yuki hold her while she had a good cry, she couldn't give up that much control. She suddenly needed Wyatt, wanted him by her side, wanted him touching her and making her feel alive. Memories of their time together by the lake flew through her mind and she silently cursed herself for using him so roughly. He had feelings and she shouldn't have pushed him like that without having even kissed him.

God, what was wrong with her?

Yuki must have sensed her change in mood

because she left the couch and went across the room to the cupboard, pulling out two mismatched mugs. "Did I ever tell you how unfair it is that you look pretty when you cry?"

Michelle giggled, allowing Yuki to draw her away from her dark thoughts. "You are such a sadist."

"Much to James' relief, my tastes don't run in that direction." She poured them two mugs of coffee, no sugar and no cream, then moved across the room before handing Michelle her mug. "Look, I'm not trying to tell you how to train your sub, but give the guy a bone."

Laughing, Michelle raised her cup to her lips. "I think he's the one that wants to give me a bone."

"So let him knock the cobwebs off your pussy."

"You are so foul."

"I'm just saying that it's not natural to go this long without dick. If I didn't know for certain you didn't swing that way, I'd swear you have a female sub hidden in your closet."

"I still want to take things slow with him...but maybe not this slow. You're right, I need to show him some honey tonight instead of vinegar."

"You give a man one good, toe-curling, I-rocked-your-fucking-world blow job and he'll never leave you."

"I'll take that under advisement."

Chapter 6

The muscles along either side of Wyatt's spine groaned in protest as he hauled another bag of feed into the stables. Thankfully, he regularly worked out his abdominals to regain the strength he'd lost from his injury so he wasn't worried about re-injuring himself. James had given him a pair of thick leather gloves and a long shirt to wear and then they set to work at cleaning up the stables.

It had been a long, long time since he'd done physical labor on a ranch, not since his grandparents got too old to run their farm and retired to Port Lavaca off the Gulf Coast. The scent of hay and sweat brought back a lot of good memories and he let himself relax into the work. It was nice having something to do, something that made a visible and instant difference. He'd never be happy as a desk jockey, sitting in a cubicle day after day, doing tedious work that would grind his soul into dust. Lifting the last bag from the wagon behind the ATV he used the sleeve of the shirt to wipe the sweat off his face. Once the last bag was in storage he cracked his neck and wandered back out.

"Catch." James tossed him a bottle of cold water.

Wyatt caught it, cracked the seal and took a big swig. Sweet and cold, the liquid rushed down his throat, clearing away the dust. "Thanks."

James straddled the ATV and looked over at him with a smile. "Thanks for your help today." He hesitated and the smile left his face. "Look, I know what goes on between you and Michelle is none of my business, but...well she's had a rough time the last couple years."

"What do you mean?"

"Take it easy on her."

Confused, he capped the water bottle. "Okay. What are you trying to tell me? Just spit it out. I'm not good at this beating around the bush bullshit."

"No can do. Not my story to tell. I only wanted to let you know that even though Michelle comes off strong, she really has a very gentle heart and can be easily hurt." He licked his lips and glanced at the barn where his wife was and back at Wyatt. "I just thought you might want to know that you're the first guy she's brought home in four years."

"Excuse me?"

James turned on the ATV, the roar of the engine flooding the air. James raised his voice to be heard over the engine noise. "When things get tough, and they will because that's life, you need to hold onto that idea. I'm not saying she hasn't dated, but she's never brought anyone home to meet us, and we're pretty much members of her family. Don't let her push you away, 'cause she's gonna try even if she's not consciously aware that she's doing it. The more real things become with you, the more vulnerable she feels."

Wyatt shook his head and a drop of sweat creased down his face. "I don't understand what the fuck you're talking about."

"I know. Just know that Yuki and I will give you

guys your space, and we're here if you ever need to talk. Make sure you wash up in the bathroom off the mudroom before you go into the rest of the house. Michelle is death on anyone tromping crap all over her floors. I bet she hasn't eaten yet, either."

"So, I should make her lunch?"

"Never hurts to show women you appreciate them."

James revved the engine and waved, leaving Wyatt standing in the late afternoon sun. He looked at the main house, his gaze searching the windows for some hint of the female inside. She confused the shit out of him. On the one hand, she made him want to throw her up against a wall and fuck her until she couldn't walk straight, and, on the other hand, he wanted to sit at her feet and worship her.

Or both.

Man, was he one fucked up *hombre*.

If he was thinking with his big head instead of his little head he'd ask James to take him into town then call his sister to come pick him up. Surely that was what any normal guy would do. He wouldn't be thinking about how good it would feel to finally make love to his Domina, to have the intimacy between them that came from the act. And if he was being honest with himself, the thought of her tying him up and having her wicked way with him made his already hard dick jerk in his pants.

His boots scuffed along the earth and he had to keep himself at a casual stroll. Not that anyone was around him, but a man had to have some pride. Part of him was scared at how much he wanted to be with her, but then again when he thought about who she was, what they had been through together...well, fuck, if the woman who saved his life wasn't good enough to be worshiped like a Queen he didn't know who was. The memory of her looking down at him as she and a corpsman tried to save his life flashed through his mind, complete with the phantom smells of acrid smoke and fresh blood.

He saw movement from the corner of his eye and he tensed, his mind instantly shouting at him that he was under attack. The spot between his shoulder blades began to itch and his primitive brain screamed at him to run to the house a hundred yards away or dive behind the nearest solid object and seek cover. The fight or flight instinct tried to overwhelm his rational mind and turn him into a thoughtless animal.

Fuck, why does this have to happen now?

There was no stopping the fear or his body's response, but he knew how to ride it out now and began to employ the techniques he'd been taught to make his stupid animal brain stop trying to take over. Because it was still daylight he was able to use one of the orienting tricks his therapist from the VA had taught him for dealing with panic attacks. He stopped and focused on the house, keeping his arms at his side. This position left him totally vulnerable and his fear ramped up another notch. Every muscle in his body trembled and he fought an internal battle against himself, forcing his body to stay still even as his mind screamed to flee. His muscles locked up tight and a sick feeling of dread filled him until it felt like the world was ending.

His breath came out in rapid pants but he stood still, part of him waiting for an enemy bullet to tear into him, fighting the irrational fear. Thank God he was alone. When his panic attack had struck in the middle of the mall while shopping with his sister, it had been a humiliating experience. He'd been on the edge of a complete meltdown, surrounded by too many people, when a teenage boy bumped into him.

Instead of brushing it off Wyatt had turned on the kid and had been about to kick his ass when his sister stepped between them, pleading with him to back off. She later said that what had scared her the most was that at first he looked at her like he didn't even recognize her and she'd been really afraid of him for the first time in her life. That event was the one that spurred him to seek help from the over-stretched and understaffed local VA. Turns out he wasn't the only one having problems adjusting to the real world, and the government had vastly underestimated how many would need assistance holding their shit together enough to just get by.

Now he employed a couple of the ways to get out of panic attack that worked for him. First, he began to tap his fingers against his thumb and picked three things to look at. From his vantage point he immediately locked onto the porch leading to Michelle's house, and what to his animal self signified safety. The brass door handle of the backdoor leading to Michelle's house, the potted red geraniums at the bottom of the steps of the porch, and a set of silver and wood wind chimes hanging near a pair of rocking chairs. In no real pattern, he made his gaze go from object to object, naming each and making himself see it. Chimes, door, plant, then plant, chimes, door. Over and over, faster and faster, focusing his mind to stay occupied with both the object identification and keeping his fingers tapping against his thumb. He used to worry about looking like a fucking moron while doing the hand thing, but it was better than losing himself.

A few moments later, the panic began to recede, going down the scale from an eight on a scale of ten, slowly back down to his normal state of two. Yeah, he always felt jumpy now, and while he didn't like it, he'd rather be jumpy than stoned out of his mind on the drugs they threw at vets. While that worked great for some guys, it turned one of his buddies into a zombie, and that scared the shit out of him more than freaking out in public.

He continued his walk to the house, his head down and praying that no one had noticed. Soon he reached the back door and sprinted the last three steps, that itchy spot between his shoulder blades still insisting a bullet with his name on it was on its way. The cool air in the house brought an instant sigh to his lips and helped him push the memories back. Once inside in the quiet house, it became impossible for his mind to insist that bad guys were going to ambush him from the laundry room. The familiar scents of detergent and fabric softener filled his nose and he took another deep breath, grounding himself in the present.

Sighing, he leaned back against the door and felt most of the tension dissipate, leaving behind the metallic taste of the adrenaline that flooded his system during his attack. The muscles of his back were still tight, and his arms were sore, but that was more from the workout he'd gotten while cleaning the barn with James. Wyatt had forgotten how good it felt to be physically worn out. He had to admit that other than lifting weights he really hadn't done much to keep in shape other than the occasional bout of physical therapy. He'd done some sporadic jogging, but he worked most of the day with his dad and didn't like going outside at night unless he was with someone. With a frown he tugged his boots off and headed into the bathroom, banishing the thought of what it would be like to have someone try to mug him as he jogged before it could fully form.

Cool blue glass tiles mixed with different shades of green gave the room an almost iridescent look. He quickly stripped and stepped into the oversized shower, glad to see a bar of regular soap among the bottles of feminine washes and shampoos. Being inside Michelle's home was strangely intimate, as if everything he looked at hinted at hidden part of her personality and mind that he'd wanted to explore for a long time.

The taste of salt rolled over his lips as the water pounded down on him, scouring away the dirt. He'd lost count of the times he'd fantasized about Michelle over the past two years. When he'd been assigned to the base outside of Kabul, he'd been relieved to finally have a post with at least some of the comforts of home, like electricity and running water. He'd just come off of rotation with the EOD unit and his nerves were past strung out. Guarding a stationary object was like a vacation.

Even if he hadn't been assigned to watch over Sapphire, he always took a personal interest in the medics. It didn't take a rocket scientist to figure out that if you wanted to live, you needed to keep your doctors and nurses as well supplied and guarded as possible. He made sure that his men treated them with the utmost respect, even when they were prima-donna assholes, which most of them were.

Except Doc.

Humble, kind, and one of the most beautiful women he'd ever seen in real life, she had the kind of presence that made people around her want to work with her. He'd seen her take control of chaotic, bloody, terrible situations and snap everyone into shape. To say that he admired her was an understatement. That didn't mean he wouldn't give her shit, or that she was perfect, but they had an almost instant rapport with one another.

Rinsing off the last of the soap he turned off the water and grabbed a towel.

As time had passed, things in the sandbox had gotten infinitely more interesting and annoying at the same time. He could tell she wanted him, there was no way he was wrong, and he certainly wanted her, but nothing inappropriate ever happened other than being there for her the only time he'd seen her cry.

Giving his reflection a rueful grin he opened the vanity again and took out the stuff he needed to shave. At some point he'd have to go back to his place to get some clothes, but right now he didn't want to be away from her.

There was something fragile about her trust.

He hadn't needed James to tell him that Michelle was vulnerable. He saw it in her eyes every time someone had died despite her best efforts. When she lost someone it cut her soul-deep, and he wondered how she could live with so many emotional scars. God knows he remembered and mourned the face of every man he'd lost in combat, but the injuries, the suffering she'd seen probably surpassed his experiences in the field.

His stomach began to knot up again and he stopped thinking about the war, instead focusing on the little basket of dried flowers adorning the sink. Some of them he recognized and he began to list the flowers in his head, forcing himself to think only about that plant and if he'd ever seen it in his mother's garden. Soon his mind wandered back to mundane, safe thoughts like spending time with his extended family in his parents' massive backyard, sipping homemade lemonade and discussing whether or not it was too hot to play a game of flag football.

It never was.

He rinsed his face after he was finished shaving and glanced at his dirty clothes on the floor. There was no way he was putting those things back on, the shirt was stiff with dried sweat. Looking down at the towel around his waist he grinned and began to plot a seduction.

*****

Twenty minutes later, after a trip to the kitchen, he finally found Michelle in a large study at the back of the house. The rustic decor extended to this room as well with its open beam ceiling and off-white plaster walls. Floor to ceiling bookcases took up two walls while a sliding glass door led out onto a concrete patio festooned with pots of brightly colored flowers. Beyond that mature trees stretched out as far as he could see, a lush burst of green beneath the gorgeous blue Texas sky.

Her blonde hair glowed in the light streaming through the window and her brows scrunched down as she typed something on her computer. She'd changed into a pair of loose white pants and a matching shirt that had started to slide off one shoulder. Embroidered flowers in reds and oranges trailed around the neckline of her shirt, bringing out her tan. To his amusement she sat cross legged in the computer chair, as tempting as an ice cream sundae.

"Hey, you hungry?"

She looked up and the tension melted off her face as she smiled at him. Her bright blue eyes widened as she caught sight of the tray he held and she licked her lower lip. "Famished."

He brought in the tray he'd loaded down with food scavenged from her fridge. He knew how to cook well enough to not starve to death, but had stuck to simple chicken sandwiches and fresh cut fruit. Setting the tray down on the edge of her desk, he surreptitiously checked to make sure the towel was staying in place.

Now he had to figure out how to hit her hot buttons.

"Where should I sit?"

She clicked something her screen and turned to him. "At my feet."

His dick jumped and he quickly knelt before her, his cock now pressing fully against the soft terry cloth. He wanted so much to lean forward, to place his mouth on her sex and bite through her pants. He wondered if she wore panties beneath the white cotton, because she certainly wasn't wearing a bra.

She handed him a sandwich and took one herself, sighing as she took the first bite. "Thank you. Sometimes I forget to eat when I'm distracted."

"Me too," he mumbled around a mouthful of food. "What are you working on?"

She looked away and a hint of pink colored her cheeks. "I was ordering some things...for you."

He narrowed his eyes at her. "I don't want you spending your money on me."

She rolled her eyes. "I can spend my money however I want, and if I chose to spend it on you the polite thing would be to say thank you."

God, this woman threw him off his game. "Thank you, Domina. May your lowly slave ask what you bought him?"

Using her foot, she began to tug at the towel around his waist. "Some clothes and such."

If that towel moved another inch his dick would be poking out to say hi. "Can you pass me a strawberry, please?"

She smirked, obviously enjoying his discomfort, but she did as he asked. After selecting one she held it before his mouth. "I want you holding the strawberry between your lips."

He opened his mouth and held the delicate fruit between his teeth.

She leaned closer, the shoulder of her shirt dipping lower, giving him an unimpeded view of the lush curve of her breast. His heart threatened to pound right out of his chest when she closed her eyes and opened her mouth. With slow movements she began to eat the berry from his lips.

He wanted to move, to kiss her back, to touch her but he knew from their time earlier that she wanted him still. Sweet juice flooded his tongue and he swallowed, wishing it was her honey he was eating. The soft brush of her lips against his drove him wild and even the friction of the terry cloth towel against his cock was almost too much.

She pulled back just the slightest bit. "You may have the rest."

He quickly chewed and swallowed the fruit, aware of how close she still was, how her berry-scented breath blew across his lips. Tension hummed from her and he groaned in frustration. Just one little move and he would finally get what he craved, what he needed more than air.

"Wyatt, please kiss me."

With a growl that vibrated through his chest he grabbed her from her seat and pulled her down onto the floor with him. The moment their lips touched he wanted to howl with triumph. She fit against him perfectly, her soft mouth slanting against his in just the right way, her arms wrapping around him and her hand fisting in his hair, holding him while she kissed him back.

Their tongues met and stroked along each other. Fuck, could this woman kiss. Raw hunger burned through his body, his dick aching as he pressed against her. Unable to help himself he grabbed a handful of her ass and tugged her forward, groaning against her mouth when she parted her legs and pressed up against him.

Not breaking their kiss, she reached between them and ripped his towel away. Before he could protest she had her hand around his cock and everything went white. He became lost in her, the silken slide of her fist squeezing tight as she jerked her hand up and down his length. The burn started in the base of his spine and he pulled away enough to say, "I'm going to come."

Immediately she stopped touching him and moved back on her knees. Lust blazed through her beautiful blue eyes and her swollen breasts pressed against the thin fabric of her shirt. She had long, thick nipples that he wanted to suck on and her heavy breathing made her breasts tremble.

He reached forward to reclaim her lips, eager to taste her again, unable to get enough, but she held up her hand. "I want you on your back."

All kinds of dirty thoughts flew through his head at the things they could do together while he was on his back. Maybe she'd sit on his face, finally give him some of that pussy he'd been craving. There was something so sexy about being with a woman who knew what she wanted and wasn't afraid to demand it. Hell, he found everything about Michelle sexy. In his Domina was as if someone had brought the essence of his every wet dream to life, only better.

To his shock she pulled off his towel completely and gave a pleased, hungry sounding purr. "You really are a big boy."

She moved between his spread legs and grabbed his dick. Holding his gaze, she slowly lowered her head. As her mouth neared his prick, she leisurely stroked up his shaft, milking him with her thumb along the thick vein on the underside of his erection. Pre-cum wet the mushroom tip and he thought he was going to spurt all over her face when she delicately licked it away with feather soft brushes of her tongue.

"Oh fuck, please, let me touch you."

"No." She gave him a wicked grin and ran the nails of her free hand down his stomach, hard enough to leave red marks. The burning sting mixed with the ache of his dick, somehow making the drive to fuck, to come hard and long double until he trembled with the effort of obeying her. "Stay still and don't come until I give you permission."

Her soft mouth captured the tip of his erection and he fisted his hands to keep from grabbing the back of her head and shoving her down on his cock until his dick filled her throat. No way was he going to do anything that would make her stop the unbelievable feeling of her mouth sliding all the way down his shaft until her nose pressed against his pubic hair and her throat convulsed around him. It felt even better than he imagined, a pleasure that made his eyes roll back in his head.

The silken glide of her mouth back up his cock made his spine bow, and when she cupped his sac he thrust up into her mouth. She pulled back and gave his shaft a series of teasing licks until he settled back down. He needed to come so fucking bad, but he wouldn't let her down. She resumed the long, slow slide of her mouth up and down his dick. Every now and then she would add her teeth and he found himself looking forward to her nips, to the addition of a different kind of ache.

Fondling his balls, she picked up her pace, the up and down slide of her mouth the closest thing to heaven he'd ever felt. The more aroused he became the less clearly he could think until his world became only her fucking sexy mouth sucking him off. His balls drew up tight and he struggled to hold it. The burn in his balls spread through his body and he reached out to touch her but stopped himself just in time.

"I can't...you're so fucking good...gonna come."

She made a pleased sound and nipped his hip. "Count to thirty and you can come once you hit thirty."

The next thing he knew he was buried in her mouth up to his balls. Her clever tongue flicked the sensitive spot beneath the head of his cock as he reached ten. By fifteen she was doing a twisting hand motion at the base of his shaft, and by twenty he was back down her throat. Moving just the tiniest bit, she swallowed and as her throat convulsed around him and he lost the battle five seconds short of his goal. With a roar that started somewhere in the pit of his stomach he shot the first load of come down her throat.

His hips thrust up and she rode him, her tongue laving his tip, her hand coaxing more of his seed out, seed that she swallowed with erotic little moans. He buried his hands in her hair, loving the silk of it, watching her beautiful face as she gripped him and licked the sensitized head of his dick like a lollypop. She'd pulled more come out of him than he thought possible and a deep relaxation settled over him, his body turning into boneless mass against the floor.

Leaning up, she wiped a trace of his cum off her chin and sucked it off her finger. "Some Dommes don't do this."

His pleasure-befuddled brain barely processed her words. "What?"

"Give their submissive oral sex. They say it's demeaning. I say your body is mine to play with however I wish, and if I wish to have you come in my mouth I will." Her voice grew husky and he noticed how she squirmed a bit, her nipples rock hard against her shirt. "You taste delicious."

He motioned to her. "Let me return the favor."

She smiled and stood, briefly passing her hand over her pussy with a soft groan. "No."

"Why the hell not?" He sat up and tugged the towel back around his waist before standing.

"Because you came before I told you to."

He flushed and rubbed his face. "I thought I was close enough to count."

"Nope." She moved closer to him, her arms curving around his waist. "And it really is too bad, because I'm so very, very wet. In fact I've soaked my pants where they press against my pussy. Did you know that I keep the lips of my sex shaved?"

He swallowed hard, suddenly parched and unbelievably his dick started to get hard again. He'd never been ready to go this quick after an orgasm that good, but sure enough, his blood began to rush south as he imagined burying his face in her slit.

"Domina, please let me take care of you." He leaned down and brushed his lips against her neck, tracing the pounding vein of her pulse. "Let me lick you clean, suck on that hard little clit of yours while you ride my face."

She trembled against him and turned her head to his nipple, licking the metal then tugging it with her teeth before releasing him. "I have work to do. You can stay here and read a book if you like, or go explore the house."

She stepped away and he tried to tug her back, but the look she gave him had him dropping his hands. Frustration drew his stomach into a hard knot. "Why won't you let me make you come? Most women would be more than happy to have me go down on them."

"Because you haven't earned it. Licking my pussy is a privilege, making me come apart and orgasm is a privilege, and it is something to be earned. I'm not one of your bitches who drops to her knees the second you smile at her." Her voice grew low and she nailed him to the floor with a glare filled with equal parts heat and determination. "You have to earn this pussy."

He grinned, unable to stop the smartass comment rolling from his lips. "Do I need to run an obstacle course, pass a written exam? Or would that be an oral exam."

"You are about five seconds from having your ass thrown out of here." Her words were stern, but there was laughter in her eyes.

"Fine, fine." He wandered over to a bookshelf. "I don't understand you, but I want to."

She sighed and tugged the edge of her shirt up. "I wish I could give you some neat and tidy explanation for why I am the way I am, but I can't. No one ever abused me and I was never exposed to BDSM at a young age or anything like that. I just...when I'm able to top a man I feel complete."

Keeping his back to her, he pulled down a random book with a tree on the front cover. "So no straight sex for you, ever? Don't you ever want to make love?"

"Of course I do. Sometimes I even like a man to take charge, but very rarely. I don't fit into any category and I don't want to. I am who I am and I refuse to be unhappy because people don't like things they can't understand. I'm not weird or a freak and I can make regular vanilla love and enjoy the hell out of it with the right man."

The hint of sadness at the last part had him at her side, hugging her in less than a heartbeat. "Of course you aren't. You are a beautiful, confusing, and fascinating woman. Why would I want someone simple when I could spend the rest of my life trying to figure you out?" He internally winced at the rest of his life comment and tried to ignore the fact that he meant it. "So you can do whatever you want to me and I promise I won't call you a freak. I might call you a pervert, but never a freak."

She laughed and pushed at his chest, her chin once again held high. "I really need to get this work done, Wyatt."

"Fine, fine."

Turning around, he went back to the bookshelf and began to actually read the titles. Lots of autobiographies, craft and hobby books, and a huge science fiction collection mixed with various genres. As far as he could tell there was no rhyme or reason to how she had them arranged so he spent a good deal of time browsing, learning more about the woman who fascinated him.

He grabbed a biography on Winston Churchill and went to an oversized couch near the window. The sun-warmed reddish-brown leather felt good against his skin as he sat down and he placed a pillow behind his head. Opening the book, he began to read and let a contentment that he'd never felt before take him over. He belonged here and he prayed with every ounce of his soul that his

PTSD would stay under control.

Chapter 7

The warm late afternoon sun combined with a hell of an orgasm soon led to Wyatt dozing on the couch. He listened with half an ear as Michelle conducted her business, making brief phone calls where her voice became nothing more than a background song to his heartbeat. The couch was wide enough that he could lie on his back without having half his body hang off the edge and long enough to equip even his six-foot-two frame.

In other words, he was in heaven.

"Wyatt? I hate to wake you up, but I need to ask you a question."

He tried to force his eyes open, but all that resulted in was his eyebrows rising up while his eyes stayed shut. "'Sup?"

"You said you did woodworking for your father, right?"

"Yep."

"Are you any good?"

That question cleared the sleep from his mind and he sat up, leaning on one elbow and looking over at her desk. "Why?"

"Just answer the damn question."

"Well, I'm not like a master carpenter like my Pops, but I can hold my own."

"If I asked you to build something, described it to you and drew some pictures, would you be able to build it?"

"What is it?"

"A piece of furniture...of sorts."

"Probably. But if you wanted it padded or covered in fabric you'd have to take it to someone else. I could do a passable job at it, but nothing I'd want to sell anyone."

"Hmm." She looked back down at her computer, chewing distractedly on her lower lip.

"Do you have a reason for your question or can I go back to sleep?"

Without taking her eyes off the screen she said, "Stand up and get naked."

"What?"

"I said stand up and take that towel off. I don't want anything hiding that fantastic body of yours from my sight. Looking at you brings me pleasure." She smiled at him and he swore that Eve must have looked the same way when offering Adam a taste of the forbidden fruit.

He would have thought that after the blow job earlier he'd be sated, but one smile from her and his cock was once again filling and pressing against the towel. After stretching the kinks out from his nap he stood and dropped the towel, waiting for her to look at him. He wanted to see the desire in her eyes, to know that his body aroused her. He felt a little odd walking around with a hard-on but he was more determined than ever to fuck her into oblivion. If that meant playing her game, well, fuck, it wasn't like he wasn't enjoying the hell out of it.

A minute, then another passed and he began to feel silly standing here. "Forget about me, Doc?"

She looked up from the screen. "What did you call me?"

"Umm, Domina."

"Hmph. No, I did not forget about you, but maybe you need something to remind you whom you serve. Come here."

He approached her, curiosity mixing with his desire. When he reached her side she reached out and clasped her hand around his cock, rubbing her thumb over the slit. "You have a beautiful dick and I want it adorned."

A lazy groan spilled out of him as she squeezed a small drop of pre-cum out and licked it off her thumb. She then opened a drawer on her desk and rooted around inside. From where he stood he couldn't really see much and wondered if she was going to shackle him to the desk. When she pulled out what looked like three connecting large gold rings he gave her a questioning glance.

"Have you ever seen these while you were researching?"

"Can't say I have."

"This large ring goes over the base of your cock and your balls so that it presses against your pelvis, this smaller one snugs down over the top of your balls right below your erection, and this ring goes over your shaft."

He gave the device a wary look. "I think my dick is too thick."

"Don't worry, they adjust." She licked her lips and he hoped she would lick his dick instead. "I'll leave it comfortable for now, but if you piss me off, I'm tightening it."

"What happens when you tighten it?"

"I could fuck you for hours and hours and you wouldn't be able to come. It would trap the blood in your erection and leave you unable to spurt your seed into my mouth."

He grunted and took a step back. "No thanks."

She crooked her finger at him with a playful smile and he hesitantly came closer. She set the rings down and he let out a sigh of relief. She picked up a small bottle of hand lotion sitting next to a potted plant on her desk and shook some out onto her palm. Rubbing her palms together, she wheeled her chair closer to his pelvis.

"Hands behind your head."

He complied, enjoying the way her breath hitched as she gave his torso a leisurely exam. While he was as green as could be with the BDSM stuff, having a woman paying almost constant sexual attention to him like this was energizing. It seemed like the more she wanted him, the more he wanted her until he found himself in a state of constant arousal.

Warm lotion coated his cock as she began to massage him. Helpless against the arousal she so easily called forth from his body, he closed his eyes and gave himself over to the sensation of her hands. When she loosely circled her hand over his cock he thrust his hips forward.

"Be still."

For fucks sake, he was becoming Pavlov's dog about those words. As soon as she said 'be still' he became even more cranked up. By forcing him to not move she opened his mind completely to the sensations of her touching him. He wanted to run his hands through her hair, to rock his cock in and out of her clever fingers. She took her time, making sure he was thoroughly slicked up and almost shaking with the need to come. When she was finished he looked down, swinging between apprehension and need as she picked up the rings.

Here came the pain, the point where he found out that it was his misery that made her come, that she wouldn't be able orgasm without causing him agony. It was gonna hurt and he would have to decide if he could take the pain for the promise of her pleasure. Steeling himself, he held his breath until spots danced before his eyes. She slid her hand along his shaft and his breath came out in a gasp of pleasure at the sensation of her skilled touch.

"Easy," she whispered as she leaned against his hip, licking a trail over the protruding bone. Leaning back with a wicked smile, she cupped his balls, rolling them gently in her palm. After releasing him, leaving him straining for her touch, she opened the rings and maneuvered his dick and balls into their grip, tugging his sensitive skin through. The first big ring enveloped both his erection and testicles then pressed against his pelvis. The second ring was secured around the base of his dick, and the third ring snugged around his sac at the very top. They were tight, making him aware of their presence, but they didn't hurt.

In fact, it felt kinda good.

He fidgeted and she slapped his flank like a skittish horse. "Close your eyes."

That part was harder, and he tensed when she grasped his cock and began to move the rings around. The one around his sac tightened, an entirely pleasurable burn shot through his pelvis. When she stroked her fingers over his testicles he couldn't help a rough groan. A second later her laughter rubbed over his skin. "There, done."

Stunned, he looked down. Sure enough a gold

ring now circled his cock, pressing up against his dark pubic hair. Relief filled him that he wouldn't have to be in constant pain to please her, that she really didn't want to torture him. A stupid idea now that he thought about it, but, fuck, for a second there he'd been worried about how dark her sexual tastes ran. He started to reach for himself, then stopped. "Can I touch it, Domina?"

She held her hands out. "Be my guest."

The metal of the ring rapidly warmed against his skin and he traced the smooth circle. Then he cupped his balls and the jolt of pleasure almost knocked him back a step.

"What the fuck?"

She sat back in her chair with a contented smile. "Congratulations, you're one of the lucky men whose balls get sensitized by being constricted."

He gave his sack another rub and groaned. "Fuuuuuuck."

She stood and brushed past him, her perfume trailing behind her. "Follow me."

He took one step, then another, getting used to the feeling of having his dick and balls constantly gripped. They left her office and he looked around, glad to see they were alone. He followed her to the stairs and got an eyeful of her tight ass as she climbed the steps before him in her almost transparent pants. The sassy sway to her hips led him to believe she was more aroused than she let on, and when he got a look at her chest, her nipples stood out like pencil erasers.

They reached the top and instead of heading left to her bedroom, they went to the right where plastic sheets hung, protecting the rest of the house from the unfinished wing. She brushed aside the sheet and he followed her, conscious of how good the edge of the plastic rubbing over his dick felt. Man, she must have some kind of magic because he'd never been this aware of his body. He usually had an itch and scratched but this...this was different.

Amazing.

They passed what looked like two guest rooms before reaching the door at the end of the hall. On the opposite end of the house lay the butterfly room and he wondered what was behind this door. Unlike the worn wood doors of the rest of the house, this door was made of a dark ebony wood that shone in the sunlight coming through the skylight overhead. She turned the silver door handle and stepped inside.

At first he couldn't see in the darkness, but then she hit a light switch and overhead recessed lighting bathed the large, empty room with golden light. The floors were covered with a lush, thick black carpet that felt like fur beneath his feet. Here and there were squares of black marble, and a black rubber mat, but other than that there was no decoration of any kind in the room.

She stepped closer and trailed a hand over his hip, her belly brushing his straining cock. "Someday, this is going to be my dungeon."

He tried to smile, but his mind was so focused on not reaching out and grabbing her that all he could manage was a bare curve of the lips. "Going to put in some iron maidens and the rack?"

She grinned and shook her head. "No...nothing like that." For a moment she looked uncertain. "I was, well, I was actually wondering if you'd build the equipment for me. I'll pay you, of course."

"Okay, hold on a second. What kind of equipment? And forget about paying me, I won't take it."

She glared at him. "I could order you to take the money."

"And I'd only find some way to give it back to you." He brushed his hand over her hair. "Shit, sorry. Didn't mean to touch without permission."

She sighed. "Wyatt, that felt lovely. Would you do it again?"

He did, slower this time and she turned into his touch with a faint smile. Her body relaxed against his and he soon found himself holding her in his arms, cuddling a very content woman against him. While his dick still wanted some action, his heart drank up her affection. He could almost feel the subtle shift from woman to Domina in his arms, like her energy had shifted and become harder, stronger.

She nuzzled her face against his chest hair. "After you build each piece of equipment, I will use it on you."

"What?"

"Hush and listen to me. I want you to be the first to use the art that you will make, and I know you'll make something good and solid...just like you." Her clever tongue flicked over his pierced nipple. "I want to have your sweat and seed on the wood, to have your essence soaked into it so anytime I enter this room and I can smell your musk in the air."

Shit, when she put it that way he was ready to pound the nails with his dick. "When do you want me to start?"

"You'll do it?"

"Doc, you know I'd do anything for you."

Her bright smile made him feel ten feet tall and God, how he'd missed this feeling. He liked being someone people could depend on, and damned if she didn't need him in some way he didn't understand. In fact, despite her being in the Dominant position, he'd never felt more like he was protecting someone in his life.

"Wyatt, what are you thinking about?"

"Well, it occurred to me that you need me."

"Duh." She tickled his ribs and he held her hands.

"I mean, you need me as much as I need you."

"Ahhh. Grasshopper begins to see truth." Her tone was glib, but her eyes were serious. "Now take that one step further. If I need you, then you have power over me, don't you?"

He didn't like thinking about it like that, it made him feel...not right. "I don't want power over you, Domina."

"Let me tell you the worst kept secret in the BDSM community. At the end of the day, with all the bullshit pushed aside, the bottom is the one who holds the power in the relationship."

"What do you mean?"

"Wyatt, if you say 'no' and mean it all play stops."

"How will you know if I mean it?"

"Why your safe word...oh, damn...which you don't have yet." She groaned and smacked her forehead. "My mentor would whip my ass for that one."

Confused, which seemed to be his normal state of mind around Michelle, he studied her beautiful face. While she kept her expressions guarded, he was beginning to know her well enough to read her slight cues. Right now the smile tilting her lips was one of fondness. "Mentor?"

"Yes. When I started into the lifestyle at twenty I joined a local BDSM club. Being as green as grass, they had me train with an experienced Dom before I got near any submissives."

"Trained you, how?"

"Well, among other things, anything I wanted to do to a sub I had to have done to me first..." Her gaze went distant and hot. "And I wanted to do a lot."

"Wait. You mean you had sex with this guy?"

"Why, Callahan, are you jealous of something I did when I wasn't even old enough to drink? Should I ask about every woman you've been with?"

"No, no, you don't have to do that." He scrambled to get off that subject, knowing women never liked to hear about men being with someone else. In his case, a lot of someone elses. "So did you enjoy it?"

"Yes, I did."

"But you don't want to be a submissive?"

"No. I can play the submissive role now and again, sometimes I even crave it, but I'm a Dominant through and through. Eventually, I'll want to be on top." She must have seen his hopeful look because she shook her head with a rueful grin. "Uh uh, buddy, that's a big treat. You're more likely to win the lottery first. Besides, I'd never let you touch me without proper training first."

"Would you train me?"

"Nope. My head wouldn't be in the right place.

I'd be more worried about your pleasure than if you were using proper technique. While my mentor was a friend, and we did have sex, there was nothing romantic between us." She leaned up and nipped his lower lip. "I'm rather fond of you and, you, my submissive, need a safeword. It's a word you use during play when something is majorly hurting you and you need it to stop. It's not a wimp-out word, I'll expect you to take some discomfort for my pleasure, but if you need everything to stop and need to talk or be held, then you will say that word. It should be something you remember, but don't use a lot."

He chased her lips with his own, the teasing sweep of her tongue in his mouth setting his blood to boil before he backed away enough to speak, while keeping her close. "Santa."

She laughed, her body moving against his in a maddening manner. "Santa as in Claus?"

"Yep."

"I guess that'll work as good as anything." She stepped away and moved to the middle of the room, her rocking ass holding his gaze. "What piece should we start with?"

He leaned against the wall and looked around the room, trying to imagine what she would put in her dungeon. "Do you have woodworking tools?"

She tilted her head to the side. "I might. Yuki has tools, but I'm thinking you'd like your own."

"I would."

"Then I'll buy you some."

"With all respect, Domina, I'd rather use mine." He steeled himself for an argument, running over his reasons in his mind.

"I can understand that. Do you have someone

who can bring them here or should I send James for them?"

He frowned. "Why can't I go get them?"

Her bright blue eyes darkened a shade, but it wasn't with desire. "Because you agreed to stay here for a month and I'm holding you to it."

He shoved off the wall, stalking across the room towards her, his erection still stiff and proud thanks to the cock ring. "So you're going to keep me fucking prisoner?"

She straightened and closed the gap between them, standing less than a breath away. Looking up at him she should have seemed less intimidating, but that wasn't the case. He felt like he was about to get chewed out by a superior officer. "No, I'm not keeping you prisoner and I'm insulted that you would even phrase it like that. You're here of your own free will and you can leave anytime you want, but if you do you can't come back."

"Oh that's fucking fair. So I have to stay here as your bitch or you toss me to the curb." He closed his hands into fists, fighting to remain calm, something that had become next to impossible since he'd gotten back from Walter Reed. His temper had become hair trigger, going from a little angry to fucking pissed in no time flat.

The anger morphed into rage and he struggled against it, but it seemed like the part of his mind that regulated his emotions had checked out for the moment. Adrenaline pumped through his body and he desperately wished there was something in here he could break, something he could hurt like he hurt. He needed to move, he needed to get the fuck out of here, he needed her to stop fucking pushing him.

He *really* needed a fucking bottle of whiskey.

Michelle calmly watched him, which added more fuel to the fire. She was the one who made him feel like this. Why couldn't she have just left him the fuck alone? Didn't she know how broken he was? How much of a danger he posed to her? A very dark, sick spot in his soul whispered that he could make her afraid, that he could drive her away so she never bothered him again. No, no he would not do that.

He would never, ever strike a female.

He had to make her leave before he did something that he would regret. Letting his emotions wash over him, allowing her to see the dark beast she'd roused, he snarled at her, "Who the *fuck* do you think you are!"

"I'm your Mistress and it's time I remind you of that." She stepped back and tilted her chin. Her voice was absolutely calm. "Turn around and put your hands on the wall and spread your legs."

"What?" God, couldn't she see that he hung by a thread? Already he was losing his struggle against his fucked up mind inch by inch, trying to hang onto sanity with bleeding fingernails. If he hurt her it would be the final nail in his coffin for sure. He could never live with himself.

"I suggest you turn around right now or you will sleep on the floor again tonight." Not even a hint of emotion behind her words.

The aggressive, scared animal part of his mind screamed at him to tell her to fuck off and get out of this crazy ass house, but his heart shattered at the thought. Caught between two impossible situations he spun around and placed his hands on the wall. He knew if the raging beast of his anger remained in control he was going to lash out and hurt her either physically or emotionally. One of these situations was going to come to pass; he knew it and his self-disgust knew no bounds. The drywall cracked as he pressed his palms against the wall, trying to channel his strength into his hands and away from Michelle.

She walked up next to him and raked her nails down his back, hard enough to sting, while fondling his balls at the same time. He groaned, at once hating her and wanting to do anything to make her continue touching him. For some reason it also helped calm him a tiny bit, though his chest still continued to heave and sweat dripped down his face.

"You get ten spanks."

"Fuck you. I'm not gonna stand here and get paddled like a kid."

"Eleven."

"You can't really—"

"Thirteen."

"That should have been twelve!"

"Fifteen. I suggest you shut up and take your punishment, Wyatt. You disrespected me, you know that, and I won't tolerate it."

"Michelle..." He hated the need, the desperation in his words but she was the life raft of sanity in the whirling vortex of his mind.

She moved next to him and ran a finger down his ribs. "I'm here, Wyatt, and I'm strong enough to take whatever you have to dish out. Trust me."

Unable to answer, he gave a jerking nod and, in truth, he had to use the wall to hold himself up because his legs had turned to unresponsive lead.

The first smack of her hand against his ass wasn't that bad. It stung, but he'd endured way worse. Then she began to stroke his cock in time to her spanks.

She'd hit, then rub the sore spot, all the while jerking his dick at a leisurely pace. He rested his forehead against the wall, widening his stance and groaning as she made a pleased murmur. Up and down slid her hand, her clever fingers driving away the anger and replacing it with passion one ball-clenching sensation at a time.

"That's right, Wyatt, let it go. Focus only on me, on what I'm doing to you. Nothing else matters right now." She gave his cock a hard squeeze that had his back bowing before releasing him. "I want you to jerk yourself off, I want to watch how you please yourself. You have no idea how much this turns me on."

"Want...to fuck you," he spat out, but he replaced her hands with his as soon as she moved away. Another slap to his ass, harder this time, bringing the blood in his lower body to a boil. She moved her hand over his ass, pinching the sore spots, driving him higher and higher. The slide of his aching dick through his hand blended with her hits and he began to anticipate the sting of her palm followed by a harsh flare of desire.

"You are doing so well, Wyatt." She smacked him three times in rapid succession, making his hips jerk as he cupped his sensitized balls and almost came in his hand.

"Not gonna be able to hold out," he said through gritted teeth.

"Oh yes you will, because if you do you'll be rewarded well."

"God dammit, Domina, have some pity." Even as he said that his brain checked out, fantasies of what she would do to him rushing through his brain in a rough burst of pleasure. He slowed his strokes, making each drag of his calloused palm against his dick an exquisite torture, his rage draining away, morphing into the need to fuck. He was almost savage with the primal urge to claim her, to establish dominance, but he had enough sense left to know that if he did that, this would end and he would shatter her trust in him.

He became lost in the slap of flesh against flesh, of her fingers kneading the muscles of his butt, making the sting a burn. Unable to help himself, he let go, became lost in her. His whole world was her. He wished he could see her, that the walls of this place had mirrors. Even the thought of his undoubtedly red ass aroused him because he knew it aroused her. He could smell her arousal, hear her unsteady breath, and he loved the little purring noise she made when she touched his ass.

"Done. You did very well, Wyatt. I'm proud of you." Her voice was husky with desire. She brushed her knuckles down his cheek. "Turn around and lean back against the wall, your hands behind your head."

His body did as she commanded seemingly without any conscious thought from his mind. Everything in him had drawn up tight, the need to spill his seed reaching a painful level, but the rest of him somehow floated. The painted wall was cool against the heated flesh of his back and he widened his stance, wanting her to see him, wanting the reassurance of her pleasure.

When he looked into her intense blue eyes his

muscles clenched at the fierce desire burning there. Holding his gaze, she gracefully folded to her knees and turned her attention to his cock. Despite their positions he felt more like a bewildered knight with his queen kneeling before him than a man with a woman on her knees. Pre-cum dripped from the tip and she licked it away with a delicate stroke from her tongue. He almost came right then, but the damned cock ring somehow kept him from having his release. Instead he shook as if he'd touched an electrified fence, the agonizing sensation of coming without being able to actually release making him shout.

"Shhhh, I'll take care of you."

Her long, slim fingers slipped around the base of his cock and the pressure on his dick and balls eased. Bracing her hands on his thighs she looked up at him. "I don't want you to come for the count of ten, can you do that?"

"Yes, shit, please just touch me, Domina, please." He'd never begged in his life but it was becoming a disturbingly regular thing with Michelle.

Without another word she opened her mouth and swallowed him whole in one long gulp. Desperately he counted, digging his nails into his palms, pressing his sore ass against the wall, doing anything he could to avoid displeasing her. He wanted to last, wanted to prove to her that he could, needed to prove to himself that his will was stronger than his animal instinct.

At the count of five she began to fondle his sac, sizzling bolts of raw lust detonating in his blood. He was hyperaware of every slide of her lips, the way her tongue stroked at the underside of his cock, how her soft fingers stroked his ball sack.

Unbelievable, the best thing he'd ever felt.

"Ten!" he shouted loud enough to hurt his throat.

She slid her mouth all the way down his cock until his dick filled her throat. Everything built and built, leaving him mindless as he fucked her face. Her nails dug into his thighs and that was what he needed to push him over the edge.

He fell, diving into an ocean of pleasure like he'd never imagined. Each spurt from his dick was more intense than anything he'd ever experienced before. Nothing existed but him and Michelle. He let himself float in the hot currents of satisfaction that her mouth brought as she continued sucking on his dick, hormones overloading and sending his mind off into some state of intense relaxation.

It was only when Michelle finally released his cock from her buttery soft lips that he realized he'd slumped down the wall at some point. Michelle stood before him, a very satisfied smile on her face. He stared at her, dazed at what she'd done for him, incredibly grateful that she'd turned his rage to lust before he'd done either her or himself irreparable harm.

It took him a few tries, but he finally managed to make his lips shape words. "Did it."

"Yes, you did."

"Reward?"

"Yes, you will be rewarded." She put her hand on her hip and studied him. "What do you want?"

Oh, he had no problem knowing right away what he wanted. His first instinct had been to say he wanted to fuck her, but right now he was feeling so drained that even the promise of being buried balls deep in her only drew a twitch from his very satiated body. Besides, he wasn't going to push her. She would let him know when she was ready and he'd wait for the rest of his life if he had to.

"I want to eat your pussy." She blew out a harsh breath, shifting so that her thighs rubbed together. "Okay."

Chapter 8

While Michelle wasn't sure if it was even medically possible, she thought she might pass out from the need to orgasm before she made it to her room. Thankfully Wyatt held her hand and dragged her along behind him, practically sprinting to her room. It would have been funny if she wasn't so desperately aroused.

The memory of his agonized cry when he finally came surged through her, making her steps falter as a rush of desire trembled through her tense muscles. He paused and turned to look at her, a rather smug smile tilting the edges of his firm lips. "Need me to carry you?"

Normally she would have done something to wipe that smile off his face, but he'd earned the right to feel a little smug. It was his reaction, his presence, his surrender to her will that had set her body on fire. "No, just hurry."

He flung open the door to her bedroom and pulled her over to the bed. Without ceremony he turned and easily picked her up by the waist, throwing her into the middle of the bed where she landed with a breathless giggle. There was something so arousing about being with an alpha male. She'd always have to work to keep the upper hand, but it was so nice to trust him to please her, to do as she wanted.

And right now she wanted his face between her

legs.

Leaning up on her elbows, she watched him crawl up the bed towards her, the big muscles of his shoulders standing out in sharp relief. His cock had grown stiff once again and she groaned at the thought of ridding him, slipping him deep inside of her where no one had been for such a long time. Owen's face ghosted through her mind but she pushed it away and focused on the very alive and very sexy Wyatt. She scooted back on the bed, still fully dressed and motioned him forward.

When he got close enough she gripped his hair in her fist and guided his face to her throbbing sex.

"Make me come." What should have been a command sounded more like a plea, but she could care less as his big, warm hands stroked her calves.

"No, Domina, you aren't going to rush me on this." He got a wicked gleam in his eyes. "Please be still and enjoy what I have to offer you. Because I'll tell you what, there is nothing I love more than eating pussy." He took a deep breath, his nostril's flaring. "And you smell delicious...ripe and sweet like a peach. Will your juice run down my chin when I bite into you?"

She couldn't respond, overcome by the erotic sensations his words drew from her body. Instead she played with her nipples, tweaking them through her shirt and sending more pleasure through her body. Hell, she was so aroused that she had to steady her rapid breathing so she didn't hyperventilate.

He growled and slipped his arms beneath her legs, his hands cupping her buttocks as he lifted her pussy to his mouth. Her toes curled in anticipation and she had to keep herself from accidentally pulling his hair out. To her shock he sealed his mouth over her cloth covered sex and blew a warm breath, making her back bow. Her hand on his head gentled, stroking the soft strands as he nibbled and licked his way over her pussy. She had no idea how his mouth on her delicate flesh could be soothing, but it was. Relaxing into his touch was a pleasure akin to slipping into a warm bath with a glass of good white wine...and then having the jets of the tub pound against her clit.

"You smell so good," he said in a low, rumbling voice that vibrated most deliciously against her.

A second later he returned to his torment, bringing her close to the edge without even having taken her clothes off. She abandoned herself to the sensations of his mouth, the hard suck of his lips against her clit. When he nibbled on that sensitive bud she cried out and clutched the pillows, unwilling to look away even for a moment.

This was Wyatt, Gunnery Sergeant Callahan, the man she'd been dreaming of for almost two years finally touching her. And he did not disappoint. He shifted and moved one of his hands from beneath her. Using his free hand, he held up the soaked crotch of her pants and bit a small hole into the cloth.

The tear wasn't big enough for his finger to fit through and she wondered what he was doing. The answer came when he carefully positioned the hole over her clit. Looking down, she could see that hard pink nub sticking out through the cloth, the only part of her flesh exposed to his touch. It was so fucking sexy, so erotic and Wyatt must have agreed because he was muttering all kinds of wickedly nasty things beneath his breath about how much he wanted to fuck her pretty pink cunt.

She wanted to make this last, but if he kept touching her like he was she'd go off like a firecracker in the next few seconds. "Stick your tongue out and don't move."

She spread her legs wide and grabbed the back of his head, easily forcing him to her sex. He was strong enough to have pulled away at any point, but he allowed her to hold him still. With a harsh cry she began to rock her pelvis back and forth on his mouth, the soft heat of his tongue dragging directly over her clit. Holy shit that felt good. Something about having just her clit exposed, the rest of her soaking sex still hidden behind a thin cloth barrier, heightened the sensation.

With abandon she rode his face, the way he let her use him tearing her apart from the inside out with joy.

"Oh...oh god Wyatt...I'm so close."

He grabbed her hips with both hands and held her still, wrapping his lips around her clit and gently suckling her. She trembled on the brink, holding onto the fistfuls of his hair, wrapping her legs around his back and tensing beneath his rhythmic sucks and licks. Then he did some kind of swirling with his tongue that blew her mind.

A scream started somewhere in the pit of her stomach and radiated outwards, followed by the blinding hot rush of all her muscles contracting at once. She writhed against him as the first strong wave of her orgasm hit, screaming out his name, inhaling his scent and reassuring herself that he was here, that she wasn't alone as she came and came. The harsh rip of cloth tearing coincided with his mouth lapping at her exposed slit, greedy sounds of pleasure coming out in a harsh growl.

Each stroke of his tongue drew another shudder from her until she tried to scramble away from him. "Enough."

Reluctantly he pulled back and looked up at her, his mouth glistening with her release. She held her arms open and he crawled up to her, wrapping himself around her, throwing his heavy leg over her hip and holding her tight. She tilted her face to his and he took the hint, kissing her while the hot length of his erection pressed into her stomach. It would be so easy to move a few inches, to slide that big dick inside of her, but she resisted the temptation.

They kissed and kissed, a sharing of something deeper than pleasure passing between them. He seemed desperate to touch her, his hand sliding over her body as their tongues met and stroked against each other. She didn't think she'd ever get tired of the taste of him, of the rough scrape of his stubble scouring her lips and chin.

It scared her how much she needed him, how she couldn't imagine ever letting him go.

Breaking the kiss, she flopped back into the pillows and pulled him down next to her. "Move that cute ass of yours so we can get under the covers."

"You mean sore ass," he muttered as he did what she'd asked, a relaxed smile on his face.

"Oh Wyatt, you have no idea how much I loved doing that."

He turned on his side, his head supported by his hand as he looked down at her. "I think I might have an idea." The faint sun lines around his eyes deepened. "I'm sorry about...earlier."

"By earlier do you mean that tantrum you had?"

"It wasn't a tantrum."

He started to pull away but she grabbed him by the back of his neck. "No, it wasn't. Why don't you tell me what really happened?"

His mouth opened, then closed and shame radiated from him. "I don't want to talk about it right now."

"Wyatt..."

"Please, Domina. I promise I'll talk about it with you, but not right now. Please let me have this moment of peace." He ran his knuckles down her cheek before kissing her forehead. "I haven't felt this good in years. Thank you...just thank you. Is this how BDSM is supposed to make you feel? All relaxed and happy?"

"Yes." She pulled him down so that his head rested on her chest, stroking his hair while he let out a low sigh. His words touched her heart and she wanted to wrap herself up in him, keep them here in this room for the rest of their lives, and surround herself with his strength. He stroked her from shoulder to hip, his touch at once reverent and possessive.

"While it's different for everyone, there is something very spiritual about it for me."

He chuckled and she rapped her knuckle against his head. "Sorry, Domina, I had some weird mental images of a BDSM church."

She snorted and resumed stroking his hair, playing with the silver strands threading through the black around his temples. "I have seen a good deal of kinky priest and nun costumes at the clubs, so I guess you're not the only one with that thought."

He stiffened, but she continued to stroke his hair in silence, waiting him out. "Do you go to BDSM clubs in Austin a lot?"

"Well, I don't know if I go a lot, but I do enjoy them. Why, do you want to come to one with me?"

"I'm not sure." He rubbed his chin against her sternum. "I don't like the idea of anyone else seeing you naked."

She giggled. "Oh honey, it wouldn't be me that they see naked. It would be you."

He gave a strangled laugh. "Well shit, that puts a different spin on things. I'm not sure if I'm up for having my dangly bits exposed to a crowd."

"Neither am I, because I'd be beating the Dommes off with a whip to keep their greedy hands off of you."

"Don't worry, Big Bertha isn't going to seduce me away from you." He ran his hand up and down her thigh, the touch at once comforting and arousing.

The thought of another woman touching Wyatt made Michelle see red, but her role as his Domme meant she would help him fulfill his every fantasy. Besides, a small part of her liked the idea of all those people watching them, seeing the magnificent male that bowed only to her. The more she thought about it, the more she wanted to take him to a club. While she'd cut any bitch that tried to touch him, she couldn't wait to show him how energizing and arousing it could be to have an appreciative audience.

There was a certain energy that flowed through a well-run dungeon, a spice that filled the air and teased the senses. She'd just have to make sure that if they went, she kept Wyatt away from some of the more hardcore, humiliation-type scenes with the female submissives and their Doms. Her knight in shining armor might be tempted to rescue some damsels who didn't want rescuing.

"Would you really like to go to one with me?"

He stilled against her, then blew out a low breath. "No, not right now. In the future maybe, but I really don't want anyone to recognize me. The last thing my Dad needs is to learn that his son is letting some little slip of a woman beat his ass."

"We could always get a mask for you." She absently ran her nails down his back, thinking through the different masks that she'd seen people use over the years.

"Huh."

His breathing grew deeper and more of his weight settled onto her. She wasn't surprised when less than a minute later he fell asleep with his head pillowed on her breasts. Cocooned by the comfort of her bed, covered by the warm heat of a strong man, Michelle closed her eyes and let herself drift off for a very indulgent late afternoon nap before dinner.

*****

It was dark when Michelle woke. She stretched out and enjoyed the smooth slide of silk against her skin, closing her eyes and enjoying the relaxation that permeated every inch of her body. Sometime during her sleep she'd kicked off her pants and she scissored her legs against the slippery fabric. Darkness had fallen while they slept and she opened her eyes again, taking in the moonlight gleaming down through the skylights. A quick glance next to her showed that Wyatt was no longer in bed and she reached out, frowning when she felt that the sheets were cool.

Sitting up, she looked around the room for him and her breath choked in her throat when she saw him by the window looking out over the back portion of her property with his hands fisted at his side. The alarm bells in her mind began to ring and her heart began to beat harder. Wyatt paced back and forth in front of the glass, pausing now and again to stare out into the night, every line of his body radiating tension. He reminded her of a lion she'd seen once at a zoo, the same restless movements and contained violence. Moving slowly, she got out of bed and grabbed her red silk robe from the back of a nearby chair. Shrugging it on and belting it about her waist, she slowly approached Wyatt, fear slamming through her veins.

Sweat stood out all over his skin. He'd put on his old pair of jeans, now dry after the bath earlier today. Shit, had it only been one day? It felt like a lifetime. Moving closer, she stopped a few feet away and swallowed hard. He didn't even notice her and she worried that he might be sleep walking. What if she startled him and he inadvertently injured her? While she would forgive him any harm he did, she didn't think he'd ever be able to forgive himself. He gave a soft, agonized moan that tore at her heart, pushing away any apprehension and replacing it with the rock solid determination to do whatever it took to help her submissive, her man, break free of his demons.

She lifted her shoulders and strapped some steel to her spine.

"Wyatt?"

He didn't stop pacing, didn't even look up at the sound of his name. She took another hesitant step forward and searched his face, her heart beating harder at the terror she saw in his eyes. He finally noticed her and froze, a tremor shaking through him.

Thank God he at least appeared to be awake.

"Wyatt? Are you okay?"

"I thought I saw something outside."

She started to step towards the windows but he swept her back, putting himself between her and the glass. "No, they might see you."

"They?"

A hint of sanity returned to his gaze as he stared at the window with his brows scrunched down. "Yeah. I thought I saw some guys out by the tree line."

She tried to put everything that made her a Dominatrix into her words, the intangible strength that she would need to really get through to him. "Wyatt, I have motion detectors all over the property. If anyone comes near the flood lights will turn on. I had them installed to keep an eye out for coyotes."

"Coyotes?"

"Yes, when I bought the ranch one of my neighbors said to watch out for coyotes. That they are a bit of a problem in this part of Texas. I don't want my cats eaten." She reached out and lay her hand against his arm, distressed by how cold and clammy he was.

"You're not safe here," he said in a low voice and turned to her, his eyes fever bright. "There are so many places they could hide."

Desperately trying to think of some way to ground him, to pull him back fully into reality she nodded. "You're right. In the unlikely event that the Native American tribes rise up against us I might have some issues."

He stared at her, confusion pushing back more of the panic as she made him think. "Michelle, the Native Americans around here are good people."

"Then who are you afraid of?"

He shuddered, hard. "There is evil everywhere."

"Of course there is, but there is also good."

He didn't say anything, just stared out into the moonlit darkness. "I wish I had some night vision goggles."

All too easily she could imagine him building up an arsenal to protect him against the monsters that haunted his mind. "I have a better idea."

"What?"

"I need you to do something for me, please. I need your help." She stepped in front of him, drawing his attention to her. Keeping her voice soft, soothing like when she was trying to calm her horses down, she tried to appeal to his natural protective instinct towards anything female. "Would you agree that a dog could sense things that we couldn't? That if someone was out there they wouldn't be able to fool a trained guard dog? Think about the guard dogs that we had over in the sandbox. Could you imagine one of them letting anyone get close enough to the property to do any harm?"

He looked over her shoulder, then back at her.

After a long moment he closed his eyes and his shoulders relaxed a fraction. "No."

"I don't know anything about dogs. Do you think you could do some research for me? I'd like you to find someplace local that trains guard dogs. I don't care what kind, as long as they are friendly with us and children."

"Children?" He blinked, almost completely back in the real world now.

She sent up a silent prayer of thanks. "I have two older brothers who, being good Catholics, seem to think it's their life's mission to populate the earth with as many children as possible. And they have been known to ship them off to Aunt Michelle's house for visits. Especially now that I have a ranch. Nina, my seven-year-old niece, is obsessed with horses. She'll be coming out for a visit with her family in a couple months."

He let out a soft chuckle. "How many nieces and nephews do you have?"

"Twelve."

With a low whistle he pulled her into his arms and gave her a hug. "Where are you going to fit them all?"

"Eventually I plan on building a bunk house nearby. I'll do it like the bunk houses they had in the old west, but styled for kids." She wrapped her arms around him and took in a deep breath of his scent, taking comfort from him even as she tried to be his rock for once. "Better?"

"Yeah." He stiffened. "Sorry about that. Sometimes...sometimes I think I see stuff that might not be there." On the last word his voice slipped off to a shamed whisper and he looked away, his discomfiture and embarrassment rolling off of him in waves.

Trying to keep her tone casual, professional, she toyed with his nipple ring as she said, "Does it happen a lot?"

"No, not back at my apartment. I live in a well-lit, and populated area. Plus, I usually don't go out at night."

She filed that information away for later and stroked his back, his skin slowly warming beneath her touch. God, he'd been exhibiting all the classic signs of shock. Unsure if she should treat him for that or continue to talk, she pulled back enough to look up at him. "I meant it about the guard dogs. Do you think you could help me with that? I don't even know where to begin looking."

His shoulders straightened and his jaw firmed. "I'll take care of it."

She had to hide her smile. One thing she'd learned about men, submissive, Dominant, or just plain vanilla, they liked to be needed. It was hard coded in their DNA to protect and defend. Stepping out of his arms, she wandered over to the table next to her bed and clicked on the lamp. "Is it the darkness that triggers you?"

While she straightened the bed she waited for an answer, the tension drawing tight between them. Finally he said in a low voice, "Sometimes."

"Good to know. I think we missed dinner, but Yuki probably left us something in the fridge. Wanna go forage for some food with me?"

"Yeah." The soft whisper of his feet over the bare wood floors alerted her to his movements. He wrapped his arms around her and pulled her hair to the side, kissing her neck. "You sure you don't want to stay here and eat?"

The sensation of his teeth grazing the side of her neck was all too delicious. She threw an elbow into his side, immensely relieved by his flirting. "Behave."

Laughing, he strolled to the other side of the bed, his swagger back in full form. They made the bed together and she filed away the information that giving Wyatt something to do, something that made him feel like he was taking care of her seemed to help with his panic attacks. Not surprising, most guys liked to fix a problem instead of talk about it like women did.

After she tossed on some pajamas and he'd donned a pair of sleep pants donated by James, they made their way down to the kitchen. The lights in the fountain were the only illumination in the foyer, throwing shifting patterns onto the walls. She had him walk down first so she could see his ass, something she fully admitted without shame. Why should she be coy about enjoying his body?

They entered the kitchen and Michelle flipped the lights on before going over to the windows facing the front drive and pulling down the blinds.

Wyatt frowned at her, his arms crossed while he watched her. She turned on her heel and placed her hands on her hips. "What's wrong?"

He nodded in the direction of the windows. "You didn't have to shut them."

She breezed past him, moving along the granite counters as she searched something edible. "No, I didn't, but I want you to be comfortable. Plus those windows can be seen from Yuki and James' house and I don't need them watching us like we're in a fishbowl." She dug through the stainless steel fridge, lifting lids and sniffing the contents inside. "What are you in the mood for?"

His warmth caressed her back before she was even aware that he'd moved. "Why don't you go sit down and let me do this."

She shot a glance at him over her shoulder. "I can reheat food."

"I know you can, but I'd like to take care of you." His lips ghosted over the side of her neck, sending a pleasant shiver through her. "You have no idea how much."

Her body went liquid and she moved out of the fridge, bumping him back with her butt so he'd give her room to maneuver. "Oh, I have an idea." She smiled at him and brushed her hands over his chest, enjoying the soft scrape of his chest hair. "That's one of the things not unique to BDSM, the need to care for those we lo-cherish."

He cupped her face with his big hands, making her aware of how much physically smaller she was than him. "May I kiss you, Domina?"

"You may."

With the utmost gentleness he brushed his lips over her forehead, her cheeks, and finally her mouth. They unhurriedly explored each other, and when she sucked on his tongue he groaned low in his throat. "This seems so surreal," he whispered against her lips. "Like any moment I'll wake up and find out this was all a dream."

Unable to help herself, she pinched his ass, making sure to squeeze on the area that she'd spanked. He startled and rubbed his butt, glowering at her. "Why did you do that?"

"Because I can." She grinned at him and gave his nipple ring a playful tug. "I meant it when I said that your body is mine to play with."

"Don't I get a say in the matter?" He rubbed his ass again and gave her rear end a speculative look. "Can I play with your body?"

"Not unless I give you permission."

"That's not fair."

"No, it's not." She swayed across the cool tiles to stand before him, conscious of how he watched her every move. "But that's part of what turns me on."

He stared at her for a moment before bursting out laughing. "Fuck me. If I'd known it would be this good to be your sub I'd have signed up the second I saw you."

Pleased more than she should be, she leaned up and placed a kiss on his cheek. "Slave boy, fetch me some food."

"Can't you call me something a little more masculine? I am more than a few years older than you."

"And I love every ounce of skill that comes with your experience." She walked over to the kitchen table, choosing a seat facing the cooking area so she could watch him. "How about...let's see...masculine manly man slave boy?"

He snorted and pulled some dishes out of the fridge. "How about no?"

"You're no fun."

"Oh, I'm lots of fun." He gave her a leering smile while putting the dish into the microwave. "I think this is stew, is that okay with you?"

"Sounds great. Check the basket on top of the fridge. Yuki usually keeps rolls up there."

They settled into a comfortable silence, occasionally broken when he asked her where things were. As they ate neither said much, more interested in filling their stomachs. She didn't know if it was all the energy she'd expended dealing with him, or the good time he'd shown her earlier, but she was starving. When the beast in her belly was finally content she leaned back with a sigh, scooping up some stew onto her biscuit.

He glanced at her and grinned. "You look as happy as a milk-fed kitten."

"Feel that way too." She stretched her legs out, putting her feet on the sturdy maple chair next to him.

"Can I ask you something?"

"Sure."

He hesitated, looking into his bowl. "Promise you won't get offended?"

"No, but I'll keep an open mind."

Shaking his head, he toyed with his spoon. "Why did you join the Navy? I mean you obviously didn't need the money, so why sign up?"

Oh, that question was loaded with places in her psyche that still cut at her soul like jagged glass. She looked over his shoulder, tracing the pattern in the painted Mexican tile border between the ceiling and the walls. "It's kind of a long answer."

"Take all the time you need."

She frowned at him. "Pushy, aren't you?"

"I told you, Doc, you fascinate me. So indulge my obsession and help me understand you."

A smile tried to break free, but she held it back. "Do you really think any man will truly understand any woman?"

"Not if they won't tell us about themselves."

"Touché." She toyed with her biscuit, breaking off small pieces onto the colorful woven placemat.

"I'm going to assume that you know some of this, but I'll tell you the whole story. Or as much of it as I can tell."

The smile dropped off his face and he reached out and stroked her calf. "Hey, if you don't want to you don't have to. I didn't realize it was a painful subject for you."

"No, I'm okay." She gave him a bright, shiny smile as false as fool's gold. "So, I was born to the esteemed Senator Sapphire and his wife, the lovely actress Hilda Sapphire, known for her beautiful blue eyes and ability to portray a quiet strength in all of her characters."

He grunted. "I never made the connection until now, but wow...you look a lot like your Mom."

"Have you seen her movies?"

"Yeah, well the western ones. Me and my sister were obsessed with westerns when we were growing up. Joy, my sister, wanted to be a cowgirl in the worst way."

His distant, fond smile helped her relax a bit. "And is she out there right now roping up calves?"

"Hardly. Well she does herd, but only her four boys."

"Four boys?"

"Yep, from the youngest who is five to the oldest who is thirteen."

"Jesus, Mary, and Joseph, how has she maintained her sanity?"

Giving her a stern look he shook his head. "No, we're not talking about me. We can talk about me later, but I want to hear your story first."

Irritated that she'd been caught unconsciously trying to steer the conversation away from what would be a painful tale she glared at him. "Fine.

Get me a glass of white wine." He raised his eyebrows at her snippy tone and she sighed. "Please. The one towards the back on the first shelf."

His look of understanding unnerved her, as if he knew it would be easier for her to talk if he gave her space. Mustering her courage, she continued her story and tried to pretend it wasn't her life that she was talking about. "After two boys their long awaited girl finally arrived. She was loved, cherished and spoiled by her family. Born into wealth and privilege, she was given the best of everything. Don't worry, she had her two older brothers to torment her and keep her humble."

Wyatt's laugher became muffled as he leaned down into the fridge and pulled out the bottle of wine.

"Glasses are in the cabinet over the sink." She drummed her fingers on the table, trying to think of how to best put the next part. "I was raised from birth to believe that the only true way to be close to God is to do his work here on earth."

Wyatt looked up from opening the wine. "You're a missionary?"

"Hardly. But I did and still do take to heart that lesson. I never feel more alive, more needed than when I'm helping someone…that is except for when I've made my sub lose his mind." Suddenly shy, she pushed away her bowl and tugged her robe closer.

"But why the military? I mean you could have found any of a thousand charities to help at home with your medical degree."

"Because I couldn't afford the degree without joining the military."

The wine gurgled as he carefully poured it into her glass. She was relieved to see that he hadn't taken down one for himself. "Didn't you say you were born with a silver spoon in your mouth? And this place ain't exactly a shack."

"My grandparents were very wise people. It was from them that we inherited our wealth. Old money and all that nonsense. Anyways, on the day we graduated from high school our parents cut us off financially, just like my father had been cut off financially by his grandfather when he turned eighteen. My brothers were lucky enough to both get sports scholarships, but I had to go a different route. We all knew it was coming so we got summer jobs, but you can only make so much money while still in high school and getting financial aid when your parents are millionaires just doesn't happen."

Setting her glass on the table, Wyatt nodded. "So you enlisted after high school?"

"No." She sighed and fiddled with her wineglass. "See, while my parents wanted me to spend my life doing philanthropic work, the thought of me going to war terrified my mother. Her grandparents had been prisoners of war during World War II and she'd grown up with war being the ultimate boogey man. The thought of her only daughter going off to battle made her sick."

"Then when did you enlist?"

She avoided his gaze. "My mother told me she would pay for my schooling if I agreed to not go into the military afterwards. My paternal grandfather got wind of this and flipped out. He'd served in World War II, and had risen to the rank of General. He considered it one of the defining pillars of his life. In his opinion, the knowledge and maturity I could potentially gain far outweighed the risk of anything actually happening to me. I think he knew even then that the family's influences would see me safely stationed in Hawaii if need be. He offered to pay for my schooling, room and board, as well as a healthy allowance if I joined the military after completing my degree."

"And that's what you did?"

"Yep."

"And your mother didn't disown you?"

"Oh trust me, she had a complete meltdown. Fortunately, I was rather familiar with her acting and could tell a dramatic fit when I saw one. Not to say that she wasn't genuinely worried, but my mom could have given Scarlett O'Hara's Aunt Pittypat a run for her money when having overblown hysterics. My grandfather had a word with her and she calmed down enough to stop fainting."

"Lord, that must have been a sight. You told me earlier that you are doing only volunteer work now. How can you afford that?"

"Because when we turned twenty-seven my brothers and I each received an inheritance of sixty-eight million dollars."

She braced herself for his reaction, but when he recoiled from her it still hurt. "Holy shit, Doc. That's a lot of green."

Feeling him distance himself from her, the edge of her temper surfaced. "What? Does that make you think less of me now? Does the fact that I didn't earn that money disgust you? Am I good enough for you when I'm poor but not when I'm rich?" She took a deep breath, trying to pull back her anger as Wyatt picked at an old wound. "Look, I know how crazy it is, but I'd be lying if I didn't say I enjoyed the freedom it gives me to do what I love."

Wyatt folded his hands on the table, his shoulders tense and his fingers tightly laced together. "Michelle, it's not you that's not good enough, it's me. I'm not good enough for you."

"Idiot." She stood and moved in front of him, pushing his chair back with her foot before straddling his lap. "Don't you understand? You have the kind of heart and soul that no amount of money can buy. You are a good man, a hero, the real deal, and I admire you more than you'll ever know."

He swallowed hard. "Can you really picture me meeting your parents? 'Cause if this, you know, thing, we have continues eventually I'd like to meet them, but I don't want to embarrass you. Fuck, look at me right now. I don't have a job, well the shit with my Dad doesn't count. I have no education other than what I learned in the Marines, and I have a fucked up mind that keeps trying to tell me I'm going to die any second."

Stroking his cheek, she shook her head. "Isn't it funny how distorted our views of you are? When you stare into the mirror you see something totally different than what the rest of the world sees. You are an amazing man, Wyatt, and I'm so very lucky to have you."

He blew out a low breath, then held her close. She rested her head on his shoulder and hugged him back, his strong body a tranquil island in the bitter swirl of her memories and emotions. It had been so long since she'd felt this good. She almost hated to break the mood but it was time she told him about Owen.

A sour lump formed in her heart, making the words hard to force out. "That's not the only reason I joined."

He rubbed his face against her hair. "What do you mean?"

Taking in a deep breath, she tightened her grip on him, afraid that he wouldn't want her anymore. "A month before I was set to graduate I became engaged to Owen, my boyfriend and longtime submissive."

He tensed, but didn't push her away. "Go on, I'm listening."

Trying to break the tension she said, "Promise?"

Instead of throwing her usual reply back at her he hugged her tighter. "Promise."

Something inside of her cracked and she clenched her jaw tight enough to ache, willing herself to spit the words out. "Fuck, this is harder than I thought." She took a breath and it hitched, sticking in her throat like razor wire. "Owen asked me to marry him and I said yes. I was twenty-four, in love, with the world before me. His proposal made me rethink my plans to enlist. I didn't want to be away from him so early in our marriage."

"That's why I never married," Wyatt said as he slowly began to rock her. "Couldn't stand the thought of leaving a wife and kids behind. It would hurt them and I couldn't deal with the guilt."

"Exactly. Well, I never had a chance to make that decision. Owen...." Wyatt stroked her, held her, gave her the strength to continue. "We had just finished playing at the Velvet Fist, a BDSM club in Chicago, and were on our way home. The club is situated in a really rough part of Chicago, but we'd never really had a problem. The parking lot to the club was fenced in and patrolled by two security officers. Before we left earlier that evening I'd forgotten to put gas in my car. I was too hyped up to really even think about it. That night we told all of our friends that we were engaged."

Bitter tears burned her throat as she relived the memories of that night, but she swallowed them back. "We stopped at a gas station two blocks from the club at a little after two a.m. I don't know if you've ever been to gas stations in the ghetto, but the person who works there is usually locked inside the building. You have to pay them from the outside, through a little slot in the bulletproof glass."

He nodded. "Yeah, I've seen that before."

"So, stupid me goes to pay the cashier and get a bottle of water while Owen pumped the gas. We'd done a lot of playing at the club and I didn't want him to become dehydrated. He didn't even want me to get out of the car but I was so damn arrogant back then and I was high. Not on drugs, but on the wave of euphoria from a really good scene and the joy we'd been surrounded with all night. I guess you could say I had my rose colored glasses on and they blinded me to the danger I was in."

Wyatt didn't say anything, just shifted her in his arms so that he held her closer. She rubbed her nose with her hand and fought to get the words out, to reveal her sin. "I was on my way back to the car when this kid comes up to me. His name was Terrance and he was thirteen years old. Earlier in the day he'd been beat into a local gang. Robbing me was his final initiation."

"Shit," Wyatt murmured.

"He pulled a gun and demanded my purse. At first I thought he was joking and I told him to go home. Owen was always smarter than I was. He recognized the danger even if I was oblivious to it. I mean I looked at Terrance and I saw a kid with a black eye and split lip holding a gun that, at the time, I didn't even believe was real." She closed her eyes, trapped in that terrible moment. "Terrance tried to yank my purse away and I jerked back. Owen ran over to help me and Terrance panicked. He shot Owen nine times in the chest."

The tears came now, she couldn't stop them but she struggled to speak, to give Owen's memory its due. "I pulled the gun away from Terrance but it was too late. The clerk inside the gas station had seen what was going on, and cops were on their way, but it was too late. Owen was dead, all because I wouldn't give a desperate kid my purse. If I had handed it over, if I had pulled my head out of my selfish ass, Owen would be alive today."

"Michelle, it wasn't your fault."

Anger, self-disgust, and grief swelled inside of her heart like a malignant tumor. "Don't you say that! It was my fault. I did it and I accept responsibility for my actions!"

"Easy, baby. I didn't meant to upset you." He began to rock her slowly, the age old rhythm that brought comfort to her body, if not to her soul.

A horrible tightness constricted her chest and she desperately struggled to take another breath, trying to get out the rest of her story. "For around a year after that I drifted through life, like my soul had died with Owen, leaving only a shell behind. I sometimes wished that I would die as well, but if I committed suicide I'd never get to see Owen, for surely he's in heaven." She swallowed hard, the admission lifting a weight from her soul. "I spent a lot of time thinking, trying to figure out what I could do as penance for my sin of pride. I needed to do something that would make up for the wonderful person I'd taken away from this world." She gave a bitter laugh. "One thing the Catholic religion gave me, besides guilt, is the ability to seek forgiveness through penance. I know it sounds weird, but for me doing an act of penance really does help soothe my soul. I knew that the sacrifice I would have to make for Owen's death would have to be something huge, something that would make a concrete difference."

The soothing rhythm of Wyatt's rocking never faltered. "Is that why you enlisted?"

Tears burned her eyes and she fought them, rapidly blinking in a vain effort to keep them from falling. "Yes. My dad tried to pull some strings so I wouldn't see combat, but I caught wind of it and told him if he didn't back off I was going to throw a very public shit fit." She gave a watery chuckle, remembering the epic fight with her poor dad. "It was an election year, so he backed off."

"Why would you want to see combat so bad?"

A logical question, one she'd been asked many times over the years. She thought about giving him her scripted answer about wanting to serve her country, do something worthwhile with her degree, etc. That usually satisfied anyone, or bored them enough to move onto a different subject.

But it wouldn't be right to lie to Wyatt.

Not about this.

Even though the memories came rushing in on a tidal wave of grief, she pressed on, forcing her constricted throat to give up the words.

"Because I could save someone else's Owen."

That was it, the emotional straw that broke the camel's back. The sobs she'd been holding back tried to pour out of her, but she kept her lips closed, refusing to let them out. Even to her the sound was horrible, a choking, keening wail that held all the pain she kept inside of her. All the terrible loneliness and guilt over wanting to be with someone, of wanting to love Wyatt with her whole heart when she swore that she would never love again. Up until now it had been an easy promise to keep.

"Oh, honey." Wyatt pulled her against his chest, smoothing her hair back. His scent filled her nose as she buried her face against the crook of his neck. His voice vibrated her lips when he said, "I've got you. Let it out."

Memories of the good times she'd had with Owen flowed through her mind now that the gates of her past had been opened. She remembered their gaze meeting across the room at a coffee shop, how his auburn hair shone like fire in the sunlight, their first kiss, the way he'd asked her to tie him up the first time, watching him brave a rainstorm to run across the street to the bakery to get her a cookie. Those and a thousand other simple things that made up the ruined tapestry of their life. No, maybe not ruined; there were still bright and beautiful spots, but the pattern ended before it was completed. It wasn't just missing what they had, but what they might have had.

"Here, blow." Wyatt pushed a napkin into her hand.

She sniffled and took a breath, or at least tried to take a breath. Her lungs hitched, giving her that he-he-he sound that she always hated from a hard cry. Blowing her nose, she let out a few more low moans, slowly relaxing into Wyatt's strength. Through it all he'd been there for her and that helped more than she could ever say.

She could only pray that he'd let her do the same for him.

Shit, he needed her to be strong for him and instead here she was, a hot mess of tears in his lap.

His embrace went from comforting to constricting and she suddenly needed space between them. "Excuse me," she started to get off his lap, but he held her hips. Glaring at him, she snapped, "I'm going to the bathroom, if you don't mind. So unless you want a puddle on your lap, let me go."

"Damn stubborn woman."

He released her and she stood. Reaching across the table, she tossed back the last of her wine with three large gulps. The rich liquid burned away the salt of her tears and soothed her sore throat.

"Take it easy there," Wyatt said in a low voice. "Don't use alcohol to try to make the hurt go away. It doesn't work."

She felt vulnerable and that made her lash out. "Oh, isn't that the pot calling the kettle black."

He stiffened, then took a deep breath. "You're not going to push me away, Domina. I'll be here for whatever you need me to do."

His words disarmed her and she scrambled to

regain her footing. "I need you to step out of the way so I can use the bathroom."

He moved aside with a sardonic bow.

Once safely behind the door of the bathroom, she leaned against the wall and grabbed a towel. Bunching it up, she shoved it against her mouth and screamed, letting out the pain festering inside of her. She wanted to wail, gnash her teeth, rend her clothing so the world could see a visible badge of the sorrow in her soul. But she couldn't, wouldn't fall down that dark well again.

Wyatt was depending on her and letting him down wasn't an option.

Strength returned to her and she stood, her legs weak and trembling. It had been a very long time since she'd cried this hard. Come to think of it, there were only two times she'd cried like this. One was at Owen's funeral, and the other was when Wyatt had been injured. Jesus, had she subconsciously thought she lost Wyatt? Is that why she kept holding back the one thing she knew would cement them together, sex?

Only it wouldn't be just sex with Wyatt.

It would be making love.

Looking into her red eyes and puffy face in the mirror she turned on the cold water. After soaking a washcloth in the icy stream she wrung it out then applied it over her nose and eyes. It was a trick her mother used when she'd been an actress and had to go from a scene where she cried to a scene where she had to look normal.

When Michelle took the washcloth off her face the swelling had indeed gone down and she chalked up another point for her mom. Her hair was a frizzed out mess, looking almost like an afro, but at least she didn't look like she'd suffered an allergic reaction. She glanced down at her pajamas, glad to see she hadn't messed them up. A knock came from the door and she suppressed a sigh.

"Come in."

Wyatt peeked his head in. "A delivery man is here with a shit ton of boxes for you."

She smiled, this time with a trace of true happiness. He smiled back and care and understanding in his gaze made her heart skipped a beat. There it was, a hint of the connection she got from making a sub fly. It was a subtle difference, like a song sung in a different key, but similar enough to warm her through and through. She cleared her throat, took a deep breath then splashed some more water on her face. He handed her a towel without being asked, anticipating her needs.

Holding out her hand, she said, "Come on. I have some toys to show you."

Chapter 9

Wyatt trailed after Michelle, amazed at how quickly she pulled herself together. He'd seen his sister cry like that a couple times and she'd looked like shit afterwards. While Michelle's hair was an adorable fluffy mess, the rest of her was as put together as a runway model. The natural grace returned to her step, and the way her red silk robe shifted over her thighs made his dick hard. Cursing, he looked away, trying to get himself under control before the delivery guy saw him.

Michelle entered the foyer first while he adjusted himself and Wyatt got to watch the delivery guy's jaw drop. He looked stunned and Wyatt had a hard time holding his laughter. Poor guy. He'd seen that look on a thousand Marines' faces. The delivery man, with a name tag identifying him as Paul Stanely, stared down at Michelle, no doubt getting a good view of her cleavage. Michelle seemed not to notice and she chatted with him while signing for her packages.

Wyatt strolled behind her and wrapped his arms around her, giving her a sound kiss on the side of the neck. "What's in the boxes, beautiful?"

She handed the clipboard back and reached behind Wyatt, giving his ass a hard pinch. "Just some toys."

Paul cleared his throat and backed up a step, his eyes going between Michelle's bare legs and Wyatt glowering behind her. "Thanks, ma'am. Uh, if you ever need anything else delivered, ask for me and I'll get it to you as quick as I can."

"Thank you." She smiled and ushered the stunned young man out, shutting the door behind him with a snick.

The gleam in her eyes at once aroused Wyatt and scared him. She bit her lower lip and strode across the foyer towards him, that sensual smile curving her lips into an image of sin. His cock wasn't worried one bit about what kind of fucked up BDSM toys might be used on him. He still wore the cock ring, never having bothered to take it off. It was loose enough right now so that he could wear it for a long period of time. In some weird way the ring around his cock reminded him of her...well, her ownership for lack of a better word. The caress of that smooth metal marked him as belonging to her as surely as the rings through his nipples.

He had a feeling that as soon as Michelle spotted the cock ring she would tighten it and make him sweat.

If helping her feel better meant he had to take some ball squeezing pleasure, he'd just have to make that sacrifice.

When she finally reached him electricity sizzled across his body. Any lingering trace of sorrow had left her eyes, leaving behind mischief and arousal. Still, he noticed how tired she looked beneath it all and he sighed internally, trying to figure out how he would get her to rest without insulting her or incurring her wrath.

"So, what's in the boxes?" He was proud that his voice came out steady, even if a bit tight.

She ran her hands up his stomach, playing with the lines between his ribs before reaching his nipples. Before he'd gotten them pierced he wasn't that into having his chest played with. But now...fuck, it felt so damn good. And Michelle seemed to love them. She couldn't be near them without wanting to touch.

"The big box holds some clothes for you."

"What kind of clothes?"

"The kind I want you to wear." She gave him an impish smile. "Don't worry, James picked them out. He wouldn't let me put you in silk harem pants."

Refusing to be distracted by that disturbing image, he nodded his head in the direction of the pile of smaller packages. "And the other boxes?"

"Well, go get me a knife from the kitchen and we'll see."

He hesitated, torn between spending an evening with Michelle, indulging her every kinky whim, and doing what he had to do in order to serve her best. As always his innate sense of right and wrong kicked in and he sighed, regretting what he was about to say. "Michelle, we've had a long night and you've given me a great deal to think about." A brief flash of hurt tightened her face and he went to his knees before her, trying to coax out a smile. "Besides, I've been put in charge of your security, Domina, and I take my position as you chief of security very seriously. And aren't you the one always telling me to go slow, to savor? I'd like some time to savor."

She stroked her hand through his hair with a bemused and almost sad smile. "While your attempts to manipulate me are as obvious as a five-year-old's, I happen to agree with you."

He nuzzled his face against her stomach, remembering James doing the same to Yuki earlier and understanding the appeal now. This portion of Michelle's body was so feminine, the belly and her hips, a soft and inviting cradle that all men yearn for. His base urges wanted him to nuzzle lower, where the scent of her musk would coat his face and tongue, but he restrained himself.

"Do you have a computer I could use? And a cell phone charger?"

"Hmm, yes. You can use my computer in the library. Log in under the guest profile, please. I have patient files under my personal profile that you can't see."

"Of course." He looked up at her. "Want me to come tuck you in?"

She laughed and tightened her grip on his hair, hard enough to slightly sting and feel good. "No, I think it's better if you stay down here right now." She gave him a gentle smile. "I find my ability to resist your charms is pathetically weak."

"No, not weak." He stood and cupped her face in his hands, stroking her satiny cheeks with his thumbs, looking into her bluer than blue eyes. "You are the strongest woman I know."

She reached up and placed her hands over his before removing them with a soft sound of regret. "You know where my study is. I suggest your haul ass there before I decide to do something wicked with it."

"You want to do wicked things with my ass?"

"You have until the count of ten."

"No, seriously, Michelle, I don't know if I want

anyone near my ass."

"Nine."

He backed up a pace, his sphincter clenching. "Is that what's in those boxes? Things you want to put in my ass?"

Her feline smile curved her lips. "Eight."

"Okay, okay."

He turned on his heel and strode past her to the hall off the foyer leading to her study. When her hand connected with his ass he bit back a groan. Damn, who'd have thought a spanking from such a small hand could leave such a lasting impression. He might have to reconsider his stance on no rough stuff with Michelle. If she could make something like a slap of the hand erotic, he couldn't wait to see what else she could do with him.

With his erection leading the way, he had to laugh at himself. Never, in a bazillion years did he think he'd be here, doing this, with *her*. All those times he'd been standing so close to her, near enough to touch if either of them shifted an inch, but neither willing to cross that line. So, he'd suffered with a perpetual case of blue balls, but what he didn't know at the time was how hot she'd been for him. Fuck, she'd hidden it well. Every once in a while he'd could have sworn he caught her watching him with a look of such desire that he'd usually fuck up whatever he was doing. He could still remember her laughter when that look had made him drop a box of wrenches, and his swearing as one hit his foot. It wouldn't have been as bad if it had been a regular wrench, but those were the big ones they used on the transport vehicles.

That shit had hurt.

He reached the smooth wood door leading to the library and paused to run his hand over the jam. Whoever had installed it had left an edge and he frowned at the shoddy craftsmanship. The contractor in charge of doing the renovations wasn't maintaining a high level of detail. His gut tightened and anger simmered in his blood at the thought of someone ripping her off. When he saw that contractor he was going to take him aside and....no. No, he wasn't going to beat some guy's ass because of the rough edge on a door frame.

Closing his eyes, he turned on the lights and walked past the door jam, unwilling to let his fucked up mind dwell on it.

He slumped into her chair and a puff of her perfume swirled around him. Immediately he relaxed, and just let himself feel. He hesitated, unsure if it was a good idea, but trying it out anyway. Closing his eyes he went still, imaging her voice whispering it in his ear, the only thing in the world his body and the scent of her perfume.

Ethereal and delicious, like spun sugar candy.

Jesus Christ, he was so fucking pussy whipped.

An image of Michelle dressed in some type of latex body suit holding a whip came to mind and his dick tried to punch a hole through his pants. Okay, that was certainly not helping him focus, but he was no longer freaked out. Pulling the chair into the niche beneath her driftwood desk he let out a soft sigh after turning on the blue and purple Tiffany lamp next to the monitor.

Now this desk was a thing of beauty. He marveled at the size of the logs needed to make a solid surface this big. Smoothing his hand over the wood he smiled in appreciation. It was smooth, silken, like a woman's skin. Someone had spent months, if not close to a year making this.

Relaxed, but somehow more awake, he clicked the mouse and began his search.

*****

Three hours and a half dozen phone calls later he had a guard dog trainer coming tomorrow with five dogs to show Michelle. If none of the dogs displayed an interest in guarding her, they'd have to try someone else. He really hoped it worked, because these dogs were amazing. The lady who trained them was a retired military war dog trainer. They'd had an animated discussion about her techniques, each trading stories about their time in the service. He'd liked it, a lot. Not because the woman reminded him of a dirty version of his Aunt Betsy, but because they'd had an instant bond because of their service.

It was nice, and he realized he'd missed that. How could he not? He spent eighteen years of his life, from eighteen to thirty-six, working for Uncle Sam. His life had been the military and he'd grown used to that atmosphere. Talking with someone who understood that felt good, and he considered taking the dog trainer, Lilly, up on her offer to show him around the local Veterans of Foreign Wars of the United States Hall. She said the VFW was actually a pretty full place now. They'd had a lull during what she called 'the peaceful years' between wars, but now with everyone coming back from the sandbox they'd had a huge uptick in members. She'd sounded sad about that and he didn't have to ask why.

War sucked.

With a long sigh he pushed himself out of the chair and stretched. His spine snapped, crackled, and popped with each breath he took. Fuck he was getting old. Maybe he'd start up yoga or some shit if he wanted to keep up with Michelle's sexual appetite. Turning off the lamp, he ambled across the dark room and went down the hall.

He'd also emailed his sister, giving her directions to Michelle's house. Tomorrow Joy would come by and bring his things. She'd immediately written back demanding to know what was going on, so he'd spent an extra half an hour convincing her that it was him, and he was indeed alive. And yes, he was currently shacking up with a woman.

Then he'd told his sister who that woman was and she'd immediately changed her tune, asking him if he wanted his truck up as well. After hesitating for a moment, he said no. He didn't want to give Michelle any reason to think that he was leaving her. His Domina was carrying around some heavy shadows on her heart and he'd realized tonight how vulnerable she was beneath her strong surface. While he would never claim to understand the way a woman's mind worked, he was pretty sure that in her own way, Michelle needed him more than he needed her. Yeah, he was fucked up with PTSD and had always been a difficult son of a bitch, but that didn't change his macho pig view that his woman's problems would always come before his own, that he would throw everything he had into making her feel better. Not just for now, but for the long term.

Helping her, serving her, being there for her made him feel whole.

The cool marble of the foyer changed to the warmer wood of the stairs beneath his feet as he climbed. The fountain was still on and he loved the golden light. There was something almost dreamlike about it. This room matched the butterfly room in the hints into the designer's beautiful soul. While he had no doubt Michelle could do shit to him that would be erotic torture, and could be cruel if she wanted to, her spirit was too gentle to truly hurt someone. His earlier ignorant views about all Dominatrices being man hating, ball crushing, sadistic bitches couldn't be further from the truth if Michelle and Yuki were any example of what a Mistress was truly like. Everything she did to him, with him, was for their mutual pleasure and never once had he felt abused. If anything he felt cherished in a weird way.

He hoped he made her feel the same way because he sure as shit recognized that she was the greatest gift God had ever given him.

Shadows enveloped him as he walked across the second floor landing to her room. The door was open and a soft golden light poured out. He wandered in, giving his eyes a moment to adjust. Michelle was an indistinct lump among the pillows of her decadent bed. When he'd been eating her sweet pussy on those sheets he'd been embraced in that same comfort and yearned for it.

He really wanted to join her up there, but he hadn't been invited. As he wandered closer the he realized the light source was a single white candle burning in a black Native American pot filled with sand. Then he got close enough to get a good look at her and his heart stopped. She'd dusted herself in some type of powder that made her skin sparkle with gold. Every breath she took made her skin shimmer, from her parted lips down to the first hint of a soft pink nipple.

She slept on, oblivious to his frantic battle against his baser instincts. Saliva flooded his mouth and his dick ached. She rolled fully over onto her back providing him a new view to enhance his obsession with her. The gold ring on his cock stretched a bit to accommodate him, but not enough to keep from driving him crazy. One of her arms was flung out to the side and the silk sheet had drawn up enough to reveal the smooth outline of her hip and upper thigh. That skin also sparkled and she wasn't wearing any underwear.

With every breath he took he became more saturated with her scent. He stood on a precipice and chose the nobler path that would leave him with only a case of blue balls, if he was lucky.

Moving as quietly as possible, taking his time, Wyatt lifted the sheet from the end of the bed. He held it up and slid beneath it until he was between the cradle of her thighs. She shifted and he stayed still, his breath warming her pussy. And, fuck, what a pretty cunt it was. Full outer lips barely hiding the pink within, bare of any of the golden hair that covered her mound.

For a moment he only looked at her, committing her body to his memory forever. Then he lapped at her, long licks that slowly parted her labia, gently working his way in. She moaned something incoherent and he moved closer, his wide shoulders now spreading her thighs, giving him greater access. He bit his way around her mound, drawing blood to that sensitive area, making her cry out softly.

He was pretty sure she was fully awake now by the way she grabbed the back of his head and pressed him harder against her now swollen sex. Her essence rolled over his tongue and now it was his turn to groan. Desire permeated every inch of his body and he paused, exploring the sensation and reveling in how fucking hot it made him. The head of his cock slid against the silk sheets with his movements and he found himself unable to stop thrusting. While it was nowhere near as satisfying as having a woman beneath him, it still felt good.

Especially when Michelle cried out his name.

He brought his thumb to her pussy and played with the soaking wet entrance to her sheath. Turning his attention to her clit, he slowly rubbed up one side of the hard nub and down the other, all the while gently pressing his thumb against her entrance, but not penetrating her. Her movements became restless and she arched her hips, trying to get him inside.

When her grip on his hair tightened to a painful degree he slid his thumb into her, and pressed down on her pelvic floor. One of his lovers had clued him into that trick and every woman he'd ever done it to had loved it. While he could give her three of his fingers to feel stretched, pressing downwards made it feel like she was being fucked by something much bigger than a thumb.

Sure enough, she shuddered against him and began to rock on his face, a liquid roll of hips that had him aching with need. The more turned on she became the more turned on he became until he was rubbing his cock in earnest against the bed. He kept up a steady rhythm with his thumb, following her lead for how much she wanted and when. She continued to writhe, to grow more aroused until her hot sheath gripped him like a fist.

He'd never been so tempted to be inside a woman in his life, but he wasn't the kind of man who took what wasn't offered. So instead he focused on driving her crazy. She bore down hard on him, little tremors stiffening her limbs. When he gave her clit an experimental suck she screamed and he smiled against her.

Seemed like his Domina was ready for her orgasm.

He held her clit gently between his teeth and lashed it with the tip of his tongue. She stilled beneath him, then exploded. Her pussy practically sucked on his thumb and his own orgasm took him by surprise, his seed shooting out onto the bed beneath him. He couldn't help imagining what it would feel like to have those delicate muscles milk his dick and he rubbed his cock against the sheets, overwhelmed by her response. Pleasure shook him from the inside out and he struggled to keep eating her, to make sure she got as much from her orgasm as she could. When they'd both stopped shuddering Michelle lifted the blanket with a lazy smile.

"Should I pretend that I invited you to do that?"

He pulled himself up her body until he lay next to her in the bed. "I was hoping that we could consider that an entrance fee."

"An entrance fee for what?"

"To get to sleep in this bed. I don't know about you, but I've slept on enough shitty floors to last me a lifetime. You can tie me up, chain my dick to the ceiling, whatever, just let me sleep next to you tonight."

She looked down at his slowly relaxing cock, at the smear of come against his lower abdominal area, and back up to his face. A flush filled his cheeks at her sudden look of understanding. "Did you come?"

Embarrassed, he nodded. "Yeah, you have a wet spot at the foot of your bed."

"From eating my pussy?"

"I told you I loved to do it. I wasn't lying."

A wicked gleam entered her gaze and she scooted closer to him, reaching down to stroke his dick. The head was particularly sensitive right now and he gritted his teeth against the pleasure/pain of her touch. "I know what I want you to start working on. It shouldn't take you too long."

"You mean for your dungeon?" Blood continued to flow back into his cock and he enjoyed the lazy way she was toying with him.

"Mmmm hmmm." She traced the metal circles of the cock ring. "I take it you don't have a gold allergy?"

"Umm, nope."

Her fingers tapped along the ring, making it vibrate in a way that stole all coherent thought. A second later the clench of the rings disappeared and he watched as she drew it off his dick and balls, a tight grip that forced pre-cum from the tip of his dick. She paused and licked him clean, leaving him with his head thrust back into the pillows, gripping the sheets. When she pulled away he groaned with frustration, wishing she'd do that for the rest of their lives.

The bed shifted as she moved and he looked up, watching her crawl across the bed, her still wet pussy being pressed between her thighs. The way her heart shape ass wiggled was a work of art and he wondered if he got to play with her ass if he'd let her play with his. Might be almost worth it if it meant someday he'd have that little pink anus spread around his shaft.

She bent over and opened her bedside drawer. This only exposed more of her deep pink cunt, and the hard bud of her clit. There was no doubt in his mind now that she knew exactly how much she was teasing him and how much it turned her on. She brought her legs close together and squeezed her thighs, her ass clenching.

"You are an evil woman, Domina," he said in a raspy voice.

She laughed and crawled back over to him, her breasts swaying with her movements in an utterly distracting way. He had no idea where she'd gotten that glitter stuff, but it made every bit of her flesh a work of art. He couldn't help but chuckle and rub at his mouth.

"What?" Michelle asked as she settled next to him.

"Do I have glitter all over my mouth?"

She looked closer and started to laugh. "Oh, dear. You look like you gave Tinkerbell oral sex." She slid closer to him, her pubic mound pressing against the head of his cock. "I like it. If we ever go to a club together I'm going to cover my pussy in glitter and make you eat me out in the car before we go in. I want everyone who looks at you to know that you are mine, and it's my pussy they smell on your breath."

He stared down at her, mildly shocked by her brazen statement. And that was saying something considering he'd spend most of his adult life around the filthiest mouthed motherfuckers to ever walk the earth, the US Marines. Well, Michelle had been exposed to them as well so maybe he shouldn't be too surprised.

Shaking his head, he gave her a mock disapproving look. "You are so kinky."

"Yes, I am." She resumed stroking his cock, now pressed between their bodies. "The cock ring I'm about to put on you can be worn at all times. You might want to take it off when you shower, but other than that you can do all of your normal daily stuff while you wear it. I like the thought of a visible, tangible reminder of my ownership being on you at all times."

Unable to respond to the depth of emotion in her eyes, the pleasure of her touch, he nodded and rolled back onto the bed, taking her nude body with him so that she landed astride his stomach with his cock resting against her ass.

"I'm at your mercy, Domina."

She snorted and moved off of him, much to his disappointment. Her warm fist gripped him and he was amazed at his recovery time around her. It seemed like she merely had to want him and his dick was hard. The wet suction of her mouth engulfed his cockhead and he looked up just in time to watch her nose hit his pubic hair. Then she slowly pulled up, catching his gaze as he watched the wet path she left behind.

After releasing the head of his dick with a pop,

she gave him a teasing smile. "Had to lube you up first."

He gave a laugh that sounded more like a wheeze as she slid the first gold ring down. Then she gently cupped his sac and eased his balls through the second gold ring one at a time. He groaned when the ring around his dick finally slid into place. Pausing, she nuzzled his balls and made his back bow as blood rushed to his cock.

She sat back on her heels, giving him a hell of a view. "There." She leaned over and switched off the light, crawling unceremoniously across him to her side of the bed.

He stared up at the ceiling, wondering if he could die of blue balls.

"Wyatt, come over here and cuddle me."

"I don't know if that's a good idea."

"Don't be a brat. You're too much of a gentleman to ever do anything that I'm not ready for. I know that and you know that, now spoon me before I beat your ass and make you sleep on the floor."

He grumbled, but rolled over next to her with a sigh, sinking into the bed. He felt embraced, cared for, and very comfortable. The ache of his cock began to fade, then roared back to life when she wiggled enticingly against him. Her soft laugh made his teeth clench, but he managed to restrain himself from spanking her.

He had a feeling that would end badly.

So he endured her teasing wiggles until she fell asleep, and he began planning his morning revenge.

Chapter 10

Michelle was rudely jerked from her erotic dreams about Wyatt when he yanked the covers off of her before opening her curtains, letting hot Texas sunshine into her room.

"What the fuck!"

"Morning, Doc. Get up, we're going for a run."

"I'm going to shoot you."

"Don't be such a whiner, get up."

Irritation rankled her spine, but she also kinda liked his shouty drill instructor voice. It reminded her of him yelling at his grunts. She'd always stop and watch the way his men scrambled to do whatever he said, intimidated as hell by this big Gunnery Sergeant. Her big Gunnery Sergeant. She stretched on the bed and noticed a restlessness about him.

"Why are you acting all odd? What are you up to?"

He winced. "Damn, I can never fool my sister either."

With a bounce in his step he came to her bedside, dressed in a pair of jogging shorts. If he planned on running without a shirt she just might forego beating him to death for waking her up at this ungodly hour. Sitting up, she tried to run her fingers through the tangled fuzz of her hair. "Jesus, you remind me of a hyperactive dog."

He growled, then lunged at her. Despite the

violence of the initial move he cradled her so she gently landed on the bed and pressed himself up on his arms. "I have a surprise for you. But you need to be out of the house for a little bit in order to get it set up."

His enthusiasm tickled over her like bubbles and she couldn't help but smile back. "Do I get to punish you later if your surprise doesn't merit a break-of-dawn run?"

"I...I guess so. I mean yes, Domina." He pressed his pelvis against her, enough so she felt his heavy arousal between her legs. "If I've displeased you, I beg for your punishment."

Holy shit.

The joy lifted from his face, a much more adult, dark desire taking its place. Their eyes met and a delicious electricity fused them together. He felt huge against her, all male strength and lust. So different from a woman's slow build-up to desire. Men could go from zero to ready to fuck in the blink of an eye. Not that she minded one bit.

He leaned down, his intention to kiss her obvious.

"Wyatt, lift off of me, then be still."

He pushed himself up on his arms and froze, only the slightest dilation of his pupils indicating that he found the order to be arousing. Well, the widening of his pupils followed by the twitch of his cock against her, with only the smooth silk of his jogging shorts separating them. She reached between them and slipped her hand inside of his shorts, playing with the body she owned. He was heavy and warm in her hand, a drop of pre-cum wetting her palm. She rubbed over the head of his cock and he tensed against her.

Oh yeah, he was feeling it.

His eyes closed half way, incredibly sexy and filling her with need. She traced her fingers down his shaft until she came to the rings around his cock and balls. He bucked into her grip when she gently squeezed and pulled his shaft.

"Shit. That feels too good." His breath came in rapid pants, each breath pressing his erection against her.

She slowly withdrew her hand, milking him and stroking out a big drop of pre-cum. Using her fingers, she caught up as much as she could. Still holding his gaze, she smeared his lips with his pre-cum, then pulled him down for a kiss.

He was a hot, welcome weight on top of her. They kissed, their lips slicked with his essence. She sucked first his lower lip, then his upper. The heady musk of his essence on his mouth had her rocking her pelvis into his. His tongue chased after hers and she sighed as he tasted himself from her mouth.

With a desperate gasp she pushed him off of her. A few more minutes of this and she'd be ready to have him bend her over and fuck her until she couldn't move, which would ruin his surprise. A little voice whispered in her head that she wasn't worried about his surprise, she was avoiding a situation that would make her break her oath. An internal battle between her past and present that was becoming increasingly hard to ignore.

"Give me a minute to throw some clothes on and we'll go for a run."

He gave her such a pained look that she had to laugh. He glanced down at his obvious erection and then back up at her. "Did you tighten the ring?"

"Ohhhh, I might have. Hmmm, we can't have you running with a hard dick now can we?"

She crawled across the bed to him. "Lift your hips."

He did with an eagerness that once again made her laugh. The mirth died in her throat as she caught sight of his beautiful flushed cock reaching to his belly button. Evidently he'd been up for a while because he'd trimmed his pubic hair back a bit, making the gold rings stand out. In fact, he'd shaved his balls as well.

Oh my.

Keeping her cool had never been harder than when her tongue touched the smooth skin of his balls, licking at him and eliciting a groan of such volume that she'd be surprised if Yuki and James hadn't heard it. With her other hand she loosened the expensive adjustable rings so that the internal springs moved just enough to let the blood flow back out. Not that her tonguing his sac was helping with that.

After making sure that everything was loose enough, she slowly took both of Wyatt's balls into her mouth, gently rolling her tongue. They tightened beneath her touch and she teased him for a few more seconds before releasing him with a reluctant sigh. He stared at her incredulously as she got off the bed and sauntered over to her walk-in closet.

"I'd be more than happy to return the favor, Domina." Then his grin turned wicked. "By the way, you still sparkle."

She turned just enough so that he could see her face and raised her eyebrows, then made a motion of wiping off her mouth. He cursed and rubbed his hand over his lips, shaking his head when he saw the glitter. "Fuck. I'm going to look like one of those pretty boy vampires."

"Come here, Wyatt. Then be still."

He gave her a weary look, but came when she motioned him with her finger. When he was standing before her she placed her arms around him and rubbed her breasts over his chest and stomach. He shifted and she dragged her nipples over his arm, placing a nip at the hard mound of his shoulder. When she reached his back she made sure to the kiss the spot where she'd ground herself onto him, then proceeded to rub glitter all over his back.

"There, now you look like a glittery vampire."

He shook his head. "You told me you weren't a sadist."

"I'm not. We'll just wash it off in the shower together when we get back."

He stepped away from the door to her closet and bowed. "In that case, time's a wastin'."

*****

Time had indeed been wasted because by the time they returned from their two-mile run, an unfamiliar truck with a trailer attached was sitting in her driveway.

"Shit, she's here early."

Breathing heavy, she glared at him and changed pace so they were running to the back of the house instead of the front. "Who's here?"

"Your surprise. Come on, I guess it's good to meet them this way. Lilly said if none of them liked the smell she'd leave before we returned."

"What the hell have you done, Wyatt?"

He grinned, looking too damned good running without his shirt on. She'd been looking forward to that shower.

"Come on, Doc, let me surprise you."

"Fine." She glanced down at her sweaty shirt and blew out a disgusted breath. "I hope whoever it is doesn't mind if I stink."

He snorted and slowed to a walk as they came around the side, the smell of cedar scenting the air as the boards warmed beneath the sun. Stretching out, she followed him and he yelled, "Lilly, we're coming over by you now."

"Okay," an older woman's voice called back.

"If you got me a female submissive, I usually prefer them younger."

His jaw dropped in shock. "You what?"

They rounded the corner before she could reply and stopped in her tracks at the sight before her.

Two of the most beautiful dogs she'd ever seen waited in front of her. One was a big German Shepard that was mixed with something she couldn't identify, wearing an American flag handkerchief around his neck. Whatever the dog's genetic mix was, it gave the Shepard a thicker coat than usual and a white muzzle. The other was an equally big Rottweiler, with a small white blaze on his black and tan chest. He was sporting a handkerchief of the Navy's emblem.

Entranced by the intelligence in their gazes, amused by the slight wiggle she detected in each butt, she crouched down and held out her hand. "Hi pretty babies."

The dogs looked over their shoulder and an

older woman with short silver hair dressed in hunter green sweats nodded. "Go ahead."

The dogs came forward and sniffed her hand, their breath tickling her as their tails wagged enthusiastically. Soon she found herself sitting on the grass next to her driveway, close to two hundred pounds of loving dogs both trying to sit on her lap.

The older woman laughed and came over, shooing the dogs away and offering her a hand up. "You must be the owner of this house."

"Yes." She took the woman's hand and stood. "My name's Michelle, and you are?"

The woman looked at Wyatt, who still stood behind them. He cleared his throat. "Is it okay for me to approach?"

"Dear me. Are you covered in glitter?"

He turned completely red, from his hairline all the way down his chest. "Uh, yes ma'am, I mean Lilly."

"Huh." She turned back to Michelle with a smile. "Is he allowed near you? Like in your personal space?"

"Of course."

"Mud, Tuba, *freund*. You're free to approach now, Wyatt."

The dogs both sat, one at Michelle's feet and one at Lilly's. Wyatt grinned and crouched down in front of them. "Hi pups."

The dogs looked back at them and both women nodded. Then there was a repeat of the enthusiastic greeting session, ending with Wyatt almost falling because of their head butts to the backs of his knees.

He looked over at Lilly. "Are they trying to

knock me down?"

"It's because you're all sweaty. They're trying to get you to rest."

Michelle pursed her lips. "Really? Do you have them somehow scent trained for it?"

"Honey, these dogs can do pretty much anything that doesn't require thumbs." Lilly fanned herself. "Not to be forward, but do you mind if we take this inside? It's hotter than a demon's pussy out here."

Blinking, Michelle looked over at Wyatt who was gaping at the older woman in a way that made Michelle want to laugh. "Yes, of course."

Wyatt held the door open for them while Michelle led the way to the kitchen. Behind them the dogs' nails clicked over the marble floor and onto the wood. She briefly wondered if they were house broken, but figured that since that's one of the things dogs didn't need thumbs for they were.

"Lovely home you have here, Michelle."

"Thanks." She gestured Lilly to take a seat and stretched out her legs while Wyatt poured glasses of cold sweet tea. "I had just talked to Wyatt last night about this, he must have called you late at night."

"Yes, it was rather late, but I was bartending at the VFW so I was still up."

"Are you former military?"

"Yes, I was part of the 341st Training Squadron over at Lackland Air Force base for many years. We trained war dogs for every branch of the military." She gave a small smile at Michelle's stunned expression. The trainers were considered an elite unit and for Lilly to have been a trainer back in what had to be the seventies was a big deal. It was pioneers like Lilly who paved the way for Michelle and her respect for the woman grew. Shoot, she almost felt like she was around a military celebrity. "But I try to keep that hush-hush. I have enough business as it is and don't want to turn into one of those guard dog gumball machine places that spit out one poor animal after another to an owner they don't belong with. I train dogs because that's what I love to do, it's part of my soul. That also means I love every one of my dogs like my furry children and I wouldn't give my children to just anyone. "

Wyatt handed Lilly her drink, a towel around his neck. "That's why I had to take you out of the house. Lilly's husband comes with her when they show prospective owners their dogs. They sniff out your house and the dogs that want to stay, do, while the other dogs get back into her husband's truck."

"And he takes them back home," Lilly finished. "I have to say, I'm surprised by the dogs that wanted to stay. Tuba, the Rottie, hasn't wanted to stay with anyone for close to six months now and Mud, the Shepherd, for even longer."

"How old are they?"

"Tuba is one and a half and Mud is two years old."

"What commands do you use?"

"One second..." Lilly dug around in the pockets of her sweatshirt. "Ahh, here we go. This is a full list of commands and what they will do. It's German."

Scanning the list, she picked one at random. "*Sitz.*"

Both dogs sat and looked at her like they were

waiting for her to tell them what to do next. "Cool. Uhhh...at ease dogs."

"Snap your fingers twice," Lilly said after taking a sip of her tea. "That's their sign to come to you for love."

Michelle came around to the other side of the counter and leaned against where Wyatt sat, using his bulk to brace herself. After snapping her fingers she soon found herself surrounded by the dogs, each whining low in their throat, trying to nudge the other out of the way for petting. She ended up scratching Tuba behind the ears while Mud went belly up for Wyatt. They grinned at each other and she looked over at Lilly. "How much do you want for them?"

"I'm sure we can come to an agreement on price. But you need to know that they'll be coming home with me today. I'll spend the next two weeks readying them for the transition to living with you. For example, if you have any other animals here I'd spend some time helping them get familiar."

"We have a bunch of barn cats, and two horses."

"That's fantastic, Tuba loves horses. If you do any trail riding he'll trot right along beside you, happy as a clam. And don't worry about the cats. The dogs will ignore them and the cats will be highly offended." She stood and the dogs reluctantly returned to her side, giving Wyatt and Michelle woeful puppy eyes. "Take a couple days then email me with any commands you'd like them to learn. Honestly, if you want them to relax when you say 'at ease' just let me know. I'll also need to go over some things with you as well, but that can wait until later. I need to get back home before my husband takes it upon himself to start weeding without me. Bless his heart but he wouldn't know crab grass from a marigold."

Michelle couldn't help the excitement bubbling through her. She'd always wanted a dog, but had never really been in a position to have one. Now it looked like she had two, and not just any dogs, but super awesome guard dogs. "Do you think we could meet up soon?"

Lilly absently patted Tuba on the head while she thought. "I'm afraid I'm going to be bartending at the VFW or with clients for the rest of the week."

Wyatt wiped his face off with the towel around his neck. "Do you think we could stop by your bar?"

"Well, considering you're both military we'd be more than glad to have you. Let's see, today is Thursday so tomorrow will be Friday. Yes, why don't you come early in the evening, say around five or six? That should give us a bit of quiet time before the loud mouths start to roll in with their stories that sound more like boasting contests." She pantomimed holding something up to her ear. "What! What! I can't hear you screaming about that time you were with a pair of Polynesian whores. Damn dirty old men."

They laughed and the dogs flanked them as they escorted Lilly to the door, sniffing around corners and keeping alert. Michelle watched them, noting how they seemed to move differently than regular dogs. If she thought about it, she'd say they moved like soldiers. Wyatt reached the door first and opened it. The dogs each paused to snuffle his hand and give him a lick before following Lilly out and Michelle fought a smile as Wyatt's chest swelled with pride.

After they said their goodbyes Wyatt turned to her gave her a small smile. "Did I do good?"

Wanting to wipe away the doubt from his mind she jumped up into his arms, making him catch her with a startled sound. She wrapped her legs around his waist and rained kisses down over his face, the salt of his sweat flavoring her lips. He made a happy noise and slowly moved them until he had her back against the wall next to the door, letting her capture his lips with her own. They melded together, breath and still warm skin pressed close, the endorphins from her run adding to her happiness.

She couldn't remember the last time she'd felt this alive.

He made a hungry noise as she toyed with his nipple ring, twisting it slowly as their tongues stroked each other. The banked fire from their earlier encounter roared to life and she was suddenly frantic for his touch, trying to take off her shirt without moving away from him. Her tank top was halfway off when the front doorbell rang. With a muttered oath she pulled her shirt back into place and gave Wyatt a narrow-eyed look.

"Did you put on a pair of briefs?"

He grinned at her and squeezed the outline of his cock through the silky jogging pants. "Yep. Sorry, Domina, but running with an erection is painful without support."

The doorbell rang again. "Stay right there. I'll deal with you as soon as I'm done with whoever that is."

She smoothed her shirt, grimacing at how her nipples stuck out. Wyatt chuckled and she shot him a death glare. After taking a deep breath she opened the door and saw a middle-aged woman standing on her steps. She had dark hair pulled back in a ponytail and around her eyes and bracketing her mouth were laugh lines. Dressed in a pair of faded jeans and a bright blouse she looked like the epitome of a soccer mom. Michelle looked into her hazel eyes and knew who the other woman was before she said a word.

She had her brother's eyes.

"Let me guess, you're here for Wyatt?"

"Yes. I'm his sister, Joy. He asked me to bring him some tools?" She pointed to a large black metal toolbox at her feet.

"Please, do come in. My name is Michelle."

She held her hand out for a shake, but Joy surprised her by pulling her into a hug then kissing both her cheeks. "I know who you are. You're the woman who saved my brother's life. Thank you. Just...thank you."

Michelle blinked back unexpected tears, her throat burning at the naked relief and gratitude plain her face. "I-you're welcome."

Joy blinked rapidly and fanned her face, looking back to what had to be her minivan. "Look at me, getting all weepy. Where is that brother of mine? If he thinks I'm hauling the rest of his stuff up from the minivan he's crazy."

Wyatt's voice came from behind Michelle. "As if I would ever do that."

"There you are!" Joy looked at his bare chest and frowned. "When did you get those done? If mom sees them she's going to have a litter of kittens."

Michelle watched Wyatt hem and haw, amused by his sudden bashfulness. "I don't know, a while ago."

With a sniff Joy put her hands on her hips. "Well that's it. You can't take your shirt off around my boys anymore. Bad enough they want tattoos like Uncle Wyatt, I'm not about to deal with them trying to pierce their own nipples as well."

"Awww, you're no fun." He moved out onto the steps with Joy. "You want to come in and have a drink?"

Joy sighed and shook her head. "I wish I could but I have to pick up Adam's band uniform before the game tonight and Jason has an orthodontist appointment and-"

"Okay, okay, I get it."

"Your stuff is in the trunk."

He nodded and meandered off towards the minivan, looking hot as sin in the full sunlight.

Joy moved next to her and lowered her voice. "Please don't take offense to this, but my husband, Officer Phelps, let me know that you're aware of what's going on with Wyatt. Did my brother tell you about the PTSD attack at the mall?"

Keeping a pleasant smile on her face, Michelle shook her head. "No, what happened?"

Joy spoke rapidly while Wyatt began to dig through the trunk of the minivan. "Something set him off, what I don't know, but that's not important. He was about to beat some guy's ass for bumping into him and I stepped between them to try and stop it." Wyatt grunted as he lifted a red metal tool box out and set it on the ground. "He almost hit me."

"What?"

"He didn't see me. His brain checked out and I was another enemy. Thank God he came back to the real world. He's coming. Look, be careful. He would never hurt you, he worships you, but if he did he'd never forgive himself."

The trunk slammed and both women jumped. Michelle pulled Joy into another hug and whispered in her hear, "Thank you."

Wyatt must have been coming near because Joy held her back at arm's length with a smile that looked as fake as Michelle's felt. "Well, he's my little brother. As disgusting as he is we'd still love to have you both over for a bar-b-que next week."

"Sounds great. I'll check my schedule and get back with you."

"Please do. You can get my cell number and email from Wyatt."

He climbed up the steps next to them, the muscles of his shoulders bulging from carrying the heavy toolboxes. "Michelle, where can I put these?"

Joy started down the steps, her dark ponytail flipping behind her. "Have fun, you two. Call me if you need me. And Michelle, it was a real pleasure meeting you."

Michelle waved and Wyatt sighed. "Sorry about that. Joy is a touchy feely person."

Using both hands, Michelle lugged the third tool box as she followed Wyatt into the foyer. "She seems really nice."

"Oh, she is. She's just very nosy." He gave her a speculative look. "What was she telling you on the steps?"

Giving him a sweet smile she said, "Girl stuff. Follow me. I'll set you up in the man cave."

"The what?"

"You'll see."

She led him down the hall to the right, past a small sitting room and to a pair of swinging doors. Using her butt, she nudged them open and Wyatt followed her inside. As she set the toolbox down on one of the massive slate counters he let out a soft whistle.

"Wow, Doc, I never would have pictured you having a man cave like this."

She grinned and turned around, looking around the big room with its various cabinets, racks, and peg boards. "This used to be the hobby room for the previous owner. I was thinking about turning it into something else but hadn't quite decided what yet."

Wyatt ran his hands over the cupboards and smiled. "Now it makes sense."

"What makes sense?"

"Well, some parts of your house are beautifully crafted...while others are...not so beautifully crafted."

Her spine stiffened. "Like what?"

"Now don't go getting all offended. It's just that some of the work on your renovations is sloppy."

"Sloppy how?"

He drifted past her, looking out the windows that faced Yuki's cabin in the distance, then turned around and wandered back over to the peg board, running his hand down the uneven surface. "Have you figured out what you want me to build first?"

Heat instantly blazed through her and she had to resist the urge to clap with glee. "I have an idea. Do you need me to describe it or draw it?"

"It would help if you drew it."

"Okay, one second, let me go get a pen and paper."

By the time she got back to the hobby room he'd begun putting his tools away. Shiny chisels of all shapes and sizes hung from the peg board, their handles colored with the patina of use. Her heart constricted at how right he looked here, like this was his home. She tried to push that feeling away, telling herself that he was in no state to make such life altering decisions right now, but oh how she hoped that he would stay after his month was up.

"Here, let me show you what I'm thinking of."

After she drew a rough sketch, he looked from her, to the paper, and back to her again. "Is this going to be used for what I think it's going to be used for?"

She smiled and shrugged. "Maybe. You'll have to wait and see."

He frowned down at the sketch. "You wouldn't happen to have an adjustable bench, like a weight bench would you? I can do the incline, but having it pre-built would allow me to get this done by tonight."

Everything south of her belly button clenched in delicious anticipation. "As a matter of fact I do. Out in the garage is a weight set along with benches and a bunch of other crap. Eventually, it's all going to go into my gym, but I'm more than happy to sacrifice whatever you need. Just make sure you put the hole where I want it."

He leaned closer to the drawing, making notes and muttering to himself. "Do you have a truck I could use?"

"Of course I do. Really, how could I live in Texas on a ranch and not have a truck?"

He grinned, but his gaze was still distant. "In that case, I'm going into town. You need anything while I'm out? I mean, Domina, can I get you anything?"

She smiled and brushed his hair back. "Get a haircut, but leave it long enough for me to grab onto."

He laughed and ran his hands through his hair. "Yeah, it's starting to bug the shit out of me. Can't stand it when it gets in my eyes."

She leaned up on tip-toe, only the thought of the pleasure that would come once his project was complete holding her back from jumping him. "I'm going to go wash up. If you're going to be playing in here for the rest of the afternoon I might as well get caught up on my work."

"Might repurpose some furniture," he said in a distracted voice. "Do you like pine?"

Laughing, she walked towards the singing doors. "You do whatever it is you do best, Wyatt. I can't wait to see what you come up with. I trust you."

She pushed the doors open and as they swung closed behind her she thought she heard him say, "I trust you too, Domina."

*****

Michelle looked up from her computer screen, her eyes burning from staring at the monitor for so long. She'd spent the afternoon catching up on business with her financial planner, a dry, boring, long process that, nonetheless, needed all of her concentration. Her phone had buzzed a few times, but since it was just Yuki she let it go to voice mail. If it was an emergency her friend knew where to find her.

She pushed her chair back and stretched out her arms and legs, the tightening and release of her muscles making her sigh. A low growl came from her stomach and she wondered what Yuki was going to make for dinner tonight. She'd promised her friend that she and Wyatt would actually have a sit down dinner with her and James over at their cabin. While she knew that the meal would only sharpen her appetite for other things, she couldn't wait to try out the queening chair Wyatt was making for her.

Standing, she smoothed her long turquoise blue skirt and slipped her sandals on from their spot beneath her desk. She grabbed her cellphone and strolled over to the window with a view of the pasture, watching Pants run around and try to get Goddess to play. The mare pretended to be indifferent, lipping at the grass while Pants raced around her. Then Pants got a little bit too close and she nipped at him. Well she didn't actually try to bite him, her teeth were never even near his body, but Pants spazzed out like she'd taken a big chunk out of his neck.

Laughing at the horses' antics, she checked her messages. One was from her mother, one was from the plumber, and the next one made her pause. It was a message from Connie, double checking that Michelle would be able to make the wedding/collaring ceremony next week in Chicago. Connie then casually brought up that she'd talked to Yuki who'd mentioned that Michelle had a boyfriend and asked if Michelle would like to bring him as a guest.

Her heart took a sickening lurch and she closed her eyes, leaning her forehead against the glass.

She and Connie had been good friends and she'd been one of Owen's best friends. Irrational guilt hit her at the thought of bringing Wyatt to her wedding. It should have been Owen at her side, but he was gone and had been for a long, long time. Still, at times like this he felt close enough to touch, and a sickening knot formed in her stomach. Was he watching her right now? Was he mad that she'd given his place to someone else?

Trying to shake off her unreasonable train of thought she brought her phone back up to her ear and listened to the next message. It was Yuki, and she needed some ingredients from Michelle's kitchen. Pausing the message, Michelle went over to her desk and grabbed her pen and notepad, restarting the message and writing down the list of stuff Yuki needed. She was glad her friend had called, because this would give her an excuse to go visit and let Yuki tell her what a dumbass she was for feeling guilty.

Maybe if she heard it enough times she'd actually start to believe it.

With the list in hand she made her way through the quiet house to the kitchen, trying to listen for Wyatt. She paused for a moment when she didn't hear the muted rumble of power tools from the other side of the house. Then she remembered all the chisels and such he'd been hanging up in the hobby room and shook her head at her own foolishness. When Wyatt said he was going to make something by hand he'd obviously meant it. She wondered if he was one of those purists who wouldn't use modern technology to make things.

Late afternoon sunlight streamed through the wide bay window in the kitchen and she felt a contentment that had been missing from her life for a very long time. That warmth seeped through her, easing the knot in her gut and letting her take a full breath. A flash of color near the sink caught her eye and she gasped in delight at the beautiful vase full of multi-colored roses. There had to be close to three dozen and the closer she got the more their scent perfumed the air.

A white notecard stuck out from the top and she put Yuki's list to the side, eager to read it and shredding the envelope in her haste.

Michelle,

I wasn't sure what your favorite rose was; there is still so much about you that remains a mystery to me, so I got you one of every color they had.

Wyatt.

A giggle escaped before she could stop it, a light, carefree sound that tinkled through the kitchen like chimes. She read the note and giggled again, glancing down the hallway to make sure Wyatt wasn't there to see her acting like a besotted teenager. Setting the card to the side she brought the vase over into the sunlight streaming over the counter and slowly looked at each and every rose in the bouquet. After careful deliberation, she finally picked a golden rose with hints of baby pink and tangerine orange around the tips of the petals. It was so beautiful, feminine, and delicate. Something that reminded her of the way Wyatt made her feel.

She found a slender crystal vase in the cabinet below the sink and filled it with water before setting the single blossom in it. Her stomach growled again and with a reluctant sigh she left the rose in its puddle of sunlight and began to gather up the ingredients on Yuki's list. When she reached her request for a bottle of white wine she looked for the one Wyatt had opened earlier. Unable to find it, she rationalized that maybe he'd poured it out, thinking it had gone bad.

Then her gaze, almost against her will, strayed over to the beer on the second shelf and she noticed that a six pack of beer was missing.

Sour bile filled her mouth and she carefully shut the door to the fridge before turning and leaning against it. How stupid could she be? Of course he'd continue to drink, after all that had been his number one source for comfort. Drinkers didn't just stop, they'd go back to it in times of stress and she'd certainly given him a good deal of stress over the past few days.

Still, he'd been sneaking around doing it. She clenched her hands into fists, her nails biting into her palms. The betrayal hurt, cut deep and fast, easily slicing through the fragile ropes holding her heart together. She'd trusted him, in her home and with her body, and he'd snuck around behind her back. Why couldn't he have talked with her about this? Did he have so little faith in her?

Owen would have never have betrayed her like this.

"Wyatt!" The word left her mouth in an angry yell and echoed through the kitchen and down the hall.

"Michelle?" His voice sounded faint, but closer when he yelled again, "Michelle?"

"In the kitchen."

He strode in, clad only in a pair of jeans and wearing some thick leather gloves. Flakes of sawdust lay scattered about his chest and arms while the scent of wood wafted from his skin. He must have showered at some point because the glitter was gone and his hair was shorter. Cut close on the sides and a bit long on top, he looked more masculine than ever. His eyes were clear and bright, but she couldn't smell his breath this close. She'd give him a chance to explain, to right the wrong between them.

"What the fuck are you doing stealing my beer!"

He stepped back as if slapped, the color draining from his face. "I didn't steal anything!"

Oh, he looked so pissed and hurt. For a second she wondered if she'd misjudged him, but the evidence spoke for itself. Six-packs of beer don't get up and walk away. "Don't lie to me. There is nothing I hate more than a liar."

He tugged off his gloves and threw them on the counter. "I'm not lying to you. What the fuck, Michelle? Do you really think I'd feel the need to sneak anything? I'm a grown man and if I wanted a drink I'll have a fucking drink-but I didn't drink your goddamn beer!"

His shout echoed through the kitchen and his anger was swiftly turning to rage, but she was too pissed and wounded to care. "You can have a goddamned drink anytime you want, but not in my fucking house. Not until you get your shit together and I don't have to worry about you ending up sitting on your dead friend's grave with a knife."

Tears welled in her eyes and she dashed them away with an angry swipe. Wyatt clenched and unclenched his hands, his nostrils flaring. "Is that what you think I am? Some pathetic suicidal drunk?"

"No! At least I didn't think that until I found out you were stealing from me."

"I didn't take anything!"

"Yes you did!"

"Fuck!"

Wyatt grabbed the vase holding the single rose and hurled it against the wall. The fine crystal shattered and water splashed down onto the tiles of the floor. The beautiful flower landed in the puddle, its petals mangled and cut by the broken glass.

They stared at each other for a brief moment before Yuki's voice cut through the air. "Well, I can see now would be a good time to borrow Wyatt for some sketches I wanted to do."

Michelle looked over to the doorway of the mudroom and found Yuki glaring, but not at Wyatt, rather at her. "This is not a good time."

"Oh yes, this is the perfect time." Yuki motioned to Wyatt, the golden bangles on her slender arm clicking together. He closed his eyes and breathed hard through his nose, a fine sheen of sweat covering his skin. "Come on, Wyatt. I need your help and your Mistress needs a moment to realize what a fucking bitch she's being."

"What!?" Michelle whirled around to fully face Yuki.

Her best friend shook her head, anger and sorrow mixing together on her expressive face. "Michelle, James took the beer."

All the strength went out of her legs and she slumped against the side of the refrigerator. "Why?"

"When you didn't answer your phone I sent him over for the stuff I needed. He grabbed some beer figuring that Wyatt wouldn't want to drink chocolate martinis with you and me."

She couldn't look at Wyatt, couldn't face him after her accusations. "Wyatt...I..."

He walked past her without responding, and she felt cold in his wake, like she'd been sprayed with icy water. She slumped to the floor against the refrigerator, staring at the broken vase and damaged flower.

It had been so beautiful and she'd ruined it.

Chapter 11

He didn't think he'd ever been so insulted in his life. Here he was, bowing to her every whim, doing everything he could to make her happy…and it wasn't enough. How could she possibly think he'd steal from her?

Yuki's smooth voice cut through his thoughts, "Because she's afraid to love you, not realizing that she's probably already in love with you. Now stop moving before I strap your ass."

He glanced over at Yuki where she sat at a drawing table near the barn wall, busily rubbing out something with her eraser. "What?"

"You were thinking out loud." She blew off the eraser dust and looked up. "I need you to put your arms back up again." Her gaze flitted up and then back down. "By the way, love the cock ring."

Fighting against the need to cover himself, he raised his arms above his head and tried to ignore James' chuckles from the other side of the workspace. He laced his fingers together and stretched upwards, the muscles of his body straining as he reached as high as he could against the wide wooden beam sunk deep into the barn floor beneath his feet. They were in Yuki's sketching room, a warm, quiet place where she liked to start her projects.

James sat in a nearby giant bean bag chair, his computer on his lap as he 'played the market'.

"Take it easy on him. He's not used to holding positions for so long."

Yuki shot her husband a glare that he didn't see and turned back to Wyatt. "Do you need a break?"

His shoulders groaned in protest, but he held the position. "No, I'm good."

She shook her head. "So in guy speak that means your arms are about to fall off. Throw on your pants and come here. You can take a look at what you've been suffering for."

James shut his laptop and wandered over to his wife while Wyatt jerked on his pants. He'd been here for the last three hours, being put through one torturous position after another as Yuki sketched him from different angles. In that time his rage had drained away, leaving him feeling raw and battered inside. Michelle's accusations hurt more than he'd thought possible and he really wanted to see her, but Yuki was making him wait, saying Michelle needed to do a little scraping and come to him.

James let out a low whistle. "That is going to be fucking awesome."

Intrigued, Wyatt walked across the bare floor, standing behind Yuki's shoulder. "Holy shit."

Without a doubt she was one of the most talented artists he'd ever met. She'd drawn a giant tree with small, barely formed leaves like one would see in spring. She had him bound against it, every muscle and detail of his body captured, right down to his tattoos and nipple rings. He looked closer and realized that his image wasn't bound to the tree trunk by ropes, but by vines twisting down from the branches above. An even closer look revealed the faces and shapes of three women, nude and rising out of the tree to curve around him.

"Who are they?" He pointed to one of the women, being careful not to touch the picture.

"Wood nymphs, and you are their human sacrifice."

"It's...I mean I've never seen anything like this. The way you have the bodies of the women forming out of the bark, it's just amazing."

With a pleased smile Yuki nodded. "Wait until you see the sculpture. I think I'm going to do it in a mixture of copper and bronze. With the right lighting it will look as if the nymphs are rising up out of the tree, a great, ethereal contrast to the solid, masculine presence of your body."

James moved over to the side, looking at it from a different angle. "You know, it might be cool to have little flowering vines coming from one of the nymph's fingers and trailing through his nipple ring. Maybe pulling outwards a bit?"

"Hmmm, that would be interesting." She glanced up at Wyatt and back down to the picture. "I've managed to capture his anger, but if I did your suggestion I'd need to temper it with some pleasure. Can you give me your 'O' face Wyatt?"

He laughed, the hollow feeling in his chest easing a bit. "Sorry, but I'm not really in an 'O' face mood at the moment."

Yuki swiveled her chair around to face him. "You ready to talk about Michelle now?"

He frowned and glanced at the closed door. "Look, I don't really feel right talking about her behind her back."

"I understand that, but you need to understand what's going on."

"Oh, I understand." He began to wander around the room, trying to keep his temper under control. "She thinks I'm a thief, liar, and an alcoholic."

"Well, she might have considered that notion for a moment, but I don't really think that's what her outburst was all about. Sit down on the couch, your pacing is making me antsy."

He grumbled but did as she asked, lounging back on the wide black leather couch. "Better?"

"Yes. Let me think of how to put this to you best. I don't want to keep you here all night with the entire story, not when Michelle will be here any minute."

He glanced at the door, hope mixing with his sadness. "How do you know that?"

"Because I know Michelle. She's spent the last five years with one foot in the grave, Wyatt." He started to speak but she held up her hand. "Just listen. Has she mentioned Owen to you yet?"

His heart constricted when he thought about her agonized crying. "Yeah."

"And she told you how he died?"

"Yeah. He got shot in a robbery by a kid while trying to protect Michelle."

"After his funeral James and I had to physically carry her away from his grave where she'd been promising him that she'd never love another like she did him. I love Michelle more than anyone in the world aside from James, but I'd about given up on her. Did you ever wonder why we moved down here with her?"

His chest hurt at the knowledge that Michelle would never let herself love him. "She said something about you wanting more space for your art."

"That is partially true, but the real reason is we were afraid about what would happen to Michelle once she was truly alone. While she was in the military she was constantly surrounded by people whether she liked it or not, forced to live and participate. I thought it was good for her, especially after she started talking about you in her letters. There was an excitement, a joy that I hadn't seen from her in years."

James sat on the opposite side of the couch and picked up where his wife left off. "Then the attack that almost killed you happened and she started to slip back into her guilt again, but this time guilt about failing you. I've never met a woman who loves her guilt as much as Michelle."

Yuki's voice cut through the air like a whip. "James, you shouldn't say that. Think of how you would feel if you ever lost me like she lost Owen."

He shook his head, a stubborn set to his jaw. "It's not the same. Oh I know she loved Owen, hell we all did, he was a great guy, but they'd only been together for two years."

"Time doesn't mean anything when it comes to the heart," Yuki insisted.

"Mistress, you have to stop enabling her."

To Wyatt's surprise Yuki nodded and her shoulders slumped in defeat. "I know I do, James, but it's so hard seeing her sad."

Wanting to get to the point before Michelle got here, Wyatt said, "So what does this have to do with me?"

James sighed. "In you, Michelle sees a chance at a new life. I think she's loved you for a long time though she'd never admit it to herself. In her mind loving you would mean betraying Owen's memory, breaking her oath to him sworn on his grave. So she can't have what she wants most in the world without eviscerating herself with guilt."

"That's fucked up." He ran his hand through his newly cut hair. "But she seems so...like she has her shit together."

"Of course she does, she's being strong for you." Yuki stood up and moved over to the couch, taking a seat on James' lap. "It's easy to ignore her own issues when yours are there to distract her."

"Wait, are you saying that she only wants me as long as she thinks I need her help?"

"No, I wasn't bullshitting when I said she loves you. You should have read the letters home about you. She was always going on about what a good, kind, strong, and honorable man you were."

James ran his hand down his wife's braid. "And we're really hoping you stay. Not because Michelle needs you, but because you guys have a shot at something special...if you can help her move on."

He slumped back against the couch, staring at the ceiling. "How the fuck am I supposed to do that?"

"Be there for her. Don't let her push you away."

"Time heals all wounds," Yuki added. "I think on some level she's already let Owen go, but she's afraid to open herself up to that kind of heartache again. It's an automatic reaction from her mind to push you away. Think of it like your PTSD."

"She told you about that?"

"Not everything, but enough so that if you had a panic attack we'd be ready."

James kicked at his foot, drawing his gaze back to them. "Don't be mad at her. She was trying to save me from an ass beating. Let's face it, if we were in a fight I'd walk away looking like I got gored by a bull."

He shook his head and gave the couple a weary glance. "You're not afraid of being around me?"

Yuki shook her head. "No. I saw you in that kitchen. You were as mad as I've ever seen anyone, but you didn't hurt her. Instead you turned your attention to an inanimate object and made sure to throw it somewhere it wouldn't hurt anyone."

Something lightened in his heart as he realized the truth of her words. He'd been harboring the fear of hurting those around him for so long. "You said her thing with Owen is like my PTSD, how so?"

"Well, in your mind whatever sets you off feels real, right? Even though your logical mind knows it's bullshit, it doesn't matter because some part of your brain tells you it is real."

He gripped his hands into fists, fighting off unwanted memories. "Yeah."

"Well it's kinda the same with Michelle. In her logical mind she knows Owen is gone and never coming back, that it was a senseless act of random violence..."

James continued, "But way down deep she still believes that she is not only responsible for his death, but that she must atone for it for the rest of her life. By allowing herself to love you, something she really can't stop, she feels like she's betraying his memory."

He sat forward on the couch, staring at the closed door. "How the fuck can I compete with a ghost?"

"You can't. The only thing you can do is be there for her and remind her that she is still alive, that the world has joys to offer and that you will be there for her and love her like she deserves to be loved. Basically just do what you're already doing, but don't let her guilt drive you away."

A dinging sound rang through the barn and Yuki quickly stood. "Wyatt, take those pants off and get back into position. James, strip and get next to him."

James flushed. "What?"

"I need some eye candy to keep her here. She probably wants to come in, tell Wyatt that she's a horrible person and he should leave. I need you two being all yummy. She's a voyeur so you two will be impossible to resist."

Both men shucked their pants and avoided eye contact. Yuki had enough time to position them as she wanted, almost back to back and both with their arms extended overhead, but with one of their arms crossing over the others.

A knock came from the door and Yuki took a deep breath before saying, 'Come in."

The door opened and an ashen faced Michelle entered. Her eyes were sunk into her head, rimmed with red and her movements were hesitant, like she was afraid that at any moment she might be struck. Wyatt immediately went to go to her but Yuki snapped, "Don't you fucking move. If you ruin your position I'm going to be pissed."

He might have gone anyway, but James clasped his hand on Wyatt's upraised forearm. Michelle looked from him, to James, and back to him. Some of the sorrow went out of her gaze, replaced by the faintest spark of heat. Still, she wouldn't meet his eyes.

"May I come in?"

"Sure, have a seat on the couch. I'm almost done."

She nodded, a slope to her shoulders that hurt Wyatt's heart. When she sat she looked down at her clasped hands and didn't raise her head as the minutes ticked by. Yuki continued to sketch and as he watched her expression smoothed out and she soon 'spaced out' as James liked to put it, becoming wrapped up in her own world.

"Michelle, silver or bronze?"

"What?"

"Look at the guys and tell me if you think this statue would be best in silver or bronze."

She looked up, her gaze darting over their bodies, then skittering back to Yuki. "I'd go with steel."

"Really?" This made Yuki look up and she considered the men. "Oh for fucks sake, put your arms down before you dislocate your shoulders. I can see you both shaking."

Both men did and Wyatt bit back a groan as the pins and needles sensation in his arms became a sting.

"James, come here. You suffered for me so let me make it all better."

Out of the corner of his eye he caught Michelle flushing, then sitting up straighter. "Wyatt, come here." Her words came out in a whisper, and it hurt his heart at how afraid she sounded, like she fully expected him to walk away.

He approached her, trying to make her see in his face that he forgave her, but she wouldn't look at him. "Where would you like me, Domina?"

Now she did look up, and the naked relief in her eyes showed him more than anything that she did indeed love him. God, how could he have not seen it before? Unable to stop himself, he leaned down and brushed his lips over hers. "I'm still yours, if you'll have me."

Her eyelashes fluttered as she blinked back tears. "Turn around and sit so I can rub your shoulders."

With a much lighter heart he did as she commanded, letting out a low sigh at the first touch of her hands on his skin. Yuki said something about a wedding coming up for a mutual friend and the women began to chatter animatedly about who was going to be there, what to wear, other normal things that became a background drone. Her thighs parted wider to accommodate his shoulders and he scooted back, surrounding himself with her warmth. Strong and steady, her touch soothed him more than he could imagine and he gave himself up to her silent apology, closing his eyes when she laid a gentle kiss on the back of his neck. Somehow, he'd make this confusing, beautiful woman that drove him crazy realize that she loved him...and that he loved her.

*****

The stars were out by the time he and Michelle said their goodbyes to Yuki and James. After they'd left the barn they'd gone back to the couple's house and had dinner with them. It had been so normal, so comfortable, that he allowed himself to forget about the impossible task waiting for him.

Slipping his hand into Michelle's, he pretended

not to notice how she flinched, then clenched his hand tight enough to hurt. "I love how clear the sky is out here."

She didn't respond, just walking next to him like a silent shadow. The tension thrummed from her and he wished he knew what to say to make her open up. Instead he started talking about the different stars as they strolled back to the house, the first hint of autumn slightly cooling the air, and with it the promise of change.

They reached the side door and he opened it for her. Before she could enter he knelt at her feet and looked up at her. With the light from the kitchen illuminating half of her face his heart skipped a beat at her beauty. She'd swept her hair up in a loose bun, but a few curling tendrils had escaped, softening her aristocratic features and giving him the urge to touch.

"Domina, I would be honored if you would see what I've built today."

She flushed, then whispered, "Wyatt, I'm sorry I didn't trust you. I'll understand if you want to leave."

He looked up her, holding her gaze and drowning in the melancholy blue of her eyes. "I'm not going to say you didn't piss me off, but I'm not going away because of one spat."

Her hand shook as she reached out to touch him, but grew steady as she combed her fingers through his hair. "I don't deserve you."

Giving her a teasing smile, he nipped at her wrist before saying, "No, you don't, but you're stuck with me anyway."

She seemed to gather herself, to once again draw that mantel of authority around her that made his balls draw up tight. The atmosphere changed, became charged with the first flashes of lighting from the erotic storm to come. She slowly licked her lips and his gaze followed the path of her tongue, imagining what other wicked things she could do with it.

"Did you make the hole like I requested?"

He nodded. "I did, but I don't know why."

The savage gleam flared in her gaze and his cock jerked against his pants. "Go get ready for me. I want you kneeling next to the door in the hobby room, naked, with your hands behind your back."

He watched as she walked into the house, the silhouette of her bare legs visible through the light shining through the thin fabric of her skirt. Anticipation coiled his muscles tight and he practically leapt to his feet. Not wanting to keep her waiting, he raced to his work room and tried to clean up the space as quickly as possible. Thank God the ceiling of this room was a good fifteen feet, he'd need all of it if she planned on using her chair tonight...and he hoped she did.

He tossed his shirt into the corner and struggled with his jeans, his fingers fumbling in his haste and forgetting that he still had his shoes on. After hopping around in an undignified manner while trying to remove his shoes with his pants around his ankles, he was glad Michelle wasn't here to see this.

Women didn't usually want to have sex when they were laughing their ass off.

Throwing his shoes into the same corner as his pants, he then removed his black boxer briefs. The moment his cock was free he groaned and looked down at his engorged shaft. A drip of wetness already clung to the tip and he was afraid to wipe it away, unsure if he could resist the temptation of jerking a quick one out.

Since he had no idea how long she'd keep him waiting, he grabbed one of the old, but clean towels out of a cupboard and placed it next to the door. A second later his ass hit his heels as he knelt, arms behind his back, waiting. As he sat there, his mind kept going over his conversation with Yuki and James, trying to piece it together with what he knew of Michelle.

Could guilt really be the reason she didn't want to sleep with him? Maybe he could push her a bit tonight, test her reaction. While he didn't mind waiting, and would endure as long as she needed, he had to know that getting his reward was a possibility. He wanted Michelle, all of her, but he had to figure out how to wrestle her mind and heart away from a dead man.

More time passed and eventually his thoughts began to drift and his heartbeat settled into a slower rhythm. His knees had started to ache and his cock remained stiff, but he ignored that discomfort just like he ignored the hurt of every heavy pack he'd hustled during a long march. He'd learned a long time ago to compartmentalize pain, to push it away in the back of his mind until it became a dull ache.

The doors pushed open and he kept his eyes on the floor, but man, oh man, did he want to look up.

From what little he could see, Michelle wore a pair of shiny black boots that appeared as if they'd been painted onto her legs. While pretending to look at the floor he watched those very sexy boots move to stand in front of him. The scent of her soap reached him next, peaches with a hint of vanilla.

She turned away and her boots walked out of sight, but the click of her heels against the tile echoed loud in his ears. Judging by the direction she'd gone, she was looking at his...well his offering now. That word seemed to fit better than chair. For as surely as any sacrifice had been offered up to a Goddess he now offered himself to her, doing what he could to elicit her pleasure rather than incur her wrath, but also to give her a moments happiness in her difficult world.

"Wyatt, this is beautiful. Look at me."

He did and he slowly let his gaze take in the scene before him, trying not to rush, trying to be still. She wore a pair of black boots that went all the way up her thighs as if painted on, held in place by shiny black latex garters against the smooth cream of her thighs. No panties hindered his view of her sex and he bit back a groan as he noticed how flushed and swollen her pussy lips were. He didn't think he imagined a shine of moisture on her inner thighs as she turned to walk around the queening chair. Her hair was still swept up, and she wore a tight black latex vest that barely concealed her plumped up breasts. The combination of minimally hidden breasts and exposed sex drove him wild.

"I like this...I really do." She stroked her hand up the incline bench, now tilted at a steep angle. One end of the bench rested against the ground, braced by additional struts, while the other end led to the back of an old, ornate wooden chair fastened to the top of a box. It was just the right height for him to lean against the bench and have his mouth at the top, where her pussy would be.

She ran her fingers through the white rabbit fur that covered the box where she'd be sitting, with her legs over the side and her beautiful cunt right up to his face. Well, almost to his face. He'd carved a little niche out of the front so he could move his mouth around without hitting his chin on the edge.

"Where did you find this fur?"

"It's part of a jacket. I got it at the same antique store where I got the chair."

"Hmmm." She strode around to the other side on her long, long legs and laughed. "Is this the step stool from my kitchen?"

He grinned and shifted, trying to relive the discomfort of his knees. "Yes, Domina."

Her gaze cut to him. "Wyatt, please stand up. While I admire your devotion, you being unable to walk would put a large crimp in my plans to enjoy the fuck out of this chair."

Holding in a groan, he stood and tried to shake the pins and needles out of his legs. "Thank you, Domina."

The edges of her full, pink lips curved into a sensual smile. "Are you wondering why there is a hole here? And why I had you make it this size?" She traced the area in question in the center of the modified weight bench.

He shrugged. "I wondered, but whatever is your pleasure is my pleasure."

Her gaze narrowed. "Nicely said. Has James been coaching you?"

Suppressing his smile became difficult. "Domina, can I plead the Fifth?"

Her hips rolled as she strolled towards him, her beauty making his breath catch in his throat. He'd heard of this happening before, of men losing their breath at the sight of a woman, but he'd never experienced it before himself. It was like his entire focus was on her, to the point where breathing became unimportant, a small thing that was easily dismissed. Everything about her captivated him, like she was the essence of all that was female.

The soft scrape of her nails over his nipple rings brought his breath out in a rush, but she continued to walk past him and took something off the counter.

Holding it up, she slowly turned a black painted tube that reminded him of one of those big utility flashlights. "Know what this is?"

"No idea, Domina." He tried to keep his gaze on her face, but damn, her delicious cunt was so exposed, tantalizingly framed by the black latex of her boots and garters.

She must have noticed because she put the black thing in front of her sex. "Eyes up here, big boy."

He returned his attention to her face and tried not to grin. "Yes, Domina."

She strolled up to him again, her legs working those boots, until she was only a few inches away, the heat of her body caressing him. "Having you come from eating my pussy has to be one of the most erotic things I've ever experienced...but I think we can make it better for you."

"You can't improve on perfection."

She smiled and gave his ass a sharp pinch. "Cute, but don't interrupt me. As I was saying, this should help make things more intense for you.

Follow me."

He walked behind her, close enough to smell her shampoo, but she didn't object. When she reached the converted incline bench she screwed the top off the tube, revealing what looked like a pink plastic vagina.

"What the heck is that?"

"Don't masturbate much, do you?"

He moved forward the slightest bit so his cock grazed over her heart shaped ass. "When I do, I don't use disembodied vaginas."

With a soft laugh she placed the tube into the hole he'd cut into the bench, pushing down until it fit perfectly. "I've already put lubricant inside of it." She slipped her fingers into the toy's opening, sliding just the tips in and out. Despite himself, he was curious as to what it felt like. "And it has a remote."

She stepped to the side and fished a little black plastic square from the top of her boot, giving him a nice view down her cleavage.

"With all respect, Domina, I'm not sure if that's my kind of thing."

She gave him a feral smile. Oh yeah, all her earlier doubt was gone and she was back on her A game.

He didn't know if he should be happy or terrified.

"It doesn't matter if it's your 'type of thing'. Watching you fight the urge to come, strain against your arousal while you pleasure me is *my* thing. And knowing that resisting your base nature is double hard because of that toy sucking on your cock is even more my thing."

He almost reached out to grab her right then, to

lift her until she straddled his face and hold her in place with his hands, lips, and tongue. But if he did he would break the trust between them, something he wasn't willing to do. "Yes, Domina."

"Good. Now I want you to put those feet in those clever foot rests you made, but don't slide into that toy yet. I want you to hold yourself a few inches from it."

With his heart pounding he took the few brief steps to the padded bench, glancing up at her before stepping into the holes he'd made for his feet. The toy was at the perfect height for him and despite his earlier trepidation he found his arousal and curiosity outweighed the embarrassment of using a sex toy.

She went over by the doorway and turned off all the lights, except for the ones beneath the cabinet. They gave him enough light to see by, but left everything around them in shadows. With a new moon resting in the sky far above, no additional illumination came from the windows. She grabbed a bundle of black rope off the counter, slapping it against her thigh before she returned to him. Her breath whispered across his shoulders as she walked behind him.

"I'm going to tie you up, Wyatt. This rope is a nylon cotton blend that won't hurt you, so feel free to struggle."

He grunted and looked over his shoulder at her. "You don't need to tie me up to hold me in place."

"I know, but I must confess that I do love a man tied up in rope. There is an art to it, called Shibari, that some people spend their whole lives mastering. While I'm not a Shibari master, I admire that dedication, and I know enough to safely secure you in a variety of positions for my pleasure."

Then she moved to reach around his waist, down over his lower belly, and she teasingly ran her fingers over the veins of his cock, making him gasp and twitch. It seemed like whenever he was around her he became as sex-starved as a Marine coming off a nine month deployment to the Antarctic. Right now he'd chew through steel to get to her, break down a concrete wall with his dick for a chance at her cunt, drag himself across a desert with his tongue for a chance to lick her sweet pussy.

"Mmm, Wyatt you are so hard." She rubbed her thumb over his tip, smearing the fluid dripping from the slit in his cock. "I love your dick. Nice and thick, big enough to please any woman."

Her light touch became a slow stroke, driving him higher and making him brace his hands in front of himself. Pulling him slightly forward by his dick, she ran the tip of his erection over the toy, drawing a startled exclamation from him.

"Fuck, its warm."

"This is a top of the line sex toy, Wyatt. It heats up and does all kinds of other wonderful things." She continued to rub him over the soft, warm surface and if he closed his eyes it almost felt like she was rubbing him against another woman. "That's it. Feel how nice that is?"

His answer became a rumbling growl when she placed one hand on his ass, keeping a firm grip on his dick with the other, and began to ease him into the device.

"Shit."

He involuntarily flexed his hips forward, the toy

sucking on his cock as promised. She continued to push him down, watching his face as he started to breathe harder, inch by inch of his dick sliding into the slick sheath. While it didn't feel like a real pussy, it was certainly better than his hand.

Then she began to wind the black rope around his chest and back, securing him to the bench intricate loops and knots that did indeed looked like artwork. She constantly checked with him to make sure he was okay, that nothing was too tight or straining. Her reassurance, her need to make sure he was comfortable, helped ease the apprehension of being literally tied to the bench.

It also helped that it felt as if he was buried to his nuts in a warm pussy.

She paused and jerked the end of the rope around his hips. "Try to move your pelvis."

He did, only managing to rise up three or four inches, just enough for the toy to stroke a groan out of him. His arms were still free and his face was at the perfect level of her pussy, but his torso was bound in place by the rope. He raised his head up now to give her room to sit, then pushed up with his feet to see how far he could move to reach her.

She pushed something cold between his chest and the bench. "Here's a box cutter. When we're done I'll expect you to free yourself, because if you do your job right I won't be able to get off this thing without falling."

He reached down and adjusted the box cutter, moving it so it wasn't pressing against his nipple ring. "Yes, Domina."

"There we go. Now stay here and keep your eyes closed while I get onto my...throne." Her voice held a trace of a laugh on the last word, but he could smell the sweet musk of her arousal. Knowing that she was turned on by him doing this gave him the freedom to let go of his inhibitions, to embrace the situation in which he found himself.

The bench shifted a bit as she climbed up to her perch, but held and didn't wiggle as she arranged herself.

She made a pleased sound. "This rabbit fur feels divine against my pussy. I better not let Yuki see this, she'll have you making one for her in no time."

"I'm glad it pleases you, Domina." His words came out tight and strained as he fought the urge to thrust, to fuck.

"Open your eyes, Wyatt."

Saliva immediately filled his mouth when the first thing he saw as her pink sex, all open and waiting for him. She now sat above him, cradled from behind by the chair back, but with enough room on either side so that her legs could easily fall over the edge. This allowed him complete access to her and his dick jerked inside of the toy, drawing a groan from somewhere deep in his stomach. Her clit was hard, a pink bud waiting for his lips and her arousal did indeed coat her inner thighs, proof of her need.

"Domina, if you scoot a little more forward it would be perfect."

With a bemused smile that didn't chase the heat from her eyes, she did as he asked, then reached down to feel the indentation. "What is this for?"

"So I can reach as much of you as you want. If you tilt your hips I can take all of you in my mouth." He swallowed hard, his next words coming out in more of a growl than speech, goaded on by the scent of her filling the air, of the faint light giving the golden curls above her mound a shimmer. "If you tilt your hips even more I can lick your little pink anus, feel it grip my tongue while I serve you."

Her breath came out hard enough that it blew over his shoulders. "Wyatt, show me what you've got."

He lunged forward as much as he could before the ropes held him back. He reached up and clasped her slender thighs, spreading her wide in order to better pleasure her. Without preamble he buried his face into her swollen sex, licking up every drop of honey her body gave him. When her hands fisted in his hair his cock throbbed to the beat of his heart. When she held him to her sex and rolled her hips his hips jerked, and when she cried out his name he groaned against her.

"Work that beautiful ass, Wyatt. I want to see you fuck."

A very primitive part of his brain was pleased by how breathless she was, by the trembling in her thighs as he rubbed his nose against her clit while licking her below. This wasn't about teasing, or drawing it out. This was about bringing his Mistress pleasure, as much as she could take, so he did as she asked and began to thrust as much as he could. Oddly enough the restraints made him hotter, made his whole body fight against them even while his mind accepted the rope.

Now it was his turn to twitch and moan, the combination of having his face buried between her legs and the toy wrapped around his cock quickly driving him to the edge. The very air became saturated with sex, his skin burning and too tight, everything in him coiled to explode. But he held it back, resisted that pleasure for her.

He began to nibble his way up to her clit, pausing to suck on one puffy labia, then the other, gently sinking his teeth into her delicate flesh. She groaned deep in her throat, rubbing herself against him, as shameless as a cat in heat. At the exact moment that he gave her clit the first swipe of his tongue, something happened to the toy around his cock. It began to vibrate, then it felt like little balls were massaging his length.

He started to jerk back in surprise, but she held his face to her pussy with surprising strength. "Don't stop until I come, Wyatt. If you do, if you take your pleasure before mine, I'll make you fuck yourself dry with that toy."

Anger mixed with his arousal, giving his emotions a sharp edge. He took that frustration out on her, teasing her pussy, winding her up until she began to make little helpless noises that squeezed his cock harder than any toy.

"Fuck it, Wyatt. I want to see you move. Show me how you would take me if I was spread beneath you right now."

With a snarl he did, his hips thrusting in and out while he ate her, becoming a mindless animal with need. Everything faded but her pussy, making her come, tasting her and licking her and making her scream. After one big lick from her perineum to her clit he latched onto that little bud and sucked - hard.

Her scream split the air, almost as sweet to his ears as the flood of moisture from her pussy tasted on his tongue. Not feeling at all kind, driven mad her refusal to let him come, he shoved three fingers into her, stretching her and fucking her hard, as hard as he was pounding into the sheath vibrating around his dick. Her delicate inner muscles clenched down and she froze against him. He gave her one final suck, then nipped the tip of her clit.

"Oh god, Wyatt, come with me."

He rubbed his face back and forth against her quivering sex, licking her frantically while she thrust against him, saying his name over and over again, giving him another rush of her liquid arousal which he devoured. Unable to hold out anymore, he slammed into the sheath and the force of his orgasm had him throwing his head back, roaring his pleasure while he sank his fingers into her soft thighs. Each shot of seed scoured him, purging him of his anger, his thoughts, everything but the taste of his Domina on his lips.

When he'd finally stilled, the device stopped vibrating and he shuddered.

She started to move, but he gentled his grip on her thighs and rasped out, "Please, Mistress, let me clean you."

Her pleased murmur was like a soothing balm and she settled back into the chair, idly slipping her hands through his hair. Being as gentle as he could, he licked her until every trace of her arousal was gone, well as much of it as he could get. He was sure the second she stood up more would drip out of her, but if he didn't move soon he was going to collapse.

When he pulled his mouth away she literally purred with pleasure. "Good god, Wyatt. If word about you got out I'd have to keep you locked away in a cage for your own safety. Cut yourself free."

He pulled out the box cutter and set to work slicing through the rope. After three cuts the rest fell away from him, a testament to her bondage skills.

"Now, come over here and help me down from this wonderful chair."

He pulled out of the toy and got off the bench, then glanced down at his wet, still semi-hard shaft. "You know, I think I might like that thing." He reached up and easily plucked her down, sliding her body against his as he lowered her to the floor. "Thank you, Domina, for the pleasure of servicing you."

"Oh Wyatt." She looked up into his face, her gaze searching him. "I promise in the future I'll hear you out, not just assume the worst."

Tears filled her beautiful blue eyes and he hugged her close. Or at least he tried to, as soon as she touched his lube covered dick she jumped back with a laugh, teetering on her heels. "Yikes, you are rather slippery still. Come on, let's go take a shower and hit the hay. I don't know about you, but I've had about enough excitement for one day."

He followed the seductive sway of her ass and wondered if he might persuade her to let him give her a tongue bath in the shower.

Chapter 12

Lips softer than satin kissed over his jaw, the faint scent of toothpaste and perfume reaching his nose. When he turned and opened his eyes, he saw Michelle standing next to the edge of the bed, dressed in pale blue scrubs.

"I'm sorry to wake you, you look so cute when you sleep, but the clinic begged me to come in. One of their regular surgeons is out with the flu. He has kids so he probably got it from the germ pit that is schools."

He cleared his throat, reaching out to grab her hand and lace their fingers together. "Damn, Doc, you make schools sound like plague incubators."

She laughed and ran her thumb over his hand, happiness sparkling in her gaze. "They are. I should be back by around 3, so if you want we can go to the bar after that?"

He frowned up at her, remembering their fight yesterday in which she accused him of stealing beer. "Is that supposed to be some kind of joke?"

Her brows drew down in confusion. "What? I thought we'd made plans to visit Lilly over at the VFW bar so we could talk about our dogs."

Any trace of bitterness left him and he couldn't help but smile. She hadn't said her dogs, or the dogs, but our dogs. While he didn't know if he could face fighting like they had last night all the time, it seemed to have broken down one of the many walls between them. "Sorry, totally forgot about that."

She gave his hand a squeeze and let go. "I really need to leave. *Mi casa es su casa*. Feel free to use the truck to go get more supplies. I set up an account for you at Howard's Hardware off of Main Street."

His pride bristled and he sat up fully. "I have my own money, Michelle. I'm not some bum off the street."

She paused on the other side of the bed and put her hands on her hips, looking entirely too adorable in her scrubs. "Listen, Mr. Macho, you are making me beautiful works of art for free. In the real world you could charge thousands, tens of thousands for the kind of work you do. My paying for the materials is the least I could do. Besides, Mr. Howard needs the business. He's the last independent, family-owned hardware store and lumber supply in the area. Spend as much money as you want, it is all going to good people who really need it." Giving him an impish smile she turned and started for the bedroom door. "Think of it as a redistribution of unearned wealth."

*****

After a long day of researching what he wanted to make next, along with a trip to the lumber store that resulted in him having lunch with Mr. and Mrs. Howard in their home above the store, he was freshly showered and waiting for Michelle to come home. He kept checking the clock, bemused at how he was the one waiting for his woman to come home from work, and not the other way around.

Still, it tweaked his pride that he didn't currently have a job and a steady source of income. Going back to work for his father wasn't an option. Michelle was right, he loved his parents to death, but they let him get away with pretty much everything. Besides, he had an idea forming that if it worked out, could not only give him a job he loved, but also an income that could support both himself and Michelle...just in case she went on a 60 million dollar shopping spree and needed him to pay the bills.

He wandered through the house to the media room, a large, dimly lit space with cream leather reclining chairs and a huge wrap-around sofa deep enough to almost be called a bed. Everything was done in shades of brown and gold, mute colors that wouldn't detract from the enormous flat screen TV. With a grateful sigh he grabbed the remote and sat back in one of the comfortable chairs, reclining it and turning on the big screen. Nothing like kicking back with his feet up after a full day's work. A beer would be real nice about now, but he didn't dare tempt fate.

As he flipped through the channels he hit a news report from overseas about an ambush that killed four soldiers.

He froze in the chair, sweat breaking out all over his body in a harsh sting. The voice of the newscaster faded to useless chatter and he watched, unable to close his eyes as they showed combat footage. Suddenly the air he drew into his lungs seemed thick with dust and smoke, the acrid tang of gunpowder coating his tongue as he struggled to breathe.

On the screen talking heads droned on about inconsequential political bullshit while good men and women died. The faces of all his friends began to burst into his mind, little explosions of pain and regret. All those wonderful lives, gone forever. Friend's graves, empty boots, mothers clinging to him at the funerals of their sons. Tears burned in the back of his throat but he fought them, fought everything.

Panic gnawed at him, tightened his muscles to painful paralyzed mounds. He was not an animal, he would not run, he would not turn that fear to rage. Because if he was honest, that's really what the rage was. Fear. Much like a frightened dog he would snap at anyone that poked at him, hoping if he fought back hard enough they would leave him alone. No, he was better than this. He'd never quit anything in his life, no matter how hard, no matter how many times he threw up, or passed out, or cursed his drill sergeant up one side and down the other in his mind while he did pushups in the sand pit.

Slowly, the memories of the things he'd overcome bolstered him, gave him strength. Then he thought about Michelle, for in his mind she was the epitome of strength...and yet she was strangely vulnerable. He didn't know how it was possible that he felt both protective of her and admiring, but that was how it worked.

The more he thought about her the more the panic began to fade, but they still teased around the edges. He'd think about running with Michelle and a memory of running through the stinking sewage-filled streets of Fallujah would try to take its place. He tried to turn his thoughts to carrying her to bed, but his mind threw up the image of carrying the dead body of one of his men to the chopper waiting to take them away from the mortar site. While he couldn't stop the unwanted memory flashes completely from happening, he was able to keep one step ahead, always with a good memory to counteract the bad.

A soft hand pressed over his eyes and the voice of an angel whispered in his ear, "Be still. Let it wash through you and pass away."

Her perfume filled his nose, chasing back the phantom scents, helping him choke the part of his mind that insisted he was about to die into silence. The terrible memories receded, leaving blessed darkness in its wake. He concentrated on the feel of his whole and healthy body, the peace that reached into his soul from her presence, and his own strength. She removed her hand and took with it the taste of gunpowder, leaving him shaken and sweaty, but still in control.

He grasped her wrist and pulled her onto his lap, burying his face against her chest, surrounding himself with her. It didn't take him long to realize how near his mouth was to her nipple, how if he just moved a little bit he could coax that pert nub to life with his tongue. Blood rushed to his cock in a pleasant burn. Her arms wrapped around his neck and she let out a contented murmur as she stroked her fingers through his hair.

Squirming, Michelle softly laughed. "Well, I guess an erection is a good sign."

He nibbled at her breast, still covered by her clothes. Leaning back, he took in her outfit and smiled. She wore a pair of faded jeans that clung to her long legs, and a plaid shirt that was similar enough to his to look like they were one of those couples that dressed alike. It made sense, after all she'd bought the shirt he wore right now. Obviously she was a fan of green plaid. The unexpected humor chased away the last of the shadows.

"Nice shirt, Doc."

She glanced down, then back at him. "Is this like both of us wearing the same dress to a party?"

"Now you know I'd do pretty much anything for you, but I draw the line at wearing women's clothes."

"Hard limit?"

"Hard limit."

"You're no fun."

"Oh, I can be lots of fun." He moved his hand to cup her jeans-covered ass, groaning at how tight it felt behind the thick fabric.

She placed a quick kiss on his lips and scooted off his lap. "As tempting as it is to spend the rest of the night with you in chains, we need to get going."

He stood, a remarkable buoyancy filling him as he realized he'd beaten his panic attack. Yeah he'd freaked out for a little bit there, but he didn't go postal like usual. On the TV screen behind her some entertainment show was gossiping about someone who wore a scandalous dress, or some other inconsequential bullshit, and he let the tension drain from his shoulders.

Michelle wound her arms around his neck and pressed fully against him. Their lips met and each of them made a hungry sound. He was suddenly ravenous for her and shifted his grip to her ass, pressing her closer against his erection. She responded by biting at his lower lip, then sucking it, their breath mingling. She fit so perfectly against him and inside of him, his heart now completely filled with her and his soul strengthened by her. In fulfilling what she needed he'd found his purpose, the reason he'd been put on this earth.

Their kiss gentled, deepened, but neither of them broke it. He was hers, heart and soul, but, would she have him? That thought kept him from saying the words ringing through him with absolute truth. He loved her. She was the only one for him and always would be. All other women paled in comparison to Michelle, as complex and wounded in her own way as she was beautiful. For her he would be strong, he would be a rock that would never break beneath the weight of her guilt. He would do whatever she needed to feel whole again, to be able to accept love into her life again.

They broke apart, their breath coming fast as they looked at each other in the flickering light of the television.

Against his better judgment he almost told her about his revelation, wanting to share his joy with her, but fear flashed through her eyes and she pressed her finger to his lips when he opened his mouth.

"Wyatt...don't, not yet. Please."

Her voice broke on the last word and he glimpsed the pain that she carried inside of her and the immense guilt. God, how could she function with all that darkness constantly dragging her down?

He gently bit her finger and she removed it from his mouth. "You know what I was going to say, and just because I haven't said it doesn't mean it's not true."

Agony and yearning battled across her features, but finally she looked away and nodded. "I know. But please, please give me some more time."

"Domina, I'll wait until we're both old and gray, chasing you around the retirement home while pushing my walker if that's what it takes."

She didn't laugh at his joke, just sighed and slipped out of his arms. "Come on, Wyatt. Let's go see what the VFW club is all about."

He followed after her, wanting to fight her demons for her, but she was the only one that could slay them.

*****

Wyatt looked around the inside of the VFW Hall and the place reminding him of his grandparents' game room in an odd way. The social hall area was huge, big enough to host the weddings and other parties that frequently happened on the weekends. Three pool tables stood at one end of the room, while the other held tables and two big screen TV's playing sports. A long cherry wood bar took up most of the far wall and a good portion of the seats were taken despite the early hour.

Men and women from their early 20s to their late 80s sat around in small groups, talking and playing pool or watching TV. Many of the older men wore baseball caps with the different companies, ships, and military campaigns they'd been on. The flags of different military units hung from the walls and he quickly found the Marine flag, good memories about his service for once popping up instead of bad. Michelle slipped her hand into his and smiled up at him.

"Kinda feels like coming home, doesn't it?"

"Yeah, it does. I can't put my finger on it, but there is something about this place that reminds of me being in the military." He shook his head, unable to put his feelings into words. "Come on, let's go say hi to Lilly."

They made their way across the room, curious eyes following them. Part of him wanted to search the faces of the people here for his military friends he knew that were still in the area, but he was kinda hoping no one here recognized him. Inevitably, they'd bring up Aaron and Wyatt really didn't want to think about his best friend right now. While he felt stronger than he had in a long time, it was still a fragile strength. Like freshly poured concrete that could still be marked.

Before they made it halfway Lilly looked up, a bright smile splitting her wrinkled face. "Wyatt, Michelle, welcome to the VFW." She flapped her clean bar towel in their direction. "Gentleman, may I have the pleasure of introducing Gunnery Sergeant Wyatt Callahan and his lovely lady, Lieutenant Michelle Sapphire."

The elderly men seated near Lilly turned and gave them both welcome smiles. Their instant warmth and acceptance eased something in Wyatt's gut.

An old man with bushy grey eyebrows and a baseball hat showing that he served on the USS *Hornet* gave them a devilish grin. "Managed to win a beautiful Officer's heart? Lucky bastard."

Michelle gave her husky, fucking sexy laugh and now all the men at the bar turned to look at them, as entranced with her as he was. "Actually, I'm the lucky one."

Pride swelled Wyatt's chest and he grinned down at her. "Damn straight."

She elbowed him in the ribs, then took a seat at the bar. "Thanks again for inviting us, Lilly."

"You're most welcome. I have to tell ya, Tuba and Mud have been pining for you. That towel that you gave me with your scent on it? The dogs have been fighting over who gets to sleep with it. They finally tore it in half and both carry their scrap around with them, afraid the other one is going to steal it."

Pleasure suffused Michelle's face and Wyatt couldn't resist stepping behind her and wrapping his arms around her. "I know how they feel."

A man's voice came from behind them. "Wyatt? Wyatt Callahan?"

He tensed, then turned to find his old buddy, Clive Mercer approaching them from the pool table area. He'd put on about twenty pounds since Wyatt had last seen him in Afghanistan around four years before, but Clive looked good. Dressed in a pair of faded jeans and a flannel shirt, the balding man clasped Wyatt in a hug.

He thumped his friend's back as he returned Clive's embrace. "Mercer, you old devil dog. How are you?"

Clive pounded him on the back in return in that guy version of a hug then pulled away. "Doing good, man. I got married after I got out and have a two-year-old son." He gave Michelle a smile. "Who's the pretty little woman with you?"

Michelle arched a brow in that imperious, aristocratic way she had. "Lieutenant Michelle

Sapphire. Nice to meet you, Clive."

The old men around them hooted with laughter as Clive turned nine different shades of red. "Sorry, ma'am."

She grinned, the haughty look dropping from her face. "No worries. If no one ever salutes me again I'll die a happy woman."

Lilly slid two pops across the bar. "Why don't you guys go rhapsodize about your glory days over at one of the tables? Michelle and I are going to talk dogs."

Michelle gave him a questioning look, but he ignored it. "Sure, come on, Clive. Let's go talk about all the women we've done."

He managed to dodge Michelle's kick enough that it hit him in the back of his thigh rather than his ass. "Behave."

Grinning, he popped the top on his soda and took a seat with Clive at one of the battered tables near the big screen TVs. Moving his chair so he could keep an eye on his woman, and the randy old sailor flirting with her and Lilly, he smiled at Clive. "So what have you been up to since you got out?"

"Right now I'm working at a car dealership. Nothing special, but it pays the bills. What about you?"

"Kinda still figuring out what I want to do." He sighed and stretched his legs out. "I'm playing around with the idea of making custom furniture."

"Oh yeah? You any good at it?"

He thought back to Michelle's reaction to his creation and grinned. "Not too bad."

Clive glanced over at Michelle. "Pretty lady. Did you meet her after you got out?"

"No. We served together over in Afghanistan."

Clive's eyes widened. "Were you together then?"

"No, not at all. Nothing happened until we both got out."

"Man...that sure is something. What'd she do over there?"

"She's a doctor so she..." His stomach clenched memories of the comrades they'd lost and those she'd saved. "She saved a lot of men."

His skin prickled and a hot then cold sensation flashed over his body as if he'd been roasted in the sun and frozen in ice at the same time. The conflicting sensations made him shiver, made his muscles tense, and made the frightened animal of PTSD roar inside of his fucked up head.

No, not here, not now in front of all these people.

Please, God.

Clive gave him an odd look. "Sorry, man, I didn't mean to pry."

The can he held gave a metallic crinkle as Wyatt struggled to regain control of himself. Fuck, one mention of Afghanistan and his mind slipped right back into insisting that he was in danger. For a moment he could smell the blood, hear the moans of the dying. What many people didn't realize is that if someone is well enough to scream, they'll probably live. It was the men that could only moan incoherent, soft sounds of anguish, or worse, those who remained silent who were in real trouble.

"Callahan."

He closed his eyes, struggling to take a steady breath. "One sec."

"You got it too, huh? PTSD?"

The sorrow, the understanding in Clive's words

reached out to Wyatt like a lifeline. He took a deep breath then choked down a mouthful of soda, chasing away the lingering phantom flavors of gun smoke and blood from his mouth. "Yeah."

Clive let out a low sigh and moved his chair closer. He grabbed Wyatt's hand in his own beneath the table and squeezed hard. "I'm here with you, Callahan. We're in the United States, at the VFW hall in Austin, Texas. Right now you're sitting at a beat to shit table with an uncomfortable chair under your ass in a place that smells like old people. Your lady is looking pretty worried, so unless you want her coming over here you better snap your shit back to the present."

He opened his eyes enough to confirm that Michelle indeed was watching him with a very worried look. Using up all the energy he had left, he shook his head. She stared at him for a moment longer, then nodded. While she talked to Lilly, she continued to keep an eye on him.

"Unless you're gonna try to get in my panties, Mercer, you can let go of my hand now."

"Thank God. One more second and I wouldn't have been able to hold myself back from jumping you and dry humping your leg."

The mental image startled a harsh laugh out of him. "Thanks. Sorry I got weird on you."

Clive shook his head. "Like I said, you're not alone. This shit is like the fucking plague sweeping through the military. You never know who it's going to hit and how hard. Shit, I have to deal with the fucking bullshit of PTSD as well. I don't want to go into details and trigger a freak-out, but most of the people here struggle with it in their own way." He leaned closer and lowered his voice. "I've talked with the old timers about it, and man, they had it way rougher than we do. When they came back from Korea and Vietnam there was no diagnosis for it back then. It was something that got swept under the rug and ignored. Shell shock was the term most often used, but there wasn't any treatment for it."

Rubbing his forehead, Wyatt looked at the old men at the bar and tried to imagine what it was like for them to come back home to a country that didn't support the war they'd fought or value the sacrifices they'd made. "How did they deal with it? How do you deal with it?"

Clive let out a low breath. "I was in a real dark place for a while, but refused to admit it. You know, all that leftover mental bullshit from the military that if you go seek help for anything you'll end up killing your career or will be labeled as a head case. My wife suffered with me, in some ways I think more. She saw me slipping away but didn't know how to help. Luckily she had a good support system from the Ladies Auxiliary here at the VFW. She talked to them about the problems I was having and convinced me to seek treatment. That thing I did with you? Pulling you back to the present? She's the one that taught me that." The admiration and love Clive felt for his wife was evident in the way he talked about her.

Wyatt's gaze fixed on Michelle and his heart let go of some of the grief. "A good woman makes all the difference, huh?"

"I wish it was that simple, but my wife helped. No one, absolutely no one, wants to live with the bullshit of PTSD, but it never really goes away. One day I had kind of an epiphany. While I couldn't be strong for me, I had to be strong for my wife. She needed me, and then when she got pregnant I knew that I couldn't let my kid grow up with a fucked up father. I couldn't let the war screw up another generation of my family." He took a drink and set the can back down, rolling it on the table's surface. "Does that make any sense?"

He thought about Michelle, and how in their relationship they were both trying to be strong for each other. Each had their own demons, their own version of PTSD that might have eaten them alive if they were alone, but together they had to be strong enough for each other.

"Yeah, I understand perfectly." He gave himself a mental shake, flinging off the nasty remains of his barely averted panic attack. "So coming here helps?"

"Fuck yeah. Despite what some people think we don't just come here to talk about the war. In fact, most people don't talk about it. Instead we talk about the good times, the bullshit that we went through and the bullshit we put other people through. We were all there, we all lived it, and we'll never forget it. We talk about what the Cowboys are going to do, what politician is an asshole, what movie star we'd like to screw. Normal stuff." He leaned back in his chair and grinned. "Man, did we do some fucked up stuff in boot camp together or what?"

Wyatt smiled back at him. "You mean like the bullshit we put Drill Sergeant Hump through?"

Clive barked out a loud laugh and smacked the table hard enough to rattle the cans. "Oh man, I haven't thought about that motherfucker in years!

God, that man had a hard-on for your ass, Callahan. I've never seen someone do as many pushups as you."

They talked for another hour or so before Michelle came to collect Wyatt and head home. Walking out of the VFW Hall, she looped her arm through his and rested her head on his shoulder.

"You did good in there."

He placed a kiss on top of her head. "Thanks to you." She flushed and tried to pull away but he held her close. "I mean it, Michelle. You give me the strength to fight it off, to keep it from overwhelming me. At the risk of sounding cheesy, you're like my candle in the darkness." Embarrassed, he cleared his throat. "Now I'm going to stop complimenting you before you get a swelled head."

She looked away, but he caught the small smile curving her lips. "Funny, I like it when your head swells."

He chuckled and resumed walking to the truck. "I think I might come back here sometime."

"Me too. If you turn out to be a dud I have a whole list of handsome silver foxes that want to sweep me off my feet."

"Kinda hard to do when they use a walker."

She giggled and placed a kiss on his cheek. "Well, there is that."

Looking down at her, he thanked God for bringing her into his life and hoped that he could be everything she wanted, needed, so that she would never leave him alone in the dark.

Chapter 13

After five blessedly normal, well as normal as they got around Michelle, days, Wyatt found himself shoveling one of Yuki's amazing omelets into his mouth, letting out sighs of appreciation. He'd only had a few small, manageable panic attacks and Michelle had been with him every time, letting him fight for himself, but providing her strength and support if he needed it. "Man, I forgot how hungry you get when you work at a ranch."

James held up one of his sausage links in a toast. "It was nice having an extra pair of hands for a change. God knows I don't get any help from...err...from the horses."

Yuki snorted and snatched his sausage out of his hand, bit off the tip, and handed it back to him. "Keep that up and I'll be doing a Shibari demonstration on you at the Connie's wedding reception. If you really piss me off I'll hang weighted clamps from your balls and hang *you* from the ceiling in a rope harness."

Wyatt paused in his chewing and looked over at Michelle. "I thought you said this was an old friend's wedding in Chicago that we were going to?"

Michelle swallowed hard and dropped her gaze, one of her avoidance techniques he noticed she used when something really bothered her. "There is a collaring ceremony afterwards, during the reception. It will be held at a BDSM club in the area. I-I thought maybe we would leave before that so you wouldn't be uncomfortable."

He chewed slowly, noticing the minute tremble of her lower lip. "Why would I be uncomfortable?"

She set her fork down. "Because all of these people were Owen's friends and they probably won't want you there."

Yuki stared at Michelle. "What are you talking about?"

Michelle flinched, but kept her gaze on her half empty plate. When she spoke, her voice had a fragile, almost childish quality that he wasn't used to hearing from his strong and brave Mistress. "I don't want anyone being mean to Wyatt for taking Owen's place."

Yuki started to speak, but James put his hand over hers. "Honey, they are your friends, and more than anything they want you to be happy. All of them. Wyatt makes you happy; anyone with a brain can see it, and no one will think of it as anything but a long overdue blessing that you richly deserve. Owen's dead, Wyatt is alive and so are you. Wherever Owen is he wants you to be happy."

Michelle made a pained, choked sound before she finally looked up at Wyatt and her eyes shimmered with tears. "I have to go feed the horses."

Her chair scraped roughly over the floor as she stood and walked quickly out the back door.

Yuki smacked James in the back of the head. "Way to go."

"What? We can't keep coddling her, Yuki. She

has to move on and we are not helping by letting her avoid any mention of Owen, ever." He scooted back his chair and set his napkin on the table. "You ever heard that phrase, 'You have to be cruel to be kind', Mistress? You know we aren't going to stay here forever. At some point we will leave and she will be alone with her ghosts."

"Not alone," Wyatt spoke up, cradling his coffee in his hands. "I don't plan on going anywhere."

Yuki tossed her braid over her shoulder, trying affect a cool expression that was ruined by the strained lines around her eyes and mouth. "Shit, I'm sorry, Wyatt, but you two haven't been together long enough to know if things will work, regardless of the issues you both bring to the table."

He shook his head. "No. I know. I'm not going anywhere, ever. I'll chase her to the ends of the earth if need be." He took a sip of the bitter brew, choosing his words carefully. "I feel like my whole life has been leading up to this point, that everything that has happened to me had to happen so I would be ready for her. I love her."

Yuki placed her hand against her mouth while James gave him a shrewd look. "Does she know that?"

"You mean did I tell her outright?" He gave a rough laugh. "She was sitting at the breakfast table this morning, wasn't she?"

Yuki's shoulders relaxed a fraction. "Do you think she knows?"

"Absolutely." He looked Yuki in the eye, willing her to see his sincerity. "I will be whatever she needs, whenever she needs it. And I don't just mean as her submissive. I'll be there to guard her when she needs a protector, to hold her when she wants to be held." He ran a hand over his short hair. "I'd marry her today if I didn't know the mere thought of it would send her screaming off into the night."

James laughed and pulled his chair back up to the table. "Good, we wanted to make sure you were aware of the...unique obstacles you will have to overcome with Michelle."

"Don't get us wrong," Yuki added. "Michelle is an amazing woman -- if I was gay I would have married her a long time ago -- but she is a difficult, high maintenance bitch even in the best of times. You've done a great job of not letting her push you away, but I think going to this wedding in Chicago might stir up some shit. You need to be ready for the breakdown that both James and I think she'll have once she's back on her old stomping grounds. This will be the first time she's been to the club since Owen died."

Wyatt frowned. "The club?"

"Owen wasn't just her submissive, he was also big in the Chicago BDSM community. He co-owned a fetish club called the Velvet Fist with Petrov, who is one of Michelle's best friends. I'm sure she's told you about him."

Yuki saw his confusion. "Petrov was the Master who trained Michelle on how to be a Dominatrix."

Irrational jealousy scoured through him. "Do you think Petrov will give us a problem?"

Stretching his arms above his head, James said, "Absolutely not. He's been trying to set her up with a new submissive for the past three years. But she's never done more than a casual encounter at clubs or private parties where she gets her needs met."

Again, that stupid jealousy over the thought of another man touching her had him tensing. "I take care of her needs from now on."

With a soft laugh Yuki rose from her seat and patted his arm. "Of course you do. Now why don't you go out there and let your Mistress know that you're strong enough for her tears."

Chapter 14

With a grunt Michelle stabbed into a pile of loose hay and lifted it into the bed of the wagon behind the ATV. The sun burned down on her head and she was pretty sure she'd have a nice sunburn because she forgot her hat. Despite that, she continued to work and let the soreness of her muscles soothe her. She wanted to be exhausted, to not have to think and worry for one bloody minute. Tonight she'd sit in her bath with Wyatt, drink a glass of wine, and not feel guilty about it because she'd paid for that right with her hard work and pain.

A pair of her leather gloves hit the ground by the hay.

"Put these on or you're going to give yourself blisters, and that would really hurt my chances of getting a hand job."

What should have made her laugh instead unbalanced her, a new guilt added to the old, a bonus weight on her shoulders. He had to settle for a hand job because she wouldn't let him have sex with her like a normal woman would. "Fuck you, Callahan."

He calmly took off his shirt and tossed it onto a nearby bale of hay. The visible reminder of her claim on him shone in the morning light, the white stars on the sapphires adorning his chest glowing like a stars in truth trapped in a deep blue sky. She wanted to go to him, to let him hold her while she cried, but she was tired of being so fucking weak and messed up.

"Get the fuck out of here."

His lips quirked into a smile. "Is that an order, Lieutenant?"

She stabbed the pitchfork into the ground hard enough that it stood up on its own. "What the hell does that mean?"

"When you went to the tent to mourn the men who had died and I followed you, do you remember that?"

She crossed her arms, then nodded. There was no use in denying that defining moment in their relationship, hidden though it was at the time. That wonderful relief that he would guard her, protect her, and allow her to have a moment where she didn't have to deal with the sorrow alone. Even if back then they hadn't been able to touch each other like they wanted, his presence gave her strength.

Just like it did now.

"Well you told me exactly the same thing. If I didn't listen to you then I probably won't listen to you now." He looped his thumbs into his jeans pocket, drawing her eye to the light dusting of dark hair covering the sectioned muscles of his abdomen. "You're going to have to face the fact that I'm going to be there for you no matter what you need. So if you want to yell at me, go ahead. But I can think of something much more pleasant to take your mind off of things."

Her heart skipped a beat at the blatant sexual invitation in his tone. He stood before her, so strong, so sure of himself. That man didn't have any conflict about her. His feelings were as solid as his stance. He loved her, really, truly loved her, like Owen had. A wave of dizziness hit her and she braced herself against the pitchfork, trying to deal with her conflicted feelings, wanting him so bad the self-denial felt almost as agonizing as the heartache she'd endured over the last few years.

Trying to keep her tone light, bur failing miserably, she said, "What would that be?"

"How does an ice cream sundae sound?"

The unexpected humor helped her cross the mental bridge between denial that bordered on self-hatred and a blessing. She took a step forward, her body mirroring the emotional abyss her heart was now crossing, the dead memories that kept them apart.

"Too cold."

He smiled and took a step closer, his delectable nipples begging for her touch. Just like that her anger switched to need. She couldn't be this close to him, with Wyatt giving off his 'fuck me' vibes without wanting him. Heat settled low in her belly and she suddenly wanted his face between her legs, right now.

His gaze scorched her soul. "Hot chocolate?"

"Too sweet."

"What do you want? I am yours to command."

She closed her eyes, inhaling a deep breath of his scent, trying to make this moment last. The words stuck in her throat, a painful chunk of icy guilt. She'd sworn, on Owen's grave, to never love another. Desperate, she tried to open her mind, her soul, as much as she could and sent out a frantic prayer.

Please, Owen, if you're up there and can hear

me, please give me a sign if this is what you want for me. Please let me know it's okay.

Seconds ticked by and she opened her eyes. There weren't any signs that she could see, no hawk flying overhead, no sound of trumpets. Turning her back on Wyatt, she searched more desperately, silently begging for something, anything to please let her take Wyatt as completely as a woman could have a man.

She was so terribly lonely.

Still, nothing unusual. Grief shook her and she turned back to him, bracing herself for having to once again push him away.

When he saw her face he dropped to his knees, tall enough so that his head was only a little bit below her collarbone. "Domina, I love you. No matter what you do or say, no matter how hard you try to push me away, I love you and I'll wait the rest of my life for you to love me back if that's what I have to do."

Her mouth went dry and she stared helplessly at him. The truth of his words written on every inch of his body, but especially in his eyes. And, oh God, what beautiful eyes they were.

So warm, so enigmatic, and soul shattering.

In his eyes she found her miracle.

How could she have not wanted this? The connection between them strengthened until she felt as if she was drowning in him. His love rushed through her in a physical wave, leaving goosebumps on her skin in its wake. He waited, no doubt wanting her to say the same, but all she could do was whisper his name, trying to put everything she felt into it, every ounce of love that he'd poured into her doubled, tripled, and she tried to send it right back to him.

"Make love to me, Wyatt. I need your strength. Right now, we aren't Mistress and sub, we're two people who belong to each other. I want you to do what you want. I want you."

He didn't even bother to ask, instead standing and scooping her up into his arms. The moment his lips touched hers the rest of the world vanished, and she closed her eyes, drinking up his affection, starved for it. The more she gave the more he took, his teeth biting her lip, the firm roll of his chest against her body, the faint taste of apple in his mouth.

She threaded her fingers through his hair, holding him closer, unwilling to break their kiss even for a moment. Sucking on his tongue, she jerked his hair in time with each pull and he groaned. With a harsh gasp he tore his mouth from hers and she was stunned to see that they were on the wrap around porch at the back of the house.

"Where."

"Here."

She tried to pull him back down but he shook his head. "Don't want you or me to get splinters."

Almost snarling with frustration, she looked around. "The porch swing."

She didn't have to tell him twice. He almost ran to the wide and comfortable padded swing hanging from the thick exposed rafters by sturdy chains. It was actually more like a daybed than a chair, big enough so that she could lay out here and read a book while watching her horses in the far pasture. Now she was more glad than ever that she'd found it, because when Wyatt set her down on the soft surface he had a feral look in his eye that confirmed she would have been the one with splinters in her back.

"Take off your shirt before I rip it off, Michelle."

Her hands shook, but she managed to jerk the shirt off over her head. Before she'd even gotten it fully off Wyatt was on her, tearing down the cups of her white lace bra, exposing her tight nipples to his mouth. His wonderful tongue laved her breasts with long strokes as if licking away a wound. And it did feel like his touch was healing her, making her warm from the inside out. A memory of making love with Owen tried to capture her attention, but she managed to push it away and focus on Wyatt.

A clatter made her open her eyes and she realized he was taking off his boots without releasing her breast. Then he gave her nipple a sharp bite and held it between his teeth, his tongue flicking the tip. Before he'd been amazing in bed, but the unleashed Wyatt was devastating.

He got onto the swing with her and crushed his body atop hers, forcing her legs wider to accommodate him. The rough callouses on his hands felt like heaven against her skin. He mounded her breasts together, the hot pleasure of his mouth going from peak to peak making her arch her back, offer more of herself to his caress. For her part, she couldn't stop touching him, couldn't stop running her hands over every inch of his flesh.

Finally he released her nipples and leaned up on his arms with a satisfied smile. "That's how I like them, swollen and extended. Such a pretty, hot pink color."

Groaning, she reached for him, wanting his kiss but he shook his head and rolled off the swing.

"Wait! Wyatt—"

"Hold on a minute, darl'in', I need to get out of my pants and so do you."

Desire contracted her lower belly. She reached for the button of her jeans but he shook his head. "That's my job."

Captivated, she turned on her side, propping her head on her arm to watch him undress. God he was so fucking hot, so masculine. During their time together he'd started to put back on some of the weight and muscle he'd lost. His skin was a delicious deep brown from the sun, and when he pulled his pants down she found his tan line irresistible.

"Come here and hold onto the chain."

He arched a brow but stepped closer. She leaned over and began to lick the delineation between dark and light skin, running her tongue over his flesh until she bumped into his erection. With a murmur of pleasure she lowered her mouth to the tip, inhaling his masculine scent as she slowly took him into her mouth, being careful to keep her teeth off of him.

Sure enough the chain he held rattled when she had him fully down her throat, and when she pulled back equally slow he trembled.

"Oh, fuck no." He grabbed her hair and pulled her off of him. "You will not make me come in your mouth."

She grinned and then yelped when he pushed her over onto her stomach. "What are you doing?"

"Be very still. Don't move." He squatted down to dig around in his pants and came back up with his big pocket knife. "I'm going to cut your pants off."

At the sight of the blade's sharp edge she went perfectly still, her heart hammering inside her chest. But her heart didn't speed up because of fear; no, it sped up because she liked knife play.

A lot.

His erection nudged at her as he leaned over and lifted the worn denim from her lower waist. She gripped the slats in front of her, using them to hold as still as possible. That was one of the challenges, to master her fear and anticipation, and not move a muscle. The last thing she wanted right now was an involuntary twitch leading to having to go get stitches in her ass.

He brushed the flat of the cool metal over her lower back, making her groan but not move. Then came the pulling and release as he carefully cut down first one leg of her jeans, then the other. During the entire process she never moved a muscle, but the potential for violence, the trust involved, had her soaking her panties.

"Lift your hips."

She did and he pulled the remains of her jeans off her body. The warm air caressed her and his soft murmurs of praise about her beauty caused an entirely different warmth. When he cupped her mound she moaned and shivered.

"Do you like it when I use a knife on you? Because this soft, wet pussy tells me you sure seem to."

The cool tip of the knife scraped over her right buttock. "Mmmm, yes."

He turned her over and she stared up at him, memorizing every detail of his face. "I want to eat your pussy with your legs hanging off the edge of the swing."

She was only too happy to comply, tightening in anticipation when he knelt before her. Then he held up his blade. "Spread your legs wider."

After she did he leaned over her pulsing sex and cut the strings of her panties. Unable to handle the intensity of watching him, she closed her eyes and gave herself over to the sensations he was creating. The tip of the knife traced over her skin, hard enough to scratch. He began to draw concentric circles descending from her belly button, down her lower stomach, and towards her mound. The circles became tighter and tighter, parting the hair guarding her mound until he was almost to her clit. She held her breath, every muscle quivering with the effort of holding still. With slow, deliberate intent he circled her clit with the tip of his knife, almost touching, but not quite.

"Wyatt! Please!"

"Of course, Domina."

Then he took the flat of the knife and smacked it on her clit three times, taking away any illusion that he was following her orders. Each smack sent a painful jolt through her swollen nub, but she embraced that pain as she'd been trained to do, allowing her body to switch it over to pleasure. The swing shifted and a moment later he was lapping at her, licking up her honey with broad sweeps of his tongue, growling like a starving animal the whole time.

All too quickly he pushed her to the edge of the cliff between aching need and blessed relief. She tried to slow him down, tried to pull him away, but he opened his mouth wide and licked at her like a man eating a juicy peach, trying to keep all the sweetness from flowing down his chin.

The top row of his teeth scraped against her clit and she fell into her orgasm hard and fast, grinding herself against his face, forcing her eyes open to look at him as she tumbled. His gaze met hers and her back bowed with the strength of her contractions. He eased her down with soft licks, spending his time and covering every inch of her sex with his kisses.

He pushed himself up, his erection so full it looked like it might hurt. The golden gleam of his cock ring drew her attention but he moved onto the swing with her before she could touch. Widening her legs to accept him, she groaned in frustration when he returned to her breasts, sucking hard on the tips and reawakening the burn in her belly. He shifted and the tip of his cock brushed her sex, drawing a cry of need from her lips.

Finally he released her now sore nipple and moved so that he was braced above her on his arms, looking down into her face, less than a breath from being inside of her. "For two years I've waited for this, Michelle." He brushed through her folds, settling against her entrance. "I love you."

He began to push into her and tears burned in her eyes, not of pain but of joy. The broad head of his shaft breached her and he grunted. "Fuck, you're perfect."

All she could do was whimper and wrap her legs around his waist, enjoying the pleasure/pain of him filling her, bringing his heat into her, forcing her body to stretch for him. He pushed deeper and her sheath ached from his penetration. She'd used toys over the past few years, but none of them had filled her like Wyatt did.

Inch by inch he sank into her until he was in all the way, his balls resting against her ass, both of them breathing heavily. With a groan he lay on her, still keeping most of his weight off but covering her with his body. For a long, long moment they stayed like that then he turned his head and kissed away her tears with such tenderness that she thought she might lose her mind.

His butt flexed beneath her heels and he started to withdraw, scraping across the sensitive tissues within her, setting off small explosions of pleasure that had her moaning. He sank back in, once again filling her and she tilted her hips, trying to pull him deeper, wincing when she succeeded. His arms shook when he picked up his rhythm, his breath hot in hear ear.

She turned her head and nibbled along the side of his neck, falling into his rhythm and meeting him with a snap of her hips. He pushed himself up on one arm, sliding the other hand beneath her and gripping her ass, pounding into her now with abandon. Sweat slicked their bodies and she writhed beneath him, finally giving herself to him, finally taking everything he had to offer. She buried her fingers in his hair, rocking herself against him, her clit bumping his pelvis.

"Slow down, Michelle." He said in a strained voice. "I'm not going to last if you keep doing that."

Wrapping her fingers in his hair, her inherent need to dominate returning to her, she jerked his head down and whispered in his ear, "I'm going to come, Wyatt. Can you feel it? Fuck, Wyatt, move your hips like that...you can come when you want."

He growled at her. "No, Michelle. Your pleasure always comes first."

The rough edge to his voice stroked over her soul, just as arousing as his body moving inside of her. She got closer, closer, his steady rhythm becoming harder until he slammed into her with such force that the chains shook and the bed swayed, giving his thrusts even more power. She reached her hand between them and rubbed her clit, knowing just how to touch herself to keep her desire at the edge.

"Be still."

He froze with a pained groan and looked down into her eyes.

"Do you feel how hot I am for you, how wet?" She squeezed her inner muscles and began to milk him with her pussy.

"Shit," he hissed out, his hips twitching.

"That's it, feel me."

Abandoning the need to speak, she closed her eyes, conscious that he was watching her as she took her pleasure. Moving her hips slightly, she slid up and down his shaft, only an inch or two but more than enough to drive them both crazy. She took her clit between her fingers and rubbed.

"Going to come. Go over with me."

She opened her eyes and bit her lower lip, undone by the need, the love in his gaze.

"Come for me, Michelle. Give it to me because as soon as you do I'm going to fill you up. You have no idea how fucking close I am, how much I want to fuck you until you scream my name."

His strained words set her off as much as her

fingers and she hovered on the precipice. Looking into his eyes she started to fall, a harsh cry ripping from her as she struggled to hold his gaze, to keep this connection between them, this touching of souls. His nostrils flared and he gave her a dozen hard thrusts before collapsing on top of her, his hips jerking as his cock throbbed deep inside of her, a pressure that matched her contractions and made her clench against him. Heat bathed her sheath, a warmth that traveled through her blood and into her heart.

A beautiful, amazing relief filled her and she grabbed his face between her hands, pulling him over so she could look at him. The true words still refused to come out, but she had to tell him, had to let him know. "Me too."

"What?"

"What you said. Me too.

For a moment he look confused, then a smile filled with tenderness and joy lit him from within. He leaned over and pressed his lips to hers. "I know."

All of her worries, all of her self-doubt faded beneath the strength of her emotions and for a little while she forgot about their upcoming trip to Chicago, Wyatt's PTSD battle, and her own guilt. At this perfect moment the only thing that mattered was the amazing man in her arms and she thanked God for his miracle, praying that her demons wouldn't destroy their love.

Wyatt is begging you to leave a review.

Still by Ann Mayburn

PENANCE
Long Slow Tease, Book 2
Coming December 2013

Chapter 1

Michelle Sapphire reclined back in the sumptuous leather seats of the private jet, watching the sky fly by outside and sipped on a glass of champagne. Across her lap lay a velvety soft cashmere throw the color of honey, and a tray of fresh fruit sat on the table next to her seat. Though she was surrounded by every luxury money could buy, it was the man across from her who was the most valuable thing in her world.

He wasn't pretty, like many of the men in her family's social circles. You'd never find him casually getting a manicure, or spending two hours doing his hair. Not that he needed to. She longed to run her fingers through those thick raven strands, brush it back and see the glints of silver around his temples. There was something about him that silently broadcasted he wasn't a man to be fucked with.

Probably the result of all his years in the military as a Marine...or just Wyatt himself.

He rubbed at her elbow with his sock-clad foot. "Anything I can get you, Domina?"

Yuki answered from the other side of the plane where she and her husband and submissive, James, were lounging. "Actually, yes, you can

Wyatt."

Michelle turned to look at her best friend, but the beautiful Japanese woman kept an expressionless face. Wyatt looked to her, then back Yuki. "What is it, Ma'am."

"I want you to do a little public play with us on the plane."

Michelle would have laughed at the horrified look on his face if she didn't know what was ahead of him. Shit, if he couldn't take some public play here, he was going to hate the Velvet Fist, her old stomping grounds and the BDSM club where she'd cut her teeth. They were on their way to Chicago for a friend's wedding/collaring ceremony and, afterwards, the reception at the Velvet Fist. Wyatt had insisted that he wanted to be available to her to play with, if she so desired, but to be honest, the thought of taking any man to the Velvet Fist with her as her submissive made her nauseated.

Almost five years ago her fiancé, first love, and first submissive, Owen, died in a tragic robbery attempt gone bad. He'd been co-owner of the Velvet Fist and the place was filled with memories for her, bittersweet echoes of a different time in her life when she'd been a young woman in love. Now, she would be there as a woman who was bringing a new submissive into the club her dead fiancé helped build. Yuki said no one was freaking out about it but her, but Michelle still couldn't let go of the feeling that she was somehow insulting Owen by having Wyatt there.

After all, she'd sworn on Owen's grave to never love another, and here she was, totally besotted with another man.....a man who deserved better than her. But he was here with her now, so she was going to hold herself together and be strong for him.

Wyatt looked to her, his mouth a thin line. "I don't share, hard limit."

She nodded. "I don't share either."

He glanced at Yuki. "Sorry, Ma'am, but my Domina said no."

With a soft laugh, James, Yuki's blond and blue eyed husband, and owner of the jet, leaned forward. "No, we're not talking about touching each other. My Mistress and your Domina are going to think up some terribly wicked thing for us to do to keep them entertained."

Flushing, Wyatt ran a hand through his hair, the big muscles of his arms flexing in a distracting manner. "Domina?"

She smiled at him, her heart lightening as her mind lifted to a slightly higher level. Not the point where she flew in her Top space, but to a more aware state. A more aroused state. Uncrossing her legs, glad she'd worn a loose skirt, she toed off one of her shoes and placed her stocking clad foot in his lap. Even though in her heart she was afraid of Wyatt hating public play, maybe hating her for even considering it, she pushed aside her doubt and gave Wyatt what he deserved.

A very focused, unmerciful, bad ass bitch of a Dominatrix...with a dash of sugar to go with the spice.

"You know I told you I wanted to show you off, Wyatt, and I mean it. Yuki will see you and she will appreciate the beauty of your form, the gift of your submission. And it will make her hot, make her want to fuck James hard and fast."

Wyatt cleared his throat and kept his eyes

firmly on the window. "James, you okay with this?"

The other man laughed. "Absolutely. Look at it this way. We both get to appreciate two naked, aroused, fucking sexy as hell woman while remaining true to our Mistresses. Not only that, but serving my wife in public turns me on. I know other men want to be where I am, to have such an amazing woman own them." His voice turned soft, reverent, and Michelle watched him stroke Yuki's face with a look of such love that her heart sang for them. It reminded Michelle of how Wyatt looked at her. "I will do whatever she needs to make her happy. She knows that, and I know that the same is true for her."

Abruptly, Wyatt moved her foot out of his lap. "You're right."

He stood and stripped off his shirt before bending over and pulling off his socks. She had a wonderful view of his back muscles flexing, the complex tattoos moving across his skin.

James picked up the phone on the wall next to his seat. "I don't want to be disturbed. Even if the plane is going down in flames, leave me alone."

"Yes, Sir, Mr. Henrick."

Once free of his socks, Wyatt took the tray of fruit and moved it to a table further down the sumptuous plane. When he returned he folded down the seats so that a bed formed. Finally, he turned and knelt before her. "How may I please you, Domina?"

His gaze flickered over to where Yuki and James sat and watched, but she snapped her fingers. "I'm over here, Wyatt. For someone who swears to serve me you seem far more concerned about others in the cabin."

His shoulders tensed and he looked down, but not before she saw the flash of defiance in his gaze. "My apologies, Domina."

"Yuki, do you have a blindfold?"

"Of course." She stood and went over to her carry-on, digging through it. "Blind fold, lube, cuffs, small flogger, and a variety of vibrators."

"I just need the blindfold. Wyatt, go get my carry-on and then take the blindfold from Yuki."

He stood, the evidence of his arousal straining against his pants. She hoped she wasn't pushing him to far too quick, but she had to make him ready. The Velvet Fist was no joke and she had her own small matter of pride to attend to. The part of her that wasn't wallowing in the guilt of taking on a new submissive, a new man to love, wanted to show Petrov, the owner of the club and a good personal friend, that she'd paid attention during her training and had used the skills he gave her to make a delicious Alpha male into a submissive most Tops would die to have.

And she wanted Wyatt to be proud of her, to know that his Mistress had a good standing in a community he never knew existed, that he'd chosen to serve a woman worthy of his devotion.

Unfortunately, Michelle really didn't know if Wyatt would ever be comfortable doing a scene in public, let alone enjoying it. And if he wasn't enjoying, couldn't enjoy it, there would be utterly no point in forcing him.

Hopefully having Yuki and James witness such an intimate moment between them would help desensitize Wyatt. She certainly knew she'd use every weapon in her considerable erotic arsenal to make sure it was an experience he would never forget. After all, he'd made every moment of her life unforgettable since the moment she first saw him at the base canteen when they were serving together in Afghanistan. Of course they'd been unable to act on their feelings then; she was his superior officer and any hint of impropriety would have gotten them both a dishonorable discharge.

But they weren't in the military anymore and she planned on enjoying the fuck out of Wyatt every chance she could get.

She studied his face, loving the faint lines that experience had given him, the way his gaze softened whenever he looked at her. Wyatt Callahan loved her with every ounce of his considerable heart and she would cherish that gift. If he could just trust her enough to let her take complete control, she could bring him pleasure like no other. As silly as it sounded, having sex in public was an incredibly intimate affair, one filled with emotions and passion. Something she greatly missed and wanted Wyatt to enjoy.

He took the blindfold from Yuki, swallowing hard as she grinned at him. Michelle didn't blame him; when Yuki got into her headspace she became almost feral. Indeed, her smile had a sharp edge to it, a hint of the cruelty she could wield when in the mood. James, meanwhile, was taking off his clothes while avoiding looking at Wyatt, trying to give him some semblance of privacy.

Well, that wasn't going to help Wyatt get used to people staring at him.

"Yuki, your sub seems to be afraid to look at Wyatt."

Yuki turned on her husband as quick as a

striking snake, fast enough to see James give Michelle an exasperated took. "What's the matter, James? Have you suddenly developed a useless sense of modesty? I thought I beat that out of you years ago."

James went to his knees, his hard cock flushed red and standing between his thighs. "No Mistress. This body is yours to display as you please, to use as you please. I live to serve your pleasure and, if that pleasure is looking at Wyatt, so be it."

"Then, my pleasure is for you to assist Mistress Michelle."

Licking her lips, Michelle looked between Wyatt and James, thinking about what she could do. What she wanted to do with them definitely wasn't going to happen. After all, these two men were good friends and one hundred percent heterosexual. But that didn't mean she couldn't enjoy their mutual discomfort.

She could be such a bitch.

"Wyatt, that table can be pushed down into the floor. Click the release lever beneath it." She gestured to the chair next to her. "Yuki, if you would like to join me?"

Yuki rose, her silky green and sea blue dress sliding down her body, unimpeded by a bra and probably panties. Moving past James, who gave her a pleading look, she sat down next to Michelle and drew her legs up beneath her. When their eyes met, Michelle couldn't help but smile. It had been a long time since she'd played with her best friend outside of a club. Oh, she'd watched Yuki and James have sex, they were exhibitionists and she'd walked in on them more than once, but it wasn't the same. More like watching a movie than living the story. The visual was there, but the emotion, the energy that made it special, was missing.

"Wyatt, take your pants off and kneel before me. James, I want you kneeling before your Mistress, but first take the blindfold from Wyatt and put it on him."

The background hum of the engines barely covered Wyatt's growl and he didn't meet her eyes as he knelt, his muscles rock hard with tension. She could almost see the battle going on in his head, the fight between his desire to please her and his need to prove his dominance to the other male. It was one thing to submit to her in private, but for a man who'd spent his formative years in the macho world of the US Marine Corps it had to be double hard. His struggle battling his nature for her pleasure turned her on immensely.

Lifting her skirt enough so that the tops of the pink garters holding up her silk stockings were visible, she leaned forward and brushed Wyatt's hair away while James put the blindfold on him. A trace of sweat wet his brow and he pressed his lips into a firm line, his jaw tensing and releasing once the blindfold was firmly in place.

"Thank you, James."

"My pleasure, Mistress." He knelt before Yuki and she gave him a soft kiss on his cheek.

Wyatt's erection had faded when James put the blindfold on so she nudged his legs further apart, making him widen his stance. He flinched when her stocking-clad foot rubbed against his balls, then groaned when she ran her big toe over the three connected gold rings encircling his organ, his balls, and a third ring pressed against the base of his pelvis. A constant visible reminder of his devotion to her.

Blood began to rush to his cock and she heard Yuki's pleased murmur. Jealousy struck her and she had to resist the urge to tell her friend not to look. After all, she'd seen James in much more compromising positions over the years and had enjoyed the visual treat without ever violating Yuki's strict 'no touching' policy. She needed to get into the proper headspace and stop coddling Wyatt.

"Yuki, did you know my sub has never had anything in that tight, delicious ass of his?"

"Wait!" Wyatt shouted. "I don't want anything in there."

She gripped a handful of his hair and jerked his head forward, placing her lips by his ear but speaking loud enough for James and Yuki to hear. "You do want to fuck me in my ass, don't you Wyatt?"

His dick jerked against her foot and she smiled. "Yes, Domina."

"Well I'm not going to just let you shove that big dick into me. You have to earn it, just like everything else." He trembled slightly, pulling against her grip. "Wyatt, give me your hand."

Still holding him, she took his hand and pressed it between her legs, cupping her bare, wet sex with his palm, her breath hitching when he pressed the heel of his hand against her clit. "Can you see how much the idea of you taking a small toy in your ass turns me on? I'm going to make it good for you, Wyatt, so good that you'll be fighting not to come the second I start to fuck you."

He groaned, his head rolling back on his shoulders and the thick muscles of his chest contracting. "I will stay as hard as long as you need me, Domina."

She looked over at Yuki and found her friend attaching nipple clamps to James. "Would you like to race?"

Giggling, Yuki nodded and gave the chain now dangling between James' nipples a hard yank. "I would love to."

"Wyatt, turn around and get on your hands and knees. Crawl two paces forwards."

Yuki raked her nails down her husband's chest. "I want you next to him."

Once the men were in place Michelle dug through her bag and pulled out two metal anal plugs. She gave the larger one to Yuki since James was used to having his ass stretched and kept the smaller one for herself. The plug she wanted to use on Wyatt had a slight curve to it, made to find the prostate and put a constant pressure on it.

Anticipation sizzled through her blood and she got down on the floor, moving behind Wyatt.

"Spread your legs." He did, just a little bit and she smacked his ass hard enough to leave a red handprint. "Wider."

Deep growling noises came from him but he finally complied, giving her enough room to move behind him. Gripping his hips, she pulled him backwards like she was the one with the cock, ready to fuck him. Oh she couldn't wait to use a strap-on with him, but they had plenty of time for those pleasures. Besides, she didn't want to rush it.

Laying her head on his back, she reached around and began to stroke his cock. "You have no idea how much your surrender means to me,

Wyatt. Knowing that you are fighting your nature for my pleasure, knowing that you trust me enough to do something to you that you wouldn't let anyone else in the world do is an aphrodisiac like no other. I can't wait to have this big dick inside of me, but first we need to put something inside of you."

Next to them, James grunted as Yuki poured lube down the crack of his ass. She handed the small bottle to Michelle. Squiring out a palm full of the slick liquid, she began to work it into the crease of his ass. As expected, his muscles tightened up and she gave him another slap with her hand covered in liquid.

"Either you open up for me or I will watch Yuki fuck James and masturbate myself to an orgasm with my hand instead of your body."

He shivered, his arms shaking and his breath coming out in heavy pants. "No, Domina, I can do this."

"Darling, this isn't about enduring, this is about enjoying. I know Western society is all fucked in the head about sexuality, but none more so than about sodomy. It feels good, has been enjoyed by the manliest of men for centuries, and will make you come like you wouldn't believe. Now open that sweet ass for me. My patience is just about done."

She waited for him, rubbing her finger up and down the crack of his ass. What a fine ass it was, with hard muscles extending up to his lower back. She bit his shoulder, hard, and he groaned, finally opening for her.

As she worked her hand between his cheeks she stayed away from the tempting star of his anus and just slicked the lube from the top of his butt down to his dangling balls, cupping them in her hand and gently rolling them.

Oh, this was going to be so much fun.

Resources:

Are you in crisis and need help right now? 1-800-273-TALK (8255), Veterans Press 1. This is the National Suicide Prevention Lifeline. It's free, confidential, and available 24 hours a day, 7 days a week, and available to family and friends of the Veterans as well.

Resource list taken from:

http://www.ptsd.va.gov/public/web-resources/web-military-resources.asp

• afterdeployment.org*
A mental wellness resource for service members, Veterans, and military families.

• Compensation and Pension Benefits: VA
Information on how to submit a VA compensation claim for PTSD.

• Employer Support of the Guard and Reserve*
This Department of Defense staff group is within the Office of the Assistant Secretary of Defense for Reserve Affairs (OASD/RA).

• Give an Hour*
A nonprofit group providing free mental health services to US military personnel and families affected by the current conflicts in Iraq and Afghanistan.

• Institute of Medicine: Veterans Health*
The IOM website includes information about a variety of military-related health issues.

• Joining Forces
Joining Forces is a National initiative that mobilizes all sectors of society to give our Service Members and their families the opportunities and support they have earned - find out how you can get involved today.

• MilitaryHOMEFRONT
The official DoD site for reliable quality of life information designed to help troops and their families,

leaders, and service providers. Includes links to all Active Duty Family Program Support centers on military installations.

- My HealtheVet

My HealtheVet is the VHA Health Portal created for you, the Veteran, and your family, and for VA employees. This new health portal will enable you to access health information, tools and services anywhere in the world you can access the Internet.

- National Call Center for Homeless Veterans

Homeless Veterans, family members and service providers can now use the National Call Center for Homeless Veterans to find help and resources. Call to speak to trained VA staff available 24 hours a day, 7 days a week. 1-877-4AID VET (1-877-424-3838).

- National Resource Directory

The NRD links to over 10,000 services and resources that support recovery, rehabilitation and reintegration for wounded, ill and injured Service Members, Veterans, their families, and those who support them.

- Returning Service Members (OEF/OIF)

The Department of Veterans Affairs (VA) has created this website for returning Active Duty, National Guard and Reserve service members of Operations Enduring Freedom and Iraqi Freedom.

- SAMHSA Veteran Resources

The Substance Abuse and Mental Health Services Administration provides resources for returning Veterans and their families.

- VA Facilities Locator

Use this tool to find a VA facility close to you.

- Vet Centers

Vet Centers provide readjustment counseling, a wide range of services provided to combat Veterans to help them make a satisfying transition from military to civilian life.

- Vet Success*

The purpose of this website is to present information about the services that the Vocational Rehabilitation and Employment (VRE) program provides to Veterans with service-connected disabilities.

- Veterans' Employment & Training Service (VETS)

This U.S. Department of Labor program helps Veterans to maximize their job opportunities and protect their employment rights.

- Veterans Suicide Prevention Hotline and Online Chat*

If you are in crisis, you may call the hotline any time to speak with someone who can help: 1-800-273-TALK (1-800-273-8255) (en Español 1-888-628-9454). Veterans, press "1" after you call. You can also chat live online with a crisis counselor at any time of day or night.

- Vietnam Veterans of America's Guide to PTSD Benefits*

A helpful site for information on how to submit a compensation claim for PTSD.

- Wounded Warrior Project*

The mission of this project is to provide direct programs and services to meet the needs of severely injured service members.

About the Author

Ann is Queen of the Castle to her wonderful husband and three sons in the mountains of West Virginia. In her past lives she's been an Import Broker, a Communications Specialist, a US Navy Civilian Contractor, a Bartender/Waitress, and an actor at the Michigan Renaissance Festival. She also spent a summer touring with the Grateful Dead-though she will deny to her children that it ever happened.

From a young age she's been fascinated by myths and fairytales, and the romance that was often the center of the story. As Ann grew older and her hormones kicked in, she discovered trashy romance novels. Great at first, but she soon grew tired of the endless stories with a big wonderful emotional buildup to really short and crappy sex. Never a big fan of purple prose, throbbing spears of fleshy pleasure and wet honey pots make her giggle, she sought out books that gave the sex scenes in the story just as much detail and plot as everything else-without using cringe worthy euphemisms. This led her to the wonderful world of Erotic Romance, and she's never looked back.

With over thirty published books, Ann now spends her days trying to tune out cartoons playing in the background to get into her 'sexy space' and has learned to type one handed while soothing a cranky child.

Ann *loves* to hear from her readers and you can find out more about Ann at:

http://www.annmayburn.com

https://www.facebook.com/ann.mayburn.5

https://twitter.com/AnnMayburn

CPSIA information can be obtained at www.ICGtesting.com
Printed in the USA
LVOW13s2129260314

379058LV00001B/219/P